Tales Of Myths And Fantasy

ISBN: 1-55430-017-7

To order additional copies, please contact us.
BookSurge, LLC
www.booksurge.com
1-866-308-6235
orders@booksurge.com

Tales Of Myths And Fantasy

From the Caribbean to the Universe

Darryl Gopaul

2005

Tales Of Myths And Fantasy

INDEX

The eternal past time of the human being is to pass along our stories of the times in which we live, along with those numerous tales which stimulate our imagination. Primitive man did so around the fire after a successful hunt. Today this is still done, around popcorn, coke and through the numerous novels, electronic books and visually by the means of movies, videotapes and the television. But to this author, the best communication form, which keeps the senses of attention with the input of imagination, is through the use of the verbal form.

From the primitive to the advanced, here are a few tales of Myths and Legends in the making, to thrill all regardless of age, culture or religion.

This Book Is Dedicated To My Mother Rita Nee'
Mahabal, To My Father Robert And To All My
Relations In Trinidad As Well As,to My Family In
Canada.

INTRODUCTION

The following are a series of short stories taken from those tales told to us as children growing up during the Second World War. In the absence of television, limited movie houses—called theatres, and limited story books, the world of us children growing up in the island was dominated by our parents, grandparents and those venerable folks part of the family or were associated with part of the family.

Today, when I tell my children born in Canada about the local island tales, which dealt with the dark part of the human being and then being told to go to bed, they are horrified. These folk stories took advantage of the impact of religion and if the church on our simpler society. They were invariably dealt with fear of the devil and the consequences of those who dabbled with the occult. While there was an adult secret humour, when telling us these stories with chilling enhancements, there was the merit of us using our imagination as bed time tales had an entirely different perspective.

As our imagination grew and as we developed into adults our capability to expand our intelligence now allows us to startle this generation with our bedtime tales as we send our own children to bed but with different fears and apprehensions. However, our tales today deal with the external universe because it is unknown and hence there is greater opportunity for us adults to become creative and thus, thrill them. We tell new tales to match their more sinister intelligence.

Within this framework, the Second part of the book deals with understanding this potential source and of imaginary tales in the universe. Needless to say that it is only now my own two daughters, in their late twenties, tell me of their fears as we their parents were willing to give them away to space creatures.

In Part two, of this book of short stories, imaginative space tales blend into the story telling, which takes into consideration, the possibilities of life outside of earth becoming involved into our terrean world. This is a book of stories which deal with a different era and culture when life was much simpler and our world more naïve, so they are there only to entertain and to remind us older ones of those by-gone times which will never come. The impact of our grandparents and older relations do keep us going into the future with new stories of their time. Maybe this is the best definition of immortality within the family of the human race and that is the fact that in the next generation there is always someone who remembers those who have passed on.

Thanks to Harry, Sheldon and Stephan for their support with moving information electronically from the island to me in Canada. The book cover is a mosaic of the drawings of one of the finest artists to be found in Trinidad and the Caribbean. I have known him all my life for he is my cousin Kolo Mahabal, who I thank for his generosity in allowing me to use his artwork.

AUNT LUCILLE SAW THE DEVIL

PART—I

In the wee hours of the tropical morning, the sun was not yet up but there was heavy dew on the grass and the trees seem to be damp from the night rains. In this small island there was little opportunity to be gainfully employed especially if one did not have at least a secondary education. The society was made up of blacks or Negroes who were brought from Africa during the 17 and 18 hundreds to work on the estates of the British colonists. With the abolition of slavery not many Negroes chose to work in the plantations so the British brought in the indentured labourers from India. They encouraged migration from China and the poor white folks from England came to do penal work or were left stranded by ships sailing the Caribbean.

Such was the make up of the society and, as in a crucible, there were the inevitable mixtures of the races and because of culture or lack of or because of poverty many mixtures were in the African or Negro population. The Indians from the mother country were divided into the Hindus and the Moslem groups. They did not like the black Negroes for they said that they smelt "stinky". The Negro did not like the Indian because he also smelt of garlic and curry. There was more to these superficial prejudices for the Indians were often referred to as the brown Jews since they tended to own many of the shops and businesses. They inter married within the Indian community and some even had arranged marriages as was done in the old country. The Indians were more ambitious in having their children get an education while many of the black kids just did not go to school or if they did many just dropped out.

The Chinese population, while smaller than the rest, paralleled that of the Indians as they had their own Associations, they assisted their own folks to start new businesses, they met behind closed doors to gamble on weekends and they married their own kind. These was the occasional inter-marriage but this was with either a white or Indian and rarely with a Negro. The local whites were a "hodge podge" of different types for there were Spaniards, French and of course the

British. Those Brits who came over to take care of the Civil Service held their noses high and did not mix with the locals. I guess that was policy of the British Raj in those days. Eventually, the society matured and the boundaries began to change not only along racial lines but in education and music. The literacy of the whole island began to change as many second generation well educated children came back to take over the running of the country.

It was in this setting of change when the races were in relative harmony and a very basic feel as a local national pride of the island took place. It was exciting for now their local politicians and the few well educated took the masses by surprise and the island became independent. There was however, a large unemployed population mainly in the Negro group. The Indians had taken over the agricultural industry because of the agreement that as bonded workers they could own land. As a result over 90 percent of the land was owned by Indians and the Jews from Syria and Europe who all fled after the Second World War. In such a setting many Indian girls went into the teaching professions as did many of the educated Negroes men and women. As a boy I watched as the society developed but my own destiny in an Indian family was almost pre ordained as I would also have a job and probably go away for some form of higher education. In the meantime, our family had maids usually black women. In our trucking business we hired many labourers who were strong black men. On one occasion we had an Indian driver and he did not get along with the black men and on several occasions we had to intercede and prevent petty violence. The young women who worked in the house had distinct jobs, one was to look after the children, cleaning and dressing them. One did all the cleaning of the house, changing the bed sheets daily while another did the washing by hand in the outside sink using a washing board. She also did the ironing using hot irons on heated coal for there were no electric irons at that time. The occasional young man usually a Negro came to clean the yard and sweep the drains and as the family prospered, flower gardens were made to beautify the home.

Against such a background and setting in this small island was the community of Kandahar, where there was a mixture of working class Indians, whites, Negroes and mixtures. They all appeared to get along quite well. However, as the families were singled out because of what they did socially in sports, church and their jobs, a level of stratification also developed. It was rare to see a single black person living in a concrete house with all the modern amenities and no visible means of having this wealth. Such was the case of "Mr. Creighton" who lived in a lovely two bedroom bungalow house. It was painted a beautiful cream colour on the outside; the windows surrounded with a white oil based frame also had a wire mesh to keep out the insects. The front steps were painted in a bright red colour and the roof top was made of galvanized steel plates painted in green. Around the house was a surrounding concreted path and there was a strip of a bright green lawn which was watered intensely to keep its colour and there were no weeds.

The drains were also free of the moss that covered all the moist areas in the tropics. The whole property was fenced in with a high brick wall, which was also painted in the bright almost ochre colour. The tops of the brightly coloured poinsettia could be seen over the wall and the front door was always closed. The front door was made of a bright brown mahogany wood, with opaque glass fitted into squares of the whole door. The front porch was tiled in red and yellow squares but no one ever appeared to be at home.

The postman came to our house as I was anxiously awaiting a letter from my Irish pen pal, a girl in Cork county Ireland. He had the familiar stamp which was always exciting for me but, as usual, the postman liked to chat and he would hold the letter in his hand while he chatted away on some gossip, which he had the responsibility to spread in the neighbourhood. I waited patiently as I always did as he came off his bicycle and waved at me.

"Hello boy, it looks as though you have a letter from Ireland again" he enthusiastically informed me. "Let me see, you have had two in a month. Yes, I am sure" he laughingly said to me. "She must be in love with you" he teased. This made my large deformed ears go a bright red and he obviously enjoyed my blushing and embarrassment.

I was just twelve years of age and knew very little. It was my younger sister who passed on the address of the Irish girl who wanted to have a pen pal in the Caribbean. I wrote to her and she wrote back and so began a life long love affair in wanting to meet peoples from around the world. The letters all took such a long time to come and my poor Mum always had to have the stamps to pay for my postage and she did so without any comment on this extravagance.

The postman's name was Mr. Ramdass and he was Indian, pale brown complexion but had bright black wavy hair. He had bright white teeth and he looked smart in his khaki trousers and black tie on a blue shirt. He was always smiling and pleased to have had his job which allowed him to meet so many people during the day. I suspect that he could have done the job in half the time but this was the colonial system and he was a man in uniform, which was a sign of respect. He eventually gave me the letter and went on his way. I greedily took the letter and went into the house to show my mother and to read it aloud to her. My mother also read a great deal and she had her dreams of foreign lands and peoples as part of her fantasy. She knew about their lives, their customs, their food and their culture from just reading. When I began to get these missives from actual persons abroad, much was clarified and I am sure she had me ask many questions to verify her opinions of the country and their customs.

I was so pleased but in this instance she appeared to be pre occupied as she placed the onions into the hot oil. After reading I looked up at her and saw that she had not heard a word that I had read. The meat was added and this caused a loud noise as the water of the meat hit the hot oil. "Son, put away the letter in your room and come back. I want to talk to you" "OK Ma, I will be right back." I went into the shared bed room which had four beds made up as two tiered bunk beds. I had one shelf of the old wooden dresser, where I had my shirts, trousers, hankies and my mail. There were many letters and all had beautiful stamps from around the world.

I went back into the kitchen and by then the loud searing sound of the pots had lessened and they all had lids on them. My mother had lit a cigarette and was sitting on a wicker chair outside the kitchen on the L shaped back porch which ran in front of the open kitchen door. She looked at the back garden which had a huge avocado tree and was further shaded by two large coconut palm trees and a smaller lime tree. The rest of the garden had a twin open car port which was concreted. The back yard was completely enclosed by a red hollow brick wall. "Son, do you remember Lucille who used to work for us" she asked without looking at me.

"Yes Mama we all called her auntie Lucille for she was like an aunt to us." I replied quickly. "She was a mixture of Spanish, Negro and white she had told me" I added and sat on the railing or banister of the porch facing my mother. "What has happened Ma?" I asked as mom drew on her cigarette and blew out the blue smoke.

My mother looked down at her finger nails and the cigarette was balanced between the first and second fingers of the left hand. Her wedding band had some flour from her preparing the dough to make us roti. She looked up at me and began to slowly describe the following. "Well, I do not have all the facts but she had lost her husband about three months ago. She came over and asked if I had a job for her as a maid. I was surprised by this for she had left us over ten years ago since her husband was working regularly and they had no children or any family on either side. They were doing well I thought as they had a small house up on the hill and she always seemed to be dressed well, you know. She visited us for years and she began to go to our church, where we met and chatted. I do not have a maid's job for we had a good lady now and she was very young and she needed the job. It appears that when her husband died he did not leave her very much and she was having a rough time making ends meet. I spoke to your father about her inquiry and he said that we did not need anybody at that time but he told me it was up to me to help her in the short term until she got a better job. Dad even said that he would ask around his friends who might need a good woman servant. But you know that we never heard from her again"

My mother continued looking far away into the unseeing distance which occurs when one's mind is preoccupied. She was not looking at me "I found out that she went to see that strange Mr.

Creighton down the road for she had heard from the Chinaman who owns the shop that he was not well and he needed to have some maid's help"

"You know boy that is one strange man for he has never worked and he never gets any mail. Mr. Ramdass had said to me he has never had to drop off mail to that house. This man only comes out at night for your dad has seen him when he goes for his evening walk. He just looks over the wall and he has never spoken to anybody. His house is so clean and well looked after but he does it all. No one has ever seen him shopping and only once one of the ladies who look after the kindergarten school said to me she thinks this is a bad man for she has seen him one night in the garden but he had no pants on. She had seen his naked bottom". I was so embarrassed when my mother said this to me so I giggled a bit. She looked directly at me but she was not smiling.

I looked down at my naked feet and asked "Ma did aunt Lucille get the maid's job at Mr. Creighton?" She was quiet and as I looked at her bent head still focused on her flour coated fingers she answered "Yes she did not know what to do for she really needed the job. She knew of all the gossip about that house and that Negro man but she went up to the gate and knocked from the outside for the gate through the wall was also padlocked. Then a strained voice answered through the closed front door after a long time, "What do you want?" Lucille answered that she heard that he was not well and needed to have maid service. The strained voice replied "How much do you charge?" Lucille said that she was very reasonable and asked what he was offering. There was a silence and then the reply "Could you come back around seven o'clock tonight when I will open the door and we can discuss this further. I need help at nights can you stay over, for there is a separate room for you"

"Lucille came right over and told me everything but she needed to have a job so badly she was at her wits end.. So I told her if things were so bad that she should take the job but she should not stay over night but just until midnight, then she should leave." My mother waited and I remained silent and all that could be heard was the quiet simmering of the pots, the odd bird call of the evening. She continued, "I only saw Lucille once since that day and it was to tell me that she had taken the job and the money was much more than she had expected. The job was light cooking of mainly vegetarian food and to make sure he did not fall when he was in the shower. She said that the house was very clean and she did some of the cleaning. Mr. Creighton remained in his room all day and at night he came out dressed in his white shorts and white vest. He was very black but he was very pleasant. He wore dark glasses at nights and during the day time. She said that he was developing a weakness of all his muscles and was open to falling so he stayed in bed most of the time. She went in to change the sheets, while he was showering, fluff his pillows and bring him the soup which he had in tins and ate every day. She said that he did have the Chinese man bring the groceries to the house at night time and he always paid him in cash. He also paid her in cash as well but she did not know where he got the money from for he did not go to banks since she has been there for almost two months. You know she seemed very happy and she was just about to get a small pension after such a long time from the government. Things were going well for her."

The man was deteriorating badly and he asked her to stay for the full night and offered to pay her double plus a bonus and so she readily agreed to stay. She did not get to know him too well but she had sympathy for him that was close to feeling sorry for this lonely man. He did not speak during the day but he could not get around the little house by himself. In days he could hardly move. She had a room next to the kitchen on the other side from where Creighton remained. There was no music or radio and so in the silence she soon fell asleep at around midnight. However, on the second night of her stay he had said to her that she should come only if he called out to her. Just before midnight she was tossing and turning and could not fall asleep as she normally did. But fitfully she must have dozed off but awoke suddenly to hear voices. She could not believe the talking and she sat up quietly straining her ears to hear if she was needed but it was just a conversation going on between Mr. Creighton and a strange voice, which was high pitched. She got out of the bed and moved carefully out of her own room where she had left the door open so as to hear his call to her. The voices became clearer as she looked and saw a light coming from Creighton's room. The door was ajar and light came out of the room.

She heard the foreign voice say "Well are you ready to come? I have kept my promise and I want you to come now". Creighton's voice was heard to weakly respond "Why have you given me such pain? Could you not have used a better way to take me away?"

Lucille was not sure what she was hearing and in two quiet strides she could see through the crack in the door. What she could see was the back of a big dog sitting on the foot of the bed looking at Creighton, propped up on the pillow. "Your soul is now mine and I want it now"

"Have you heard me Madam Lucille" as the head of the dog turned towards her and the door flew open. "Ha, ha" came the sound from the dog. Lucille was found in the street lying on the pavement outside the home, she had fainted. The police were called to look after Lucille, who was babbling and in shock, Creighton was found dead in his bed and the whole house was opened up and Lucille was taken to the hospital"

"Last night Dad came from work and said that Lucille had been placed into the mad house. She had a dog bite on her arm and it would not heal."

DO NOT MESS WITH THE DEVILS HAND BOOK

Darryl Leslie Gopaul

The cool breezes keep the mornings fresh as the saline mois-ture-filled air from the sea permeates the one roomed wooden homes on the shores of this small pristine island. This story takes place around the turn of the twentieth century when the roads were not well developed and the population was a lot smaller. There was a distinct lack of infra structure as far as the government involvement was concerned in developing the conditions of this essentially agricul-tural community. In the countryside the population was made up of labourers who worked and toiled in the cocoa estates, coffee and sugar cane plantations. Most of the properties remained in the hands of a few and they were invariably the East Indian population or the lands were owned by the British gentry, who were absentee landlords and hired the East Indians to run the operation. So power and the control of wealth were in the hands of a few. The roads were not paved but were clean and covered with a white almost marble like white gravel which was rolled into the roadways of the country districts. The sides of the roads were covered in a rich dark green grass or small trees, so much of the off road areas were still covered in with tropical forestry much the same mixture as that found in the Amazon basin.

In this small island, the deer were as small as the size of young lambs, while the birds had the beautiful coloured plumage similar to those of the main land of South America but they were brighter co-lours of greens, reds, blues and bright yellows. Darwinian postulates were in full observation as the mainland life forms were similar but occurring in miniature. The sounds in the forest, in a world without radios, heavy trucks, cars or heavy industry, gave a pleasant soothing sound effect as the insects, small animals and birds combined with the wind blowing through the reeds of the swamps and the trees of the dense forest into a natural orchestral composition very close to what the heavenly hosts would have designed as a place of Peace. Oc-casionally, there would be the odd crowing sound of a cockerel or the bark of a lonely dog calling during the day or early morning from a well to do but simple farm. The control of small animal farms was also restricted to those with some form of wealth either in the form of leased land or enough money to own fowl, goats or cows. Those, who had such wealth, controlled the local market economy and sold to those less wealthy folks who just laboured to survive.

From such a localized economy, parcels of land were subdivided into smaller lots and labourers of worth were allowed to rent and eventually, over time, own these lots. As a result, they could develop small vegetable gardens where plantain trees, root vegetables like yams, cassava, tanias, sweet eddoes, which grew year round, thus providing enough food for the family as well as, some left over to be sold or bartered for other goods or live stock. Sometimes pepper trees, bhaji, egg plants as well as, papayas, mangoes, plums all came to fullness in the tropical sun and ripened at the same time causing a glut and too much for a family to consume so they were sold and this brought in extra income, all of which was saved. Life was simple and although the mortality rate for pregnant women was high, there was a gradual increase in healthy children, all of whom were loved and looked after as the precious gift for the next generation.

In Guaico, there was the Mahabal family comprising of a father, who managed the estate of his own, as well as that belonging to a British owner known as Lord St Louis, who lived in England. It was said that Lord St Louis some time in the late 1890s, visited all his estates around the world ruled by the British Colonial system. He set up local managers to look after the rotation of crops and the over all management of these small estates. The money received from such possessions was left in local banks, which were drained off when a certain level was reached and sent to his accounts in England. Rampersad Mahabal had just married and he had come from a family who was in industry for several generations both in India as well as in the Caribbean. Eventually, he had two sons with well over twenty years separating the boys. A daughter was born with a difference of three years between her and the last son and that was the last of the progeny. He had as a result of shrewd business, acquired a large estate on which he had built an equally imposing house, when compared to those in the community. He had the estate of cocoa surrounding the house and the underground water from a well close to the house.

This was a very ambitious man who knew the good life and so he had several pieces of fine furniture sent over from the UK which was no mean feat in that era. However among all the fine furnishings he had one of the largest book collections on the island. Indeed with the passing away of Lord St Louis in England, he had inherited a very large library of books sent to him in very ornate wooden trunks. Rampersad was a bright young man who spent a great deal of his time reading and was inspired by the works of the great authors. His management skills in hiring workers and in the movement of capital were lauded by those whom he served abroad. If there was success in industry it was part native skill and the knowledge he received from his great library. He was a self-taught individual. His connections with the gentry in England were such that he was accepted as an equal over many years of correspondence. He read voraciously but unfortunately he had no one of similar status around in his community with the education to discuss and debate the knowledge he had found in books. This made him a bit of a recluse with others in the community. It was only through his letters to his contacts in England did he find understanding for his opinions and suggestions, thus giving him licence to be inquisitive at a profound intellectual level. Soon this correspondence took on a different slant for he had a willing audience with those who understood his emerging philosophy as well as the keen intellect in a land so far away. His letters became missives in debate and over time dealt little with the accounts and development of the business. He knew that his name came up at social functions as he began to get correspondence from others of a similar intellect. He was invited to travel to England on many occasions but he declined and never left the community or his family.

The estate business continued to produce and the marketing demands grew as well, so both combined to be very lucrative and successful business ventures. Rampersad bought more land until he felt that he had enough that he could efficiently manage. His sons and his only daughter were quite bright and they took up their father's ability to read and to store their knowledge. This also set up the children of this family to be more academic but they lacked his business acumen. The eldest son went off on his own and became an actor, which from family rumour; he lived a thespian—Bohemian life style. He was not heard of ever again by the family. The second son tinkered with the family business but did nothing to improve it. His involvement was enough to make a suitable income to keep him in drink, women, fancy clothing and to socialize with the now growing well to do middle class segment of this small population. He married a simple girl from another village and left his own community to live in the city where he could indulge his life style. He never kept in touch with his sad mother and reclusive father. The daughter was intellectually far better equipped to run the business in the event of father passing away. The mother showed no interest in the business affairs.

However, the daughter was encouraged to marry a young man who was about the age of her second brother and he also came from a large family in the neighbouring county. He was ambitious but was not in the position to live on his family estate. He took his wife who was happy to leave home and they went to the city, where he made his career in the now fledgling oil company business beginning as an employee at a retail outlet. He eventually became a leader in the company and held a management position until his retirement. Neither he nor his wife ever wanted to go back to the Guaico district, where his father and mother in law lived. It was said that old Rampersad said to his children when they left home that they should never come back home unless they had difficulties from which they could not extricate themselves. How much of this is true is difficult to understand or believe.

What is true is that the children never kept in touch and after awhile they never returned to visit their parents.

Old Rampersad found that the family had disappeared from around him and he still had to look after his business. In his large empty house, he enjoyed a quiet but strange pseudo academic life for his reading superceded all types of literature from the history of the world through to the British Colonial political system, the classical literature of Shakespeare, the essays of Samuel Johnson as well as the poems of all the great men of the thirteenth through to the eighteenth century.

He studied the work of Sigmund Freud as well as the literature of the Gita and he could read Sanskrit. He looked objectively at the religious philosophies from Christianity, through to Hinduism, the word of the Torah as well as of Islam, and the different types of Buddhism. Rampersad had one of the finest libraries that a home could have in any country. He used this as his source of companionship for he did not socialize with anyone and soon his wife was also isolated in the very large house relegated to that of a companion. She was a very simple woman who did not have any schooling other than the basic education of reading and writing. She did not understand this man who she had married so many years ago. She was the typical wife of her era and was brought up to make the man successful. Rampersad, she felt, was a genius and so she first of all idolized him as a very clever husband. With time as they drew apart she continued to look at him first as a 'Hindu God' sent to visit this earth and her attitude was that of a woman left on her own with such a strong willed man and with age she changed her relationship to one of adoration.

He rarely spoke but he was always kind to her and gentle and he read as they sat down to eat their meals. Soon he slept by himself but she could see that he read almost all night. She took on the role of the head house keeper and all that she could remember was him coming out of the house one day a rare observation. As she was placing her washing on a clothes line in the sunshine he said "Sundarkhali, my love" he used her full name as he stood tall with his grey eyes looking down next to her smiling, "You do not have to do the washing any more get a maid to help you." He walked away. Sundarkhali later on thought that he had never ever said anything to her after that for she had servants to do all the house work and Rampersad had a young man who was the son of his previous Manager take over the position when the old man had died. The young son had proven that he could handle every aspect of the estate's business efficiently and he had a lot more education than his father. Rampersad only met with the business manager once a month to be brought up to date. Sundarkhali became chair bound by the lack of exercise and work but she thanked her 'Lord Krishna' for the wonderful husband which was given to her. She died at the age of fifty three, which was longer when compared with other women of her day. She had never been close to her children for in her mind she thought it was her task to serve her husband and very little was known about what she wanted for her self, whether she was happy or not for she lived a rather stoic life as a dutiful wife.

Rampersad continued to live in the very large house after the passing away of his wife and did not appear, to others around to have missed his companion of so many years. The manager of the estate just assumed the role of looking after staff, who would serve the "Lord in his manor," who needed to be attended to by others and a routine was established. By his self-imposed isolation much more was attributed to this enigma of this man. His fame, unknown to him, had traveled across the island and it was all to do with his obsessive reading and his massive library. Rampersad, in time, became weary of the business side. He remained in his library for days without going out of the house and his obsessive reading marathon began to affect his sight. His spectacles had become thicker and thicker for he treated himself as he aged and had his spectacle lens sent to him from England. He assembled the new lens into place. His property increased as the next generation of St Louis divested them selves of this estate in the island and he was made the owner after some monetary transaction. Rampersad was an immensely rich man but he treated his workers very well. As he became older and his health deteriorated, he was even more of a recluse becoming house bound. The workers thought, in their primitive way, that they were blessed to have such a land lord as an employer. The women hired to look after the house kept the manor in order but were afraid of the man in his library. In time the water was pumped directly into the house for easier convenience. Rampersad had to have the water warmed for him to bath daily and they knew that he was becoming more obsessive about washing himself. He also enlarged the library space and had new book shelves built to fill the new room. No one came close to him but there were clean beds and clean night clothing left for him daily. As with all rumours about unknown folks like this man over those early years, eventually there is a bad turn and it was implied by the poor uneducated workers who were the majority of folks in the village, that Rampersad was studying the occult and the rumour went so far as to suggest that he had made a "pact with the devil" in exchange for his immortal soul. Indeed, that statement went further to imply that was what accounted for his wealth. No one knew how much the Mahabal Estate was worth but gossip spread that he was rich beyond what the estate could have given to him.

With every gossip there is always some semblance of truth. Towards his last years, Rampersad received a surprise large box, which was labeled as a shipment of books from the remaining library, of the St Louis estate in England. It was said that among the books received, Rampersad had a number of strange books, which had been taken from some mid-eastern tombs by members of Lord St Louis' older generations. Why these valuable books were sent by the younger generation to the Caribbean island is still unknown. The details of these books did all deal with the after life and the occult. Among this invaluable collection of leather bound books was a small black one written in words of a strange Sanskrit dialect language and it had a small lock attached to the black leather binding which also covered the book. It was like a complete safe. The key was also sent in an attached black box which had the façade of a book, but when it was opened a Gold key was indented into the pages of the book. Inside the box were a number of yellowed pages similar to those made of papyrus, which gave distinct instructions as to how to open the leather bound book and also outlined the care which must be undertaken when dealing with the contents of this book.

In one translation, before he used the key on the leather bound missive which was the centre of the collection, there were several notes outlining a set of precautions which must be adhered too. It was suggested that the book was the key to entering the world of the utmost evil and its immortality. He carefully wrote down the translation, which outlined that there was an equivalent hierarchy similar to that of Christ and his disciples but it was Satan and his followers. Scholarly intuition had prevented this book from being destroyed but it should have been left in the dead funeral vault from which it had come. The book was intended to be kept in the hands of "civilized society" by the St Louis family who would protect the rest of the world from the detailed formulae which could bring back the evil dead and destroy many human souls.

Such literature in the hands of a man like Rampersad who was intellectually strong and who did not fall into simplistic thinking of life, death and the devil and of heaven and hell, was as much a puzzle as well as a temptation. So late one night after he had read and meticulously translated all the instructions associated with what he thought was an intellectual puzzle, he continued to search for a letter from his previous boss of so many years ago. His letters to Lord St Louis covered a range of literature and these men became similar by just exchanging letters over a period of forty years. Age and understanding have a way of mellowing humans so that the superficial human traits disappear and supercede sex, race, religion and colour. All disappear and tend to bring about a most profound understanding. Human sees human as a kin rather than as individuals separated from each other by physical appearance, intellect or class. In the beginning it was just about business, the role of the British Raj, the international changes which were taking place. However, much changed when Lord St Louis, visited Rampersad so many years previously for there was a kindred link. Lord St Louis was impressed by this upright slim tall, golden skinned man with clear bright grey eyes which belied a sharp intellect and he instinctively knew a kindred spirit. This was re-enforced when he stayed overnight in Mahabal's home and they remained in the library for most of the evening after supper talking at great lengths until the early hours of the morning. St Louis was impressed at the number and quality of books in this room in this island so far away from the civilized society which was always assumed to be England and Europe in that era. He offered to increase the numbers of books from his family library in a sentimental show of spontaneous affection for this man who looked and listened with such intensity. His debating skill was gentle and lacked no subtlety just a keen honesty. True to his word part of his own library was shipped to Rampersad. The St Louis library had the history of the family all bound in leather for over five hundred years. It was a very old history dating back to the early part of the first century when the St Louis family, were travelers with the Kings of England excursions of exploration and capture of territories. The collection of artifacts, much of which was books of various cultures outlined a brief history of the world as such. There appeared to be a focus on the exotic cultures of the world and this must have been an insidious intention within the early days of these families of power in England to take an interest in some specific aspect of the lands and cultures abroad.

TOMAS FAMILY & TWINS

In the village of Guaico, the small population was comprised mainly of East Indians who had come to the islands from India in the 18 50s, to work as indentured labourers on the estates in exchange for land. There were a number of Negro families, who lived in clusters and appeared to be able to work and live without integrating into the Indian community. They attended schools but the major difference was their involvement in the Christian church. The majority of Indians built their own temples and kept to themselves. Much of their religious devotions were held in their homes and were over looked by the visiting pundits who controlled these prayer meetings known as Puja. It was also customary to take over the children of unexpected departed parents and not place them in orphan homes. Such was the case of the Tomas family. A young Negro couple had moved from the city to live quietly in the village. Soon the wife became pregnant and her parents came to stay with the couple and eventually remained in the village. Like many of the negro people of that day they also worked on the estates and did some work in the township which were invariably manual hard work. Her parents being elderly got jobs in the church, cleaning and assuming the role of care takers, while the young couple worked in the estates cutting grass, tilling, trimming the crops and collecting the produce. They remained by them selves and while the old parents went to church, the young couple remained at home awaiting the birth of the first child. .

The young wife gave birth to twin boys but she did not survive the delivery and she died from massive bleeding. The father was devastated and while the children were healthy, the grandparents took on the task of looking after these two babies. Rampersad heard of the tragedy and sent over food and money to the old parents. The young father became distraught and one day he was found hanging on a plum tree from the estate which happened to belong to Rampersad Mahabal. The sorrow in the community of mainly Indians was profound. There was a large turnout for the funeral, which was strange since there was little contact with this Negro family. There was a strange humanism, which showed itself when there was need and when race, wealth and social standing did not matter. The old couple appreciated all the assistance they were getting and the boys grew up knowing that they were special. They attended the local village school and as they entered their teen age years, catastrophe struck again. Grandma, who was the only mother they had known, died of old age. Grandfather, who was a gentle old man, depended on his wife for everything so he was also handicapped and just could not cope with the needs of these two energetic young boys. It was then that the boys, left on their own, began to stray from home and to wander off in the woods, which became their retreat when they did not get their way.

They remained in the home but their idle hands allowed them to drift into petty thieving such as picking fruits from the neighbour's garden or stealing a bunch of bananas from the estate of one of the owner planters. They stopped going to the village school and they kept to themselves as there were no other straying kids their age around to keep them company. The old man, their grandfather said nothing to them but he just left plates of food on the table daily and the boys in turn said nothing to their grand father. They left early in the morning and came home late in the evenings eventually drifting into late nights. The home of the old man began to contain more food than he could have brought for the boys were clever and stole the provisions, fruits and peppers from the local estates. The old man did not notice the stock of food for he could never remember if a neighbour had given it to him or whether the church had sent it as a gift. He was confused as happens when age takes away the faculties slowly. The folks around soon did not pay attention to the boys other than to say, from time to time, that it was a shame that they did not get a full education. "What did they do with their time?" some wondered. However, there was a low level of gossip which remained among the male population who were in charge of the estates that they were missing produce from their lands but thieving was not such a crime as it is today for the loss of a few fruits or root vegetables was tacitly accepted as necessary for neighbours who needed help. Besides all the kids did in fact was to move freely on weekends between the estates and naturally helped themselves to fruits and may on occasion take the odd bunch of thyme, baigan leaves and bhaji home to their grandfather.

This thieving of garden foods continued until one day a farm owner who had just purchased a lot of land and was beginning to become self sustaining by having a number of chickens, two goats and a milking cow lost one of his young cockerels. The boys had now advanced to the level of petty thievery where meat was essential in their home. The numbers of thefts became noticeable and the rumour mill of the small village began to spread and as a result speculation as to who was responsible also began. Essentially almost everyone focused on the two young Negro boys who were living with their grand dad at the end of the village. They did not go to school neither did they work on the farms so what did they do as they had began to grow as strong healthy well fed boys. Surely the grand dad did not have the sort of food at home. It was known that his church pension would not cover such expenses and his little garden was not large enough to bring in enough food for the three of them. It was then said that old Rampersad decided to have the boys brought over to the house by his estate Manager.

What was said to the boys remains a mystery but both young

men were given jobs on the estate and at nights they returned to the house and spent at least two hours in the library with the old Indian man. The stealing had stopped and the boys returned home late each evening to find their grandfather asleep in his old wicker chair. By this time, he was just making enough food for himself. It was said that the old man had the visitation of a church member who also brought him food. The boys remained quiet, and in fear or awe when in the presence of the old but stately Rampersad and never spoke about him in public. The Indians who lived in the village thought that the old man was just being kind to these two orphans, while others thought otherwise and was not so kindly disposed in their opinions. It seems as though one of the boys spent more time at the house and he went shopping for select items not normally found in this growing village stores. Often he was sent off to the city to collect a number of things such as a blackened shaded lantern in which a candle could burn as well as red and black candles. The boy was very silent when he traveled in the bus and he was also well dressed for a Negro lad in this village. It was found out that Rampersad gave away much of his clothing which he still had from his young days. Indeed, much of his clothing that was still unopened in their wrappings for he had ceased traveling well over forty years ago. The twin boys appeared to be the benefactor of this clothing, shoes, slippers as well as bed sheets and blankets. Their little hut had taken on some semblance of wealth as these new items were thrown on beds and chairs. Then there was a turn in events as old Rampersad had the boys go to the cemetery where his wife had been buried and they were to remove the weeds and re white wash the head stone. His grave site was also to be weeded and cleaned on the lot next that of his wife.

The fact that the boys were behaving themselves and they were now under control did not go unnoticed by the people around. The boys also weeded the grave sites of their own parents whom they did not know, as well as that of their grandmother, who they remembered as being tough on them. She was continually preaching to them as kids and she was not averse to strapping them if she thought that they had stepped out of line or did not do their home work. Grandfather tried to prevent scenes that occur in their garden for he was a shy and retiring man. He was often ignored.

Then one night the lights were on very late in the library and this continued over many nights. At the end of these late night session both boys were found returning in the early mornings to their homes. Rampersad was rarely seen during the day time but he appeared to be awake all through the night. He was found dead by the cleaning staff one morning still in his night clothes and on his day bed which he was in the habit of using full time as of late. The boys had left for their home. He was an old man and his life was in this library. The local police came and looked over the house and the doctor of the village just said that his heart was weak and he just died of old age. On his ornate desk was found half burnt candles, prayer books or so the police thought, also present was his spectacles and his half empty cup of tea.

A fresh grave was dug next to that of his wife and he was laid to rest with only a few of his workers visiting the grave site. There was no church or religious ceremony for that was his wish. His children had never visited the old man and the local lawyer looked after the estate affairs but he had to wait for six months before deciding to split up the wealth to the children if they were alive. The twin negro boys went to the library at the local police request and they had little to say other than they were taught to read and they heard him read a lot. On their way out when all backs were turned, one of the boys slipped a small black book into his trouser pocket. It was not missed by anyone. Two days later after the funeral, which the twin boys at-tended one of the boys slipped into the house through an open side door of the house and went quietly through to the now eerie library. He opened the desk drawer and withdrew a cloth-wrapped parcel and stole back out of the house.

On the third day after the funeral, two figures stood by the still freshly dug grave with shovels in their hands. As the night darkened, the two figures bent low and began to dig up the grave site. This was not an easy task and the figures were sweating from their hard work of digging. Soon the casket containing Rampersad lay within sight. One of the figures took out two black candles and placed one at the head and one at the foot of the lid of the casket which was still screwed on. As this task was done quietly in the late night, the sounds of the forest died down and there was absolute quiet. The black book was taken out of a small paper bag. The key was carefully inserted into the tiny lock, turned and the book opened. The front page shone white in the dark night and a sliver of a moon came up. A knife, the same one which was bought in the city so many months ago, was placed across the top of the book. The first two pages were turned and the boy with the book began to read as he was taught to do by old man Rampersad. At first his voice was dull but he soon began to read and to sing in the strange tongue almost parrot like. The small lantern with the red candle glowed in the dark giving just enough light for the boy to read. At about midnight, when the moon was highest, the boy turned to the page with the picture of the dagger on it and read the words like a priest.

Hardly had he completed the verse when they could both feel a chill as the wind picked up. They were well schooled in their task and they continued ignoring the changes taking place around them. He turned to the page with the lantern, adjusted the real lantern down lower and they both began to read phonetically the last verse which when interpreted went "Arise out of your grave and become the true spirit that you really are, Arise, Arise" Suddenly, the lid of the casket was pushed up but it was still screwed down tightly, then the wind began to blow strongly as the boys looked up over their heads at the disturbance taking place outside of the grave, the lid flew open.

Then as they backed away, their faces frozen in fright, old Rampersad opened his eyes but it was not the kind eyes they were accustomed to but ones that glowered with hate and malice. A voice deep and rasping shouted "Who dares awake me!" The boys were out of the grave and were standing at the side of the heap of soil, which they had left on the side. The glowing white night shirt of Rampersad rose up in the air and stood before them but they knew that it was not the old man as one boy crumpled with fright at the site the voice came cruelly to him "How dare you wake me!" The boy with the still open book was on his knees as he looked up and with a trembling voice said "But Mr. Ram—you told us to come and awaken you on the third night" The body of Rampersad floated up and was standing on air looking down at the two boys, one on his knees the other backing away. The lantern in the grave site broke and there was the sound of many voices coming from all over the grave yard saying the same, "Who called me why are you waking me up?"

The boy on his knees looked around him and was scared and paralyzed at the sounds of the dead, which were surrounding him and he collapsed in a heap. By this time the other boy had found his feet and he began to run out of the grave yard but he could feel the coolness of the voices right at the back of his head saying "You did not complete the ceremony, come back or we will all wander around eternally". His feet found wings as he bolted out of the cemetery and he could not stop from running away from the grave yard, along the unlit road through the main street of the village towards his grand father's hut, leaving his brother behind. When he rushed into the hut he found that his grandfather was asleep on the chair but when he tried to wake the old man he found that his skin was cold. He was dead. He went to his bed and collapsed and as the tears began to wet his cheeks, his chest was thumping at the excitement and physical exertion. Then, the room darkened and a cold air filled the little hut. He could be heard screaming and shouting "No! No! , please leave me alone. There was silence then the sounds of someone being whipped and screams with the same words filled the quiet country side. The next day the body of one boy was found dead at the grave side. Rampersad casket was empty. The presence of the candles, the broken lantern suggested the use of some occult service being performed at least so said the local pastor of the Christian church. The grandfather's body was also found but the local physician reported that he had been dead for quite some time. The second twin was also found but his body had the marks of a horse whip striking his naked body. He was beaten to death for his skin was ruptured all over his hands, face, chest and back. He died of traumatic shock. .

No one ever bought the Rampersad house. The estate was sold

off, the children were contacted, but only the last boy and daughter were found and shared in the wealth. No family ever came to the site of the home. Whoever were the new owners never came to the house which remained locked for over fifty years. The estate of Rampersad was always avoided when passing at night time and even during the day. The rumour was that on certain nights the lights could be seen in the library but no one ever went to investigate. There was often the sound of two old men chatting one of which was a heavy English accent. There was the occasional dry laugh but this is all gossip and many just avoided that area especially at nights.

Another of Grandpa's horror stories.

HELLO I AM BACK

Darryl Leslie Gopaul

Chandra Singh and her husband of forty years, Jugmohan, lived quietly in a semi divided house in Blue Stocking Alley. This street was in the district of St James just outside the capital of the island Port of Spain. Their children were all married thanks to the family contacts and connections, which had allowed her and her husband to find suitable companions for their son and daughter. They were the proud grand parents of three, two boys by her daughter and a girl from the union of their son. It was in 1923 that she and Jugmohan were born in transit from India to the British West Indies. As a matter of fact, as they grew up in Trinidad, it was common for the family to jest that they were "small islanders" a derogatory phrase in the local idiom but always said with great laughter by their brothers and sisters.

Like all East Indian families, their Hindu religion and close community tended to shield them from inter marrying into different races as well as into the choicest of the wealthy families. Almost all their free time and socializing occasions were done at family functions which appeared to occur regularly every weekend. Cousins became close with each other and when other friends, also of Indian families joined the functions there was ample opportunity to single out a mate and to meet folks within the community. Old aunts, grandmothers and uncles used these occasions to pick and discuss with families the opportunity to join each other through the young unaware girls and boys playing together as children. Many families became assimilated by this type of situation which was more common in the country farming districts, where there were large villages of Indians who still worked the small lots and estates on this little island. Language and dialects from India became bastardized in the new land but religion and the culture slowly metamorphosed into a different way of thinking but this occurred over a great deal of time. It was also a jest by the youth that they were linked to other Indian families by the old "pumpkin vine" and this by way of explanation, the example that "my uncle on my mother's side was married to the other cousin's daughter on the great grandfather's side et cetera." Such complexities were kept in focus by the cunning of the old dowagers, who made sure that the marriages were not too close.

With the family all settled in their own homes, Jugmohan continued working at the gas station where he had been promoted to the position of Superintendent. This entailed that he no longer wore a uniform of the oil company but rather a white shirt, white pants and a tie. He also carried a fountain pen with ink in his top shirt pocket. His tasks were to make sure that all shifts were covered and so he was in charge of scheduling the few men. He also counted all the money at the end of each shift and carefully balanced it with the reading of the volume of gasoline sold. He took the money and the log books to the bank daily. This was no hard task since the bank was across the street from his gas station. He tallied the money collected with the receipts written in the log book. He signed off at the end of each page and the bank manager or his assistant signed off that the funds were deposited. Life was simple for everyone paid in cash. Of course, Jugmohan still had to work weekends and carry a leg in all three shifts. While his salary was better than those who pumped gas and did maintenance on vehicles in the 'lift room', his position allowed him to be addressed as Mister. This prestigious position allowed him to meet a number of "well off" folks and Jugmohan understood the need to grant a few favours making his customers happy and to feel important. It was common those days to have the windshield washed, a quick wipe of smudges on any part of the vehicle as well as to check the tires and oil levels. Little details such as these added services made him singularly popular with many customers in the government civil service and with many business men. He made his work crew cut their nails, keep short hair and wear clean uniforms. They also had to keep the facilities white washed and tidy and he was a stickler for such sanitation. In response, the company inspectors awarded his station with gifts, certificates and commendations all of which, found their way to prominence on the walls of his tidy office for all customers to view and to comment.

Chandra did drop in from time to time from her shopping

excursions in the capital city of the island to visit her important husband. While she did not know exactly what her husband did, he looked good, behaved important and so she was very proud of him. Through his connections she also met the people of importance, who could be useful from the family perspective. Indian wives may look kind and gentle but beneath their big, brown eyes, shy smile and delicate features was steel and resolve of the toughest kind. They were not the gentle kind innocents that the rest of the world thought and their husbands knew who the boss was at home. He was the boss of the home because his wife made him appear as such. She had done what was necessary for them to maintain an upper class level in their society and she could use charm and other wiles to keep the necessary people involved to sustain and exchange favours for her family.

Her health problems all began when she turned seventy three when pains in her chest caused her to see a range of physicians. It was thought at the time that she had a deteriorating heart condition. In today's language she might have had the early symptoms of congested heart failure. She was told to get as much bed rest as possible with no arguments. Jugmohan went silent and spoke very little as her diagnosis was being investigated. What will happen to him if his dear Chandra ever was to die and leave him alone? He was faced with this impending catastrophe and it showed as fear on his face. He became attentive to her every need and when he was alone he quietly shed tears of sorrow for his faithful companion of so many years. She bore him two healthy children and saw that they were suitably married. They, in turn, contributed three lovely grand children to their parents who had looked after them for so long. Her bedridden status showed that she was deteriorating rapidly from the inactivity. One night, he had just fed her and went into the kitchen to do the dishes and when he returned to her bed side she appeared to be asleep. She had repeatedly said to him that if he wanted to wake her, he just had to touch her arm. This usually worked for she would open her eyes and he got her attention quickly.

He had to give her pills every four hours, so he went into the spare room to sleep which was next to her room. He got into his striped pajamas, brushed his teeth, looked in to see her in the darkened room and returned to his own room. He sat in a lotus position and prayed to Lord Krishna to make his faithful wife Chandra well again. He went to his bed and set the clock to alarm at 11.00 pm when he was to give her the pills recommended by their doctor. He had asked to have the week off so that he could attend to her. Her chest pains had grown to a high level of discomfiture. She looked so tired laying there with her eyes closed and her silvered hair splayed out on the pillow like a back ground accentuating her face and head. He fell into a fitful sleep but automatically looked at the clock just a few minutes to 11.00 pm. He quietly slipped out of his bed went into the adjoining kitchen and took a clean glass from the cupboard. He filled it from the tap and opened the small brown bottle of pills. He adjusted his glasses and re read the instructions of two pills six times daily. He went into her room where the lantern was turned down to just give a glow. He placed the glass on the small dresser in the room and sat at the edge of the bed. He reached over to stroke her arm. He found that it was cold but he just thought that she was sleeping very hard.

He tried to warm her arm with the heat from the palms of his own hands. She did not respond and he placed the pills on top of the dresser next to the water. He went back and tried pushing her shoulder but to his surprise she did not move but rather her arm fell limp next to the edge of the bed. He went to her mouth to see if he could feel her breath and panic set in as he raised his voice calling loudly "Chandy, Chand, Chandy, please wake up for your pills." There was no response. He panicked and rushed out of his front door to the porch. His mouth was dry and he was panting and unaware that his cheeks were wet with tears. He rushed out of the house to the next semi home which was attached to his own. They were his next door neighbours, who were Negro people and knocked loudly on their front door. He could see that their lanterns were still on which meant that they were still awake. The shutters opened and a candle came out followed by a black face looking out squinting in the darkness, the inquiring voice called "Is that you Mr. Singh?"

"Yes neighbour, please help me I think my wife might be dead, I cannot wake her" came the sobbing voice.

"Wait down there, I will get my husband to come and see you" It was just seconds when the front door of the semi-detached house opened and the large black face of their neighbour came out still in his white shorts and sleeveless vest carrying a fully lighted lantern. Hugh Tousaint was in the police force and he was over six feet tall and quite broad across the shoulders.

" Hello Mr. Singh, " came the dark baritone voice of Hugh Tousaint. " I know that your wife has been to the doctor and she did not look well today" came the understanding voice of this neighbour. By this time the cool air and the lantern revealed a pale faced wet cheeked Mr. Singh.

"Mr. Tousaint could you go and fetch Dr Mohan from the main road I do not want to leave Chandra alone" said the pathetic voice of Jugmohan.

" Oh Mr. Singh I will go right away. You go back and close the front door and wait for me" came the sympathetic voice of Hugh Tousaint

"Thank you, Mr. Tousaint. Thank you very much I will wait until you came back. The front door will be unlocked" answered the relieved but sorrowful voice of Jugmohan Singh.

He hastened back to his house and as he reached his front door he turned around in time to see Hugh Tousaint on his bike still in his shorts and vest pedaling away bare feet from the house along the dark night of Blue Stocking Alley.

It was less than fifteen minutes but it seemed longer to Jugmohan when he heard the voices in the street. Dr Mohan, an older Indian doctor who had trained in India but has been in practice on the island for over twenty years, still rode his old heavy Raleigh bicycle to see his house-ridden patients. He quickly parked his bicycle outside the porch of the Singh's house while Hugh waited outside. Dr Mohan went up to the front door and opened and closed it after entering. He called out loudly in the darkness of the living room "Mr. Singh can I come into the back room?" The full light of a lantern flared and

Jugmohan came out in his slippers and night clothing and ushered the doctor into the bed room where he was waiting for the doctor. Chandra lay motionless. He pushed Jugmohan aside and went directly to the bed. He took a well worn stethoscope from his worn out, black leather case. That bag could tell quite a story and it must have quite a history.

He sat at the edge of the bed and felt the wrists of Chandra. He placed his ear to her mouth. He placed the scope into his hairy ears then placed the round disk onto the slightly open neck of the night dress. He then moved it towards her chest under her left breast then onto the centre of her chest. He just muttered to himself and did not speak audibly for Jugmohan to hear. Jugmohan was sobbing quietly and his cheeks were wet. Dr Mohan went back into his bag and pulled out a small round mirror, which he placed near to Chandra's mouth and he stared at the mirror but there was no moisture traces. He repeated the process of the wrist with the stethoscope again and went through the same routine calling quietly "Chandra, Chandra wake up"

He finally stopped and without looking at Jugmohan he said to the lady on the bed "I am sorry" He then turned around to face Jugmohan, who began to cry and scream loudly "My Chandra, My Chandra—do not leave me. Please Dr. Mohan bring her back."

Dr Mohan hugged him and in a weak voice said quietly "Jug please try and control yourself. You are screaming. Chandra is dead. No one can bring her back. I am so sorry" and he moved into the drawing room which he had entered just five minutes earlier. He sat on the couch with its flowered pattern, it was well kept and clean. The loud crying in the bedroom went on for another five minutes. Then Jugmohan appeared to get himself under some sort of control. He came into the room and Dr Mohan got up to meet him. With reddened eyes now surrounded by almost black circles, he looked at Dr Mohan, who nodded and went back into the bedroom. He must have loosened the cover sheet and covered the body of Chandra Singh. He closed the bed room door and brought out the brightly lit lantern into the living room. The whole house was now lighted.

He could hear the voice of Jugmohan speaking to Hugh Tousaint outside saying "Thank you Mr. Tousaint for helping me and getting Dr Mohan" There was a quiet response and an agreeable murmuring voice of Hugh Tousaint saying, "I will go and tell the funeral home tonight but I must go in and dress myself first. Turn on all the lights Mr. Singh. I am so sorry again".

Dr Mohan had known this family for as long as he had practiced and he was responsible for bringing the two children to Jugmohan and Chandra. It was like his family and his eyes were staring and stark. He said "Mr. Singh, I shall call a taxi and have them go and collect your children tonight. You will need everyone around you. Wait for me"

With that Dr Mohan got on his bicycle and road out into the dark street. The clock in his bed room began to alarm and this shocked Jugmohan into an awareness and he rushed to turn it off and returned immediately to the porch. He was just in time to see Hugh Tousaint riding out into the dark night. From the Tousaint house, the front window opened and Nora Tousaint looked out from her house, which was also lighted with the bright lanterns. Her saddened voice came out in the darkness of the porch "Ah Mr. Singh, I am so sorry. Your wife was such a kind woman and she worked so hard. I am so sorry" and he could hear her sobbing. "My Hugh will help you, so wait in the front of the house." She quietly said to Mr. Singh. Suddenly the lights of the house across the road also came on and the female voice of the Morong family echoed "Tous, this is Louise. Why have you got your lights on? Are you speaking to Mr. Singh? What is happening?" came the concerned and inquisitive voice.

Nora Tousaint replied sobbingly "Hi Louise poor Mrs. Singh, she died tonight. Mr. Singh is alone and we are waiting to hear from the children.

"Oh My God!, Nora, Oh Mr. Singh!" came the now loud voice of Louise Morong

"Oh My God! Oh my God!" and there was more sobbing. "Poor Mrs. Singh I did not know that she was so sick Man! Oh My God!" and more sobbing

Jugmohan Singh now saw others crying for him and he said loudly "She was a beautiful wife, you know. I have lost my pretty wife" The doors of the house of Louise Morong opened and she walked across the darkened street wearing slippers and a shawl over her shoulders under which was her night dress. Nora Tousaint came down from her porch and they both stood in front of Mr. Singh's house. Jugmohan went into the house but returned with another lantern which he placed onto the porch. He could feel the chill of the night air on his cheeks and he retreated towards the back of the house leaving all the candles alight except for the bedroom in which Chandra Singh lay. It was past one a.m when Hugh Tousaint rode out of the darkness, dressed in his police uniform which he had thrown on quickly earlier. He came up the steps of the front porch and called out "Mr. Singh". Almost immediately Jugmohan came out and met with the quiet Hugh, who whispered to him "Mr. Singh I had to wake up the Funeral home owner and he said that he will come over with a man to assist him in placing Mrs. Singh into a cool casket" You better get some of her nice clothes out and wait for your daughter and son to come from across town. On my way back I saw a taxi leaving Dr Mohan's home"

At 2.00 am in the early morning the house of Mr. Singh was full of wailing relatives. Mr. Singh stood in a corner of the front living room stunned and he did not appear to have seen or heard anyone. Soon his daughter came over to him and said "Dad, we must look after these people. Chachee (her mother-in-Law) will be here to help me with washing and cleaning Ma." Her husband went off to get the Pundit and to send messages to all the family to come over to help. Mother-in-law came and she and her daughter-in-law began to bathe Chandra's cool body. They dried her off then put on one of her fancy nighties. Then they placed a pressed white sheet to cover her from her neck through to her feet. When they were finished, it looked as if Chandra was just asleep. On her hands, which was placed across her chest, were her huge engagement diamond ring followed by her large gold band. On her wrists were the gold bracelets all of which could not have been removed. In death Chandra looked quite pretty and appeared to be asleep.

The Pundit arrived and went into the bedroom where Chandra was laid out. He took out some small grass strands from his dhoti and began the Puja. He left the body and went into the living room, where the rest of the family was gathered; he then sat on the floor. The couches and arm chairs were pushed into the back dining room. A white sheet was spread on the floor and several small earthen pots were filled with Ghee and a small wick was placed into each. They lit the wicks and small whiffs of black smoke came from the tiny orange flames. The pundit opened an old Sanskrit book and began his reading and chanting. A few new persons arrived one with an accordion, the other with a tabla. There were a number of ramines, the equivalent of Hindu hymns. Then there was a small commotion on the front steps as a heavy coffin was brought in by two brawny Negro men. The looked at the gathering of people all crying and seemed to be startled by the scene in front of them but they kept their heads down and were lead through to the bedroom with the corpse. The funeral home owner, an Indian man in a crumpled black suit, found Mr. Singh and went over to him and held his hands. His head was bowed but he appeared to be genuinely in sympathy with the saddened Mr. Singh. He removed his hands and went through the crowd of folks sitting and singing on the floor of the living room. He called for the daughter and several other women to come and assist him. The women lifted the body into the white silk lined coffin which was placed on elevated legs by the two black men who left through the back door and came around the yard to the porch and remained quietly. The time was around four o'clock in the morning and so much was done. The Toussaint's house lights were still on and so was that in the house of the Morong family.

Chandra had left instructions that she did not wish to be cremated in the Hindu custom but she wanted instead to be buried and placed into the family burial site on Mucurapo road. In the tropics, funerals to be buried remained one night and so in this case Mr. Singh still mesmerized agreed to have his wife buried that afternoon. His son-in-law and his son disappeared and taxis were coming and going as plans to have a hole dug for the coffin, papers from Dr Mohan were registered in the Governments Offices on the early morning.

All arrangements were taken out his hands and he was led to the back bedroom where he remained with his eyes open but he could hear the wailing sound sof relatives as well as the chanting of the Pundit. Then he could smell the cooking of fresh roti coming from the outside kitchen. These were vegetarian people and there was no meat around. The smell of Ghee came to his nose but apart from all the movement of family, the noise was subdued. In the early morning daylight the Pundit left promising to come to the burial site around 5.00 pm that afternoon. Jugmohan Singh dropped off into a fitful slumber as the noise of people faded into the back ground. He was awakened by the bright sunshine and the face of his daughter and son who had red rimmed eyes.

He was encouraged to get up but he did not eat the proffered roti but drank the sweet warm tea. His children sat one on each side and hugged him. His body trembled and in the convulsions tears flowed silently down his wan cheeks. His son and daughter sniffled loudly without making any deep crying sounds. Just as abruptly they stopped crying and said that Chandra would be buried that afternoon. They had no relations in the country and there were no other means of calling other friends of the family. Flowers had arrived from Dr Mohan and his family which were in the living room where the furniture was replaced and the house was cleaned by the number of women in the house. The bed sheets were all changed and much food was being prepared for those who came back to the home later on after the burial. Much of this was unorthodox. Then the sister spoke to her father directly "Pa, the Negro people, you know the Tousaints, asked if they could come to the funeral. I said that I will ask you" There was silence as Singh stared into the distance unmoving. "Papa did you hear me?" asked the daughter. Jugmohan turned his head mechanically and looked with his deep brown eyes unseeingly. Then as if shocked he replied "Yes of course they must be allowed to come for they were very kind and helpful to me last night. I had no one else to call. Hugh Tousaint rode all over getting the doctor and calling the funeral home. Please tell them to come as well as, Mrs. Morong across the road. Let every one come for Mama will be missed by so many". The daughter got up and so did the son and they hurried to do their dad's bidding. Chachee came into the room and bowed before the bent head of Jugmohan Singh, "Bhapu!, Oh Bhapu! Chandra is gone" she cried quietly and her eyes were red rimmed. He looked up at the stooped woman before him who had received his daughter into her family and looked after her so well. "Achar Batie. Achar Batie. Na mar, na mar" he held her by the shoulders. She looked up at this man, who was her family by marriage of their children.

She said that he must go and have his bath so she could make up the bed and take out his suit. He mechanically went into the bathroom and found clean towels and new soap in the dish. He washed thoroughly and the cool water appeared to have awakened him and his mind cleared. Chandra would want everyone to be comfortable so he must oversee all that had to be done. He came out and he dried himself and as was his custom he kept the towel wrapped around his waist. He went back into his bedroom and all his clothing was laid out on the clean sheets. He dressed himself and noticed that it was well past four o'clock n the afternoon. He put on his jacket and asked for his son to come to him but he could not be found. His daughter came in fully dressed in a black skirt and a white top. He inquired about all the plans and every thing was taken cared of to detail. The taxis, all two of them, available in the suburbs were lined up in front of the house awaiting him and the others of the family. The trip to the cemetery was less than five minutes away. The funeral home had looked after everything and when they arrived the casket with the body was different for it was a shiny mahogany brown with bright silver clamps. Chandra eyes were closed and her face still remained a slight pink but her lips were almost blue grey.

There was quite the crowd but Jugmohan appeared to be led to the casket next to the open hole. The lid remained open and neighbours, friends and family each passed and some threw petals of roses and of marigold near to the grave site. The Pundit at five minutes to the hour began the chanting looking upwards to heaven. He had a brass lota jar and with a bent mango leaf which he dipped into the jar, he walked around the coffin sprinkling the droplets and reciting the Sanskrit prayers. After some time the people was asked to move away from the grave hole and allow the diggers to come over to close the casket and to lower by ropes the casket into the ground. An area surrounding the casket was cleared but a rush of crying folks pushed everyone back towards the casket. The wailing increased but soon the grave diggers, two burly muscled black Negro men. One was stripped down to his waist and the other wore a torn off short pants and a sweaty worn out blue shirt which was also torn in many places. In the midst of all the dressed people these men moved as they were in control. They stuck their shovels into the clayey heaped soil and went over to the casket and placed the lid on. A wail of sorrowful crying broke out by the mourners and handkerchiefs were used to mop eyes. Jugmohan stood quietly looking at the casket but he was cried out and his face was drawn and pale.

He looked as the two black men screwing on the top of the coffin but noticed they paused when the top of the face plate had to be covered over by a special square wooden slab. They appeared to stare into the box longer than usual. Ropes were slid under the coffin, one at the foot and one line at the head. The men straddled the four foot wide opening of the grave hole and began through shear muscle to slowly lower the coffin into the dank damp hole. When it had touched bottom, the ropes were drawn out by holding one end. Then the family and friends passed and each took a handful of earth and threw it down into the hole. The thudding sound of the clay bits hitting the coffin stopped as the men moved in and in a very short time they had closed the hole and heaped the rest of the soil into a mound. The flowers and wreathes were placed on the new grave. The Pundit came forward and began another ramine, when many joined in the singing. Mr. Singh did not sing but just stared as so many passed and touched his shoulder, a few threw their hands around him and he smiled mechanically and nodded.

As he turned around his daughter and son with their spouses

came towards him and waited for him to look at them. He looked up and went towards his children. None of the grand children were present. He hugged them all and a quiet tear rolled down his cheeks. He did not remember the trip in the taxis all he could remember was the Indian Music quietly being played by the accordion player. There were so many people around and as darkness fell, so suddenly large lanterns, chulas (small ceramic bowls with a short wick lighted by ghee) and candles brought some cheeriness to this somber night supper. Women in their orhni (Indian woman head covering) and long white dresses began to pass out roti with curry vegetable stuffing. One was prepared for him as glasses of fruit juices also were distributed. He walked around and for an instance he found his voice. "Hello Ram Hello Harry, Mr Lal how good of you to come, thanks" he said without smiling. He also heard "Hello Mr. Singh, Hello Jug, so sorry boy" followed by a hug and the occasional kiss on the cheek. This continued until well after ten o'clock in the evening. By this time Jugmohan Singh began to speak and he made a special effort to go over to Hugh and Nora Tousaint, who shook his hands warmly and sincerely. It was Nora who broke the chatting and said "Mr. Singh. We are right next door so if you need anything, we will be there to help". I will come over and clean the house tomorrow if you would like" Then Hugh Tousaint continued "Look Mr. Singh I will come over and clean out the yard and sweep the drains until things settle down. You need to be with the kids and the family. Leave it to us to help"

Mr. Singh smiled for the first time and said "Thanks for all you have done. I appreciate all your help. I do not know what I will do in the next few days. As the children have their own families to look after and jobs to attend to this week. I will call you. Did you have enough to eat?" he inquired.

"Yes Mr. Singh but we will leave now for you to say good bye to your relatives" They shook hands and parted.

THE COOL ATLANTIC BREEZES

The island of Trinidad is located nearest to the continent of South America and at its nearest point is only about twenty miles from Venezuela. The north of the island has a range of mountains which is just less than four thousand feet high. These are sharp forest covered. At night time the warm air from the land rises and the breezes from the Atlantic Ocean on the North end of the island rush towards the land and rises when it meets the mountain range. On cool evenings as the moisture collected from the ocean is dropped onto the mountains as mist or drizzle, the now moisture-free air becomes cooler as it flows down from the mountain communities onto the narrow flat land near to the sea.

When the moon light is late the nights are very dark. Near to the walled cemetery two figures climb over the closed gates and slip surreptitiously onto the ground. They kept to the shadows where there are no white head stones. They crouch on the ground and move directly towards the freshly covered grave site where Chandra Singh was buried earlier that evening. Then the silence is broken by a sharp whisper "Eric did you see the size of the diamond on the ring on the old Indian woman's finger"

"Yes Dave" came the quiet whisper "but I also saw the yellow gold on her bracelets. She had two on her wrists and a large heavy gold chain around her neck"

"Man Dave! These Indians bury their people with so much jewelry. They still never pay us enough for the work we do" replied the voice of Eric. "Yea Man, so it is a good job for we make the extras here" Dave replied with a silent chuckle. "Did you hide the shovels behind the tomb stone?" asked the voice of Dave

"*Oh yea Man, right next to the grave there is a head stone I placed the shovels behind it and covered them with some left over dirt. It was late and the inspector would never see them in the dark. We go take them with we, when we leave Man"* answered the voice of Eric.

The moon came out but disappeared again as the clouds covered the night sky and darkness made every thing invisible to others but there was no one around but the two grave diggers turned robbers.

The two stooped figures began to move towards the grave site. One big figure stood up and moved away a short distance and returned with two shovels. These men knew their business and they silently and efficiently moved the flowers and wreaths away onto another grave nearby. They dug fast and thoroughly. Soon they had hit the new coffin and ropes were inserted by the one called Eric who was in the hole. They both bent heir strong muscular bodies and began through physical force to lift the casket out. They carefully placed it away from the hole onto the flat surface of the road. They were puffing hard and sweating greatly and there was some nervousness judged by the giggles coming from Dave and picked up by Eric. They sat down for a brief moment to rest for awhile. Then Dave got up and began to loosen the large silver screws on the lid of the casket. He was immediately joined by Eric and with efficiency they removed the lid and placed it gently on the ground next to the open casket. In the poor light but to their adjusted eyes they could see the gold chain around the neck and Dave cautiously raised the head of Chandra and took off the chain. He raised it up ignoring the body from which it came and said "Hey Eric look at this" Eric came from the foot of the coffin where he was moving the sheet covering to see of she had worn silver bangles around the ankles but he found none. "God Man that must be worth over five hundred dollars. We could be very rich." "Yea, we could buy a lot with this and the China man will not ask where we got it from" returned the quiet voice of Dave.

Suddenly the wind picked up and there was a chill as the night air began to move the trees and the clouds allowed the moon to show for a spilt second then disappeared. Then Eric went over to try and take the rings off the fingers. After some time he got one off and called Dave to have a look. Dave said "Shit Man that is only the wedding band get the diamond ring" Eric got to the other hand as the cool wind began to blow strongly again"

"Hell Man Dave the ring cannot be pulled off" Dave said try breaking the finger I am going to have a pee in the grave.

Eric giggled and turned again to look at the hand but as he looked down at the hand and began to pull at the ring. The hand stiffened and he looked at the head and saw the eyes of the head open and look directly at him. He stared in shock and his voice did not work. Dave said "I needed that. Oh My God!" No ! She is back!" as he came towards Eric he fell over the mound of Earth. Chandra sat up and looking at Eric said "Do not break my fingers I will take it off for you."

What happened next was that Dave fell to the ground and rolled into the grave hole. Eric backed away his eyes round staring but his voice did not work. He began to run backwards, he turned and sprinted away.

Almost immediately, Chandra breathed deeply and said to her self "Why am I here?" She looked around and moved towards the gate where there was a small opening. She pulled at it and it opened for she had heard that it was often left open to allow the late visitors in the cemetery to leave. She saw that she was close to her home. It was near 11.30 pm. She walked in her slippers and hugged herself as the cool breezes blew around her. She came to the house and saw that the lights were dimmed. She opened the gate and silently walked up to the porch of her house just in time to see Jugmohan closing the front window.

She tried to open the door but it was locked so she knocked at the door and it was opened and there was her love Jugmohan standing there. "Why are you locking me out of my house?" she asked smilingly he looked at her, his eyes rolled up towards the top of his head showing their whites and he crumpled into a heap.

AFTERWORD

In the early part of the twentieth century, it was often difficult to detect life signs, especially from patients in deep comas. In the case of Chandra Singh who was in a deep coma and the cool night air and the time she spent under reduced pressure allowed her to remain in stasis but also allowed her to recover in the cool night air. The next day one grave digger was found in the hole with a broken neck. The other had lost his mind and ended a gibbering idiot. He was placed in a mental asylum and was soon forgotten. Jugmohan had a massive heart attack but awoke to find himself in bed. Dr Mohan a chastened man, examining him. Dr Mohan explained what had happened. There were more tears and a great deal of sorrow mixed with tears. Jugmohan died two months later from a massive cardiac arrest. Chandra lived for five more years before succumbing to cancer of the uterus. Her body underwent a post mortem after her death for she had changed her mind and was cremated like her beloved Jugmohan.

LA DIABLESSE
(Jablesse)

Darryl Leslie Gopaul

This is where the story begins as we, the children of my mother and those of her brother, all sat around the high bed where our grand father on mother's side was propped up looking down at us. He had a sharp nose and a golden skin. A short trimmed grey moustache sat above his top lip and it was flecked with silver/black strands. He wore gold rimmed thin wire spectacles which gave him the appearance of a Sigmund Freud, whose publications had a large collection which I am told by my mother that he had read them all. He was dressed in his white pajamas similar to a dhoti for gangrene had caused his damaged toes to be removed, making him bed ridden. His bed was made of an ornate black and gold metallic head board and each corner had metal posts which were connected to form an elevated rectangle. A white frilly curtain was hung on this rectangle. The curtains came up to a point at the apex of the bed similar to that of a tent. Hidden in this elevated roof, was a white net which was let down at nights enclosing the sleeping individual but preventing mosquitoes from getting to the sleeping 'food source' of blood protein so necessary for fertilization of the eggs and the next generation of mosquitoes.

Because of the height of the bed, I found it difficult to climb onto it but with the help of my big cousin, who was two years my senior, I was pulled up to sit next to grand dad. His eyes were a light grey-brown and he stared into my eyes and called me *"A Gopala".* It is strange for my grandmother also had a nickname for me and it was *"A Day".* When I was addressed by these family pet names I felt pleased but some of my older cousins found merriment in using these names to laugh at me even to belittle, as big boys do to little ones even today. I was just four years old at the telling of this story.

It was on such a gathering, as the house took on the darkness which was enveloping the evening outside, that we heard stories from our Grandpa. The large pitch oil lamps were lit and this in itself, while bringing about a degree of cheer, rendered the bed room with an eerie atmosphere. Grandfather began to speak or to tell us the story of his travels into the country district where he had a small estate. It began with the setting that he had to go away for three days for he had to travel into the country by bicycle to get the harvest from the land. This included, yams, Tanias, eddoes, bhaji, egg plant and some chickens. He rode his old Raleigh bike for the twenty four miles along many unpaved paths. Indeed, it was quite the challenge to balance the jute bags containing the produce of the land on his bicycle. He had made this trip many times in his life and he appeared to have enjoyed doing this labour of love to keep his immediate family and that of his son who also lived in the large house. I remember that on occasion we would have the unexpected gift of some food from his estate delivered to our home a few streets away. He explained that he traveled by bicycle at night time for it was cooler. To light his way there was a small box-like structure four inches square, made of tin in which the lower part was filled with kerosene and out of the top was a wick. This was lit and the flame shone through a small glass opening. The whole box was hung on a small 'L'shaped clamp soldered onto the middle of the bike's handle. The most difficult part of the journey was when he had to ride through the 'Jungle portion' of his trip for this was an unpaved pebble road. This was called the 'Long Stretch' and it was notorious and dangerous for there were robbers who came out at night from the darkness of the forest and stopped or 'stuck up' the travelers demanding money, jewelry and even food from their quarry. Well, this is what happened to Grandpa when he was on his journey through the Long Stretch in the wee hours of the morning for it was still quite dark. Suddenly out of the dark trees there was a shout and out ran two men with masks on their faces and flashing their short barreled sawed off guns. Grandpa said that he was startled by their appearance and he nearly fell off his heavy Raleigh bicycle.

ARaise your hands up," said one of the men. Grandpa said that he did as he was told and raised up his hands he could not see their faces or dress appearance since there was only the light of the little bicycle lamp and they looked very menacing in their ragged clothing.

The same robber continued "Well, old man what have you got for two very hungry robbers?."

"Nothing at this time" replied grandpa who was having difficulty keeping the heavy bike stationary through his legs while standing on his tipped toes and with his hands held up over his head.

The same individual continued "you know we will have to search you."

By this time grandpa said that he was slowly getting over his fear since they did not seem in a rush and were looking him over thoroughly and cautiously.

"Have you got a gun with you or any other weapon? asked the same robber.

Grandpa said that he did not have a gun with him but he did have a cutlass in his back saddle bag which also had some food and a change of clothing as well as his toilet kit.

Then Grandpa said that he felt the gun from the quiet one poke into his chest as the other robber went around to his back and began to loosen his saddle bags. It was brought around and placed on the ground in front of the light. The robber began to open the bag while the other robber and Grandpa looked each other in the eye. Each robber had a black mask over their head which revealed only the whites of their eyes. Their heads were covered with a multi coloured scarf. Their clothes were old and ragged as they both wore old coats to ward off the night time chill of the forest. His food which was made up of a roti containing potato and chick peas in a curry sauce began to give off an aromatic smell into the cool air of the dark forest. Grandpa then said to the two men, "why do you not take the food and let me be on my way. I have a long way still to travel to work in the estate and it will soon be dawn and it will be too late to ride in the hot sun."

"Be quiet old man!." said the kneeling robber with the food. "I like your thermos," which he had in his hand. It had warm tea sweetened with milk and brown sugar. Both robbers now stood up in front of Grandpa and began to eat the roti ravenously. They quietly began to wrap the bag up and said to Grandpa "Get off the bike!, we will take that and sell it."

"You will leave me stranded in the forest!," Grandpa shouted to them. They just laughed and said "Follow the path old man and in four or five hours or maybe in a day, you will come out to Guaico.

Granddad said that through out this exchange which must have lasted for 15 minutes, there was absolutely none of the forest sounds for the early birds should have begun their morning call for companionship by now. There was total silence which made this incident even more threatening. As he was about to dismount from the cross bar of the bike keeping his eyes on the pair in front of him eating his lunch, there was a snort which came from behind him. He stopped in mid movement as the two robbers began to back away from him guns lowered and was staring with large eyes even through their mask past him at his back.

"They yelled "Oh! No Papa. No Papa, No!" stumbling while backing away from Grandpa.

Grandpa was stunned as these two bullies continued to look behind him and to back away. They dropped their guns and his bag and turned away to run. Grandpa turned around to see what had changed this scene, he saw a short muscular, hairy man with a very large head run past him after the two miscreants like a horse thrashing away the bushes in pursuit. Grandpa described that this was a short muscular man with hairy legs that was snorting as it ran after the departing robbers. He was almost brushed aside by this hard muscular 'biped being' which exuded an unwashed smell of a pig barn. He controlled himself and picked up his bag quickly tied it onto his saddle again and as he did so, standing in front of him was the stocky naked figure watching him. Grandpa said he was alarmed at the huge grinning face in an equally large head out of proportion to the body. There were two lumps on his fore head, which looked like small horns. Thick lips were drawn back to reveal large crooked teeth and flaring nostrils. The whole body appeared in the dark to be covered in thick black slightly shiny hair "what do you want?" Grandpa shouted to the silent rough looking face but continued a gentler tone, he said "Thank you for chasing away those robbers. All I have lost is my food, I have no money."

The short snorting grinning muscular man bent down to pick up the remnants of the roti and curry potato with peas still wrapped in the brown paper bag and began to eat it. When Grandpa looked down on the ground where the food lay in the paper, he saw that this short big headed man had no feet but cloven hooves like that of a pig. He snorted and said little. Grandpa said to the La Diablesse (Jablesse) "Thanks for chasing away the robbers. Do not follow me!"

Grandpa then got on his bicycle and began to ride away very quickly. He never looked back but he could feel the hair on the back of his neck rise as though this devil creature was right behind him keeping pace as he was speeding away. Indeed, he said that he had even heard the odd snort but did not know if that was his imagination, but then the first rays of the sun came out to shine from a blood red dawn as he sped towards the paved road ahead, he could hear the sound of a cockerel crowing in the distance from a nearby farm. Suddenly, he could hear the calls of the morning birds and he felt that he was safe. He turned around to have a quick cautious look over his shoulder and thought he saw a darting figure disappear into the bushes of the deep forest for the sun was coming up quickly and these shadowy devils of the night fear the daylight.

Grandpa said that he made the trip to the estate and arrived later than he had wanted. He did do a full days work with two of his hired labourers. In the late afternoon, one of the labourers's wives came over to cook the evening meal. They had washed up from their sweaty hard work and had settled down to their meal when he told the three about the incident in the forest that morning. The wife said that she had heard, in the village that two "negro men", whom they had thought to be robbers, went into the police station that morning and asked to be locked up for the remaining night and confessed to being robbers. They were frightened out of their wits and the policeman on duty put them into a cell for the rest of the night for them to sleep off whatever that was wrong with them. The two labourers strongly suggested that Grandpa should start off early the next day and pass through the Long Stretch while it was still daylight. They also volunteered to stay and work late and to help him load up the bicycle with the bags of produce from the land so that he could begin the journey early or at least by mid day. He would rest when he was out of the jungle and the long stretch road. Anyway he would be riding east and the sun would be at his back.

He returned to the city as they had planned and had no more trouble on that trip back home. It bothered him that he was so susceptible to the folklore and he even began to think of himself as a coward. Anyway he decided that he will change his travel routine and will arm himself in the future. Grandpa was a very gentle man and the idea of arming himself was very unappealing. He told no one else at home or any other family member of his experience even though Grandma said that he became more wary than usual. However, once a week the local Hindu Priest or Pundit came to his shop and he usually left with a small coin contribution from the business. Grandpa thought that this was as good a person as any to relate his confrontation with the supposedly evil form of the forest that had scared him so intensely. The old pundit listened quietly throughout the whole tale and never interrupted Grandpa.

At the end of the tale, the pundit quietly asked Grandpa to describe the being again, Grandpa described the muscular physical form and the matted body hair. The pundit again asked about the feet and the form of the creature. When all was answered, Grandpa thought to himself that he was probably unintentionally adding to the description of what had really happened. If he did, it was not deliberate nor he trying to be sensational but he thought that he had related the story with out any prejudice or enhancements. However, from the questions asked by this old Hindu priest he felt that maybe he was doing some embellishing, unknown to himself and this must be happening because of the influence of the tales that he had heard as a child growing up on the island. His self analyzing of what had happened one week ago came to a sudden end, as the pundit replied after a long contemplative silence

"My Son, it was not the La Diablesse which you have met but the visitor called Papa Bois. He was sent by the creator to join Heaven and Earth. He is the gentlest of all creatures for he looks after the animals and plants and heals them when they are hurt. He has massive strength and he will never see harm done to the innocent."

SOUCOUYANT

A LIGHT IN THE BIG LEMON TREE

IN THE BACK YARD at NIGHT

It was a time in the early forties, when there was little or no public lighting of the streets at night time. In the St James District, there was a little light given off from the businesses which remained open for the late night customer. Inside of the long narrow property in St James lived our grandparents had occupied the house nearest to the main road at the front of the property. There were a number of rental one room homes in the back yard. I have always been afraid of that dark corridor of land from which emerged the tenants who lived in those old rotting wooden houses. Inter spaced among these poor homes were a number of plum trees, the occasional mango tree which hung over the fence of the neighbouring back yards, a calabash tree with very large leaves and a tall lemon tree. There was an outside shower with green moss covered galvanize walls and the water fell into a moss covered concrete sink. Further away there was an out house which was shared by all the tenants. Such was the squalor and environmental conditions, which was hidden in the daytime by the sunshine and a cleanly swept front yard. When it rained there was a swampy pathway, which was cumbersome to maneuver.

Needless to say, that at times when I was alone with Grandpa or with our cousins, the stories came alive especially at evening time. My big cousin had the imagination and the skill to terrify us younger ones by showing us his imaginary spirit friends. It was on such an evening when we were told the story of the "Soucouyant" which came on very dark nights to look down from the large lemon tree in the back yard. Grandpa had us all spell bound by telling us that the Soucouyant was the spirit of a dead woman who goes after men to get their souls. In fact he drew on a piece of parchment paper the face of a woman who looked more like an old witch, but this woman carried a lantern to trap the soul of her victim, her feet were like the claws of a chicken. It was for this reason that all the shutters on the doors of the entrances were closed as well as the windows as soon as it became dark outside, by my older cousins. From Grandpa's bedroom window, we could see the dark shadow of the lemon tree against the fading dark sky. And the shape of the house of the black tenant in one of the one room houses, which was also closed up so that no light shone from within. At certain times when the moon could not be seen a light would appear in the lemon tree and remain stationary. Towards the morning it would be seen to move down the tree and to disappear.

He had to walk home by himself along the dimly lit main road and into a very dark alley leading to his home. It was much too late to travel home but he had supper with his cousins and after the story of the 'Light in the trees and the loss of a man's soul taken away by the Soucouyant', he was a very scared and jumpy kid. He walked quickly along the main road but kept his eyes peeled on the surrounding large trees and as he crossed over the large cross road after looking both sides, he could see a light in a large mango tree just ahead of him. His eyes were lifted up to the tree which took his focus away from the road. Suddenly he ran smack into the abdomen of a big black man whom he did not see in the dark. He was startled as he looked up into the black face with a smile, which revealed large white crooked teeth. The man said to him "You should watch where you are going, bhoyo, Ho! Ho!"

Are you looking at the "Soucouyant" up in the tree? Eh!." This was followed by a deep throated giggle.

"Sorry, Sir," Grandpa said, "but I did see the light up in the mango tree and I did not see you in the dark."

"Yes, there is a 'Soucouyant' out tonight but she is only looking for young men, you are still a boy. So run on home, now"

"Thank you," he stammered and backed away. He continued to look at grandpa with the bright white teeth and eyes in the square black face, while producing a giggling and throaty sound. Grandpa turned away to run but kept his eyes on the light in the branches of the tree which appeared to come nearer. If only he could get to his street before this light comes to the ground, he would be safe, he thought to himself, as he could run very quickly home.

The light disappeared for a split second behind a branch, he thought as he came to the top of his alley. He breathed a sigh of relief but his heart was pounding and he could feel a coldness at the back of his neck as the hairs began to rise up in apprehension. He had just turned down the very dark street and could see the white lime washed walls of the front of his home down the dark alley, when he heard a cackle behind him. He stopped dead in his tracks and turned around slowly and there standing behind him was an old woman with a black face, shiny eyes all covered in black clothing, head covered with a black scarf and she was carrying an oil lantern which was turned on in her upraised hand. He stood frozen on the spot.

"Hello, young man. You are out late tonight" she looked down at him. He tried to back away toward the opposite fence as she came slowly towards him.

"Get away from me!" Grandpa screamed and ran past her but when he turned around she was following at the same distance apparently moving quickly for an old woman. He looked back to see as she gained on him and ran smack into the abdomen of the black man he had seen on the main road. He was so close to his home but he had fallen on the ground as he heard the gurgling deep throated giggling in the human face with the white teeth gleaming in the black night towering over him. He said "Pass boy, go home" and he turned away from grandpa to face the now close old woman.

"Well old lady, this is a nice child. So go away and leave him alone. Find an older man."

"No!, you go away. I have waited for a long time and no young man has passed. I might use this one," she loudly screeched. "You want him for yourself!," she screamed at the black man who was shielding Grandpa with his body.

"I do not want this child; he is no good to either of us" he replied in a deep throated baritone voice.

Grandpa said that he got up from where he had crumpled on the ground watching both these strange night travelers looking at each other. The old woman hissed loudly to the black man

"Let me pass!,"she screeched. Grandpa said that he began to run but stopped to look back quickly as the moon parted the night sky and he could see two adults away from him. The man's back was towards him and was blocking the woman. He appeared to stand on his legs which appeared to be spindly and as though he wore baggy trousers. He had his hands raised in the air to block the old woman, whose lantern began to glow. From the light grandpa said that he saw that the huge black man had feet like that of a pig, "Lajablesse," he muttered and bolted towards his home. He opened the gate and rushed through the front door. As he entered the house his father was at the supper table and he looked up at our grandpa suddenly and said "what is wrong, boy? You look as though you have seen a ghost."

Grandpa said that he was trembling and choking for air to reply, "Papa, I saw a Soucouyant and she wanted my soul. But the Lajablesse saved me just outside the house. Pa close up the house!." He panted.

"Settle down boy!," his dad said quietly as Grandpa's mother came in from the kitchen and he breathlessly repeated what had happened. She looked down at him and said "you have too vivid an imagination boy; did you have supper at your cousins?"

"Yes Ma, but I did see the man with the foot of a pig and I did see the light in the mango tree and when I came down our street she was waiting."

"Have some juice and brush your teeth. Then go to bed, Mister," his mother, my great grand mother, instructed him. "But Ma I did see…..."

"That is enough, young man!," she sharply replied..

"Yes Mama." Grandpa replied and mumbled that "I do not know why you do not believe me."

BOIS BANDY

Later that evening as I lay on my cot, I heard Mum say to my Dad "Did you have a good walk after your heavy supper?"

"Yes dear, but I met Andrew Tousaint, who was also going for a walk and he said that it was interesting but when he came out there was absolutely no sound from the neighbourhood dogs or any of the normal night sounds. He said that Nora, his wife had said that she heard the sound of a hoofed animal on the concrete steps outside the house. This was followed by a sniffing snorting sound. She thought that it was the horse from the Singh's house down the street but she could only hear two hoof beats on the road, which she said sounded quite clear since there was no noise around as though every animal and night bird was asleep. Tousaint was asleep on the sofa after supper and when he woke up Nora asked that he go out and check around the house" reported my Dad.

Tousaint was a retired Constable from the local police force and he and his wife have been our next door neighbours for many years. "You, know what Robert," Tousaint said to my dad, "There was a round ball of Light up in the mango tree between our two properties and it was too high up to be that of the city lamp post and it was not the moon. It has since gone but that was very weird to me."

Dad replied to Tousaint "My young son has just returned from his grandparent's home and said that he had seen some strange beings this night. We told him that he was imagining things from his grand-dad's stories." "Ah! Yes these kids have a great imagination," replied Tousaint, "but we never know what he has really seen, do we?" With that my dad and our neighbour parted company for the night.

I soon fell asleep. Bois Bandy had indeed visited me that night and just in time to save me.

GRANDPA CONTINUES…

Darryl Leslie Gopaul

.

My memories appear to be sharper now as a result of increasing age, when it is cast back to the time of my childhood. The tales spun by the old folks become more vivid and detailed to me now in this quirk of the aging process. As to their truth and validity I have no way of knowing other than to the fact that the intensity with which the tales were told, it was believable to my child like senses and innocence Butwith all the freshness of youth, maybe like taste, smell and feel, the intensity of an unsullied imagination was palpable. Like a branding iron these tales left profound scars on a very immature and growing brain. Maybe that is all that is really important for in those early days in a more primitive culture, folklore ruled the day. Regardless of the reasons there is a need at least my need to write these simple tales down and purge my brain of this excess baggage.

Grandpa was an apprentice to his father in the Goldsmith work shop, which was filled with several heavy pieces of equipment. Today, he was being shown how to take a small piece of gold (approx. .5 cm in length), which when passed into the grooves of the heavy threaded mill, stretched into a long wire. This was very boring and physically demanding but he loved being in the shop with his father, my Great Grandfather. When he finished this task he would end up with several feet of very thin gold wire, which would be used to make 'filigree' necklaces and ear rings. It was also the place to meet the customers. Grandpa had successfully completed his secondary schooling and wanted to be a 'Jeweler like his father and his own Grandfather. This meant that there would be perpetuation of this family trade for the third and possibly fourth generation. This was a noble trade in which to be involved and no one in the family actually knew how far back the family had been taking part in this very old profession.

It was in the jeweler's shop where he met customers from the city and several poorer ones from the country for the shop was located in the prime city business district. The folks who visited from the country were the ones who had taken a whole day to travel into the city either to place an order or to collect their completed product. It was also the people of East Indian descent who were his regular customers. Even though the Indians had most of the land in the country they also placed a lot of their wealth in precious metals and stones, often wearing bracelets of heavy silver known and ankle Chula and of gold. Such ornate wealth was also passed from one generation to the other and in some instances, was used as dowry. The country Indians also had the best stories about the folklore of this country island and while they waited, grandfather would have to keep them company as his father did the work in the back part of the shop. In those days, there was no radio or television and the newspaper, as well as 'gossip' were the ways of passing news to one another.

An older man who was a regular customer came to see Great Grand father and he had come from the country to place his order to have several pieces of jewelry made for his three daughters who were all getting married in one great ceremony to be held in one week's time. He was giving Grandpa's shop the full job of making all the jewelry and this meant that there would be a large down payment. This particular client came at least two to three times a year to place orders for the finest pieces of work to be done. This man apparently ran a grocery shop in the deep country and much of his supplies had to be transported from the city docks to his shop in the country by horse and cart. He had decided to set up his own transport by owning the horses and the carts. In his own way he was the entrepreneur of his village and as a result accumulated a great deal of wealth. His three daughters had a basic education but in such homes they were trained to be good at the house keeping duties and to make themselves look attractive as wives to be. Their main task was to be the mothers of the next generation and many such marriages were arranged by the parents of the bride and groom, a custom carried over by their parents and grand parents who had immigrated from India. Having wealth would enrich the dowry, so these girls would be doubly blessed and their chances of getting married to worthwhile spouses were greatly increased compared with daughters from poorer homes.

While in the city, the customer from the country would give his order for the work to be done and place a down payment. He would also do some shopping in the better type of city shops and on his return he would take back the lovely bales of cloth and several pieces of furnishings for his home. In a month or two he would again return to pick up either all or part of the order. Grandpa said he did not know how much was paid to his father for the jobs done but he knew that it must have been quite a lot of money for his father went to the bank with large paper bags filled with money. All transactions were paid for in cash and receipts were exchanged. This way of doing business was the norm for the day. He knew that if it was a particular good transaction he would get a bonus added to his apprenticeship wages every week. His task in those early days was to keep the customer in the front office contented and it was here that he heard all about what was happening in the country, such as who was sick or died or who got married and who was related with whom by a marriage. He listened to the customers who waited in the front part of the shop but he was also given some tasks to do such as setting fine stones into completed pieces of filigree jewelry. He also kept the glass cases clean which housed many fine pieces of work which sparkled for there were also customers who just dropped in to check out a piece and even to buy a piece. His job was to package the piece of jewelry and to write out a receipt to the customer. He was learning the basics of commerce. This was the 1920s and while the depression did not hit the island community as they did in the Americas and in Europe, there was work and an abundance of food.

Mr. Lal Beharry believed in the work done by Grandpa's family shop and he gave all his business to this establishment. When he came to town from his business and estates in the country he also brought jobs, for either repairs or request for new pieces of jewelry, required by others in his village. This was a common practice for those 'well to do' business folks who made the hazardous trips to the 'so called big city ' of Port of Spain. Today it would be considered to be the ultimate in net-working and as business spread by word of mouth it was inherently implied that the work was excellent. As a result there were many customers, which Grandpa knew only by the name given to him by Lal for he never ever met the other folks from the village where Lal came from. Mr. Lal Beharry was a customer that Grandpa had to keep happy and in doing so he had to listen to the stories and anecdotes, which Mr. Lal brought back from the village and the countryside. The absence of telephones, radio and television made the imagination of both the folks telling the story, as well as, the story teller very sharp and acute to the mind. It even included the imagination, of those who might have been the centre of the anecdote, sharper and more vivid.

It happened that Mr. Lal Beharry had a brother Ambrose who stayed with him and his wife since their own parents had died many years ago. Like the big brother that he was he found employment for his sibling, in one of his many businesses. Ambrose was a quiet man and he was grateful for all the assistance that Lal and his wife, his pretty sister-in-law whom he addressed by the Indian dialect of 'Boughie', had given to him. Lal had three lovely girl children and they loved to be with their uncle Ambrose. It was a very pleasant time for the Beharry family. However, over a four to five year period Ambrose was no longer a little boy needing to have his hand held, for he had grown into quite a handsome young man, who attracted the smiles and stares from the many young ladies in the village. He was aware of their presence and of his effect on the many beautiful young ladies who were also on the look out to get out of their parents home. He had many invitations to visit homes for suppers and to quietly have the attention of the young lady of that home shyly scrutinize him for a few hours in the presence of her family. According to Mr Lal, he knew that sooner or later Ambrose would have to have a wife and have a home of his own. He told Grandpa that he was planning to pass the full responsibility of his cocoa, coffee and citrus fruit estates over to Ambrose to be the 'Overseer'. In this way Ambrose would be able to have a good salary and develop his own business if he was that way inclined.

Mr. Lal continues as heard by Grandpa, "Well you see Bhapu, he was such a handsome brother and I knew all the good families around. They have a lot of respect for me, you know?" Grandpa nodded knowingly as he looked up from the very intricate filigree soldering of the tiny gold pieces which he had on a metal base. He looked through his thin gold rimmed wire glasses, at Mr. Lal sitting in front of him next to the work bench and he could see a great sadness descend on this normally ebullient and confident man. Looking directly at the bowed head of Lal, he quietly asked "Lal, what has happened to your brother?"

Mr. Lal broke down in front of Grandpa and began to sob uncontrollably and he was inconsolable. This came as a great shock to Grandpa who got up immediately and lead him towards the back of the shop away from where the customers and people on the street could see them. He gave Mr. Lal a glass of water from the little lead pipe where he washed his hands and was in use for the business. They both sat down on a pair of old wicker chairs which had seen better days. Lal story continues to my grandfather:

"Bhapu, I made the offer of him being the 'Overseer' of the estate to Ambrose. Ambrose was silent and asked if I would guarantee that he would have permanent work for he would like to get married as soon as possible. I told him that I would sign a paper if he wanted me to do so. I liked my little brother a lot you know, Bhapu. But he was always a bit fragile and timid and he really could not take on the cold and dampness when he would invariably become very ill. Ambrose got the paper, which he wanted to guarantee that he would have permanent employment and moved out to the estate site. He simultaneously began to overseer the estate and to court a beautiful girl from a very good family. Her name was Iris of the grey eyes and pink complexion; at least that was what Ambrose had said to me. I did not think that our family was good enough for this girl's family, so as the big brother, I went over to meet the girl's family. One of your pieces of jewelry was taken by Ambrose to give to the girl if she had agreed to the joining in marriage. Bhapu, Ambrose moved out of our house to stay on the estate where he could keep the books, hire the labourers, pick the crops keep the weeds down and deliver the cocoa and coffee to the marketplace. He lived in one of the labourers wooden shacks to save money. He cooked for himself and when I asked him to come back to the main house in the village to live, he said that he wanted to be close to keep an eye on things. Bhapu in the first three months I had a huge profit because he had stopped the stealing of the fruit from the trees by a few of the labourers and from other out of village thieves, by just being present.

But while the girl, Iris had agreed to marry Ambrose and he was free to begin visiting her, he had developed a slight cough. Although he was well groomed, dressed nicely he appeared to be losing weight but I put it down to his exercise and hard work in the fields. I came to town to do some more business and to buy some land attached to the current estate. Bhapu, I wanted to give the land as a wedding present to Ambrose and Iris, so they could build their own house and so he could be close to the business. Eventually, I would have allowed him buy the estate from me for I have other businesses to run and the estate was too much for me to handle. I did not see Ambrose for over a month and when I returned home my wife said that she had not seen Ambrose either.

She said that he must be working very hard except that Lucille the maid, whose brother works on the estate, said to her that she thought that the overseer was sick. Her brother had said that the boss slept more and was not eating very much. Her brother also said that the overseer was coughing a lot but he smiled and worked every day with the other labourers. My wife said that I should go and see him at the estate on the weekend. Bhapu, I promised to really go and see the boy but I forgot and had to attend a Puja at uncle's home in Arima. I did not get back until the Monday following. When I got home, the house was very quiet. I went upstairs and the maid Lucille said to me that my wife had gone to the estate for she had heard that little brother was bed ridden. Lucille said that her own brother had told her family on the weekend while she was visiting. She told Madam this morning and she had the horse and cart, come to take Madam over to the estate. Madam took food with her but she has been gone all day. Late that night, Bhapu, the horse and cart came back and my wife had Ambrose with her.

Bhapu, I could not believe how skinny Ambrose had become.

I sent over immediately for Dr Singh in the village. He came over that evening to the house and after examining Ambrose he said that Ambrose had 'consumption.' Bhapu before I could make arrangements to bring him to town the next day, Ambrose died in the night. "Oh!"Cried Mr. Lal, "I have not stopped crying since Bhapu for I feel as though I had sent him to his death. He never complained or asked for anything other than to work for me and my wife."

My grand father then asked, how had the girl Iris, taken the death. Mr. Lal Beharry raised his head and simultaneously raised his grey eyebrows and stared at grandpa then said "That news is even worse; Bhapu for we found out that Ambrose had been going over to see her quite regularly at least on weekends. He had not been there for two weekends. Iris told her mother and father that she wanted to be a good wife to Ambrose and to have lots of children for him. So she began to ask their maid to show her how to cook. They were using the new kerosene cookers, with a glass tank at one end and two burners in the middle. Well, while she had been cooking she saw that the kerosene glass tank was low. The maid offered to put in the kerosene in the stove from the can. Iris insisted that she wanted to do all that as well, for she said that Ambrose and she could not afford to get a maid right away. They were going to save and build their house first. We do not know what happened but the oil spilt and the stove caught fire, Iris dropped the can of kerosene and she tried to turn off the burner. Her hair caught fire and then her dress by the time the maid got to her she was on the floor burnt and dead. That happened the same day that my wife brought Ambrose home."

With that Mr. Lal began to shudder and to cry uncontrollable. Grandfather did not know what to say to him only to pat his shoulders and make clucking sympathetic sounds. Mr. Lal never came back to the shop again. When I asked grand father if he had asked about Mr. Lal, he said that his father knew something but only nodded negatively. It appeared that this customer and his business just disappeared from the shop and the island. Grandfather knew the whole story but he never said a word even on his death bed, where he quietly summarized his life and work, he never said anything about Mr. Lal.

PART—2

PROTO

By

Darryl Leslie Gopaul

It all began when the earth ship was searching for new life forms and document-ing stellar activities. The main ship seeded scientists in groups, whose task it was to visit the sites of interest, record their findings but should never interfere if there were other living life forms present. There were debriefings after every trip and all was recorded into the ship's massive computers and sent home to the collected pool of knowledge.

On one of these investigative voyages, three volunteer scientists were sent off to look at a solar system which was located approximately two weeks away from the mother ship. This was a slightly unusual solar phenomenon since the long range scans revealed that there was one sun with only one circulating planet, which appeared to have a lush carbon based flora.

The members chosen for this exploration were—Leslie Ram, Tara Luapog, and Len Denis. It was easy enough to see why these three were chosen since Leslie Ram was a qualified career space Microbiologist with speciality in minuscule life forms of the universe. Tara Luapog is a brilliant and sharp female engineer, whose specialty included the search for organic minerals, water as well as to assist with the documentation and locations of these sites. She also knew it was vital to look for habitable planets, which was a necessity for the humans from earth. She was chosen also for her leadership skills. Len Denis was so well qualified in, communications and piloting the craft but also duplicated some of Tara's skills in detecting and searching out minerals—the inorganic forms. It was not a typical crew which would cover all aspects of a true research mis-sion but it had the basic ingredients for an away team, involved in scouting out an unknown planet.

It was long before this small crew set off to check out the section of the quadrant which was been mapped by the parent ship. This was almost a routine mission. For the crew it was a chance to get out of the routine daily chores and get excited of doing anything else. The small module was provisioned for a two week stay, which was the norm. And so it passed that the three man personnel found themselves commu-nicating with each other. They were aware of each other but did not have the opportunity to officially meet or socialise with each other. It was common on the parent ships for the crew to acquaint themselves with personnel of similar interests and some go further by checking out the entire crew including the senior leadership team. This could be quite the task since at times the crew contingent could be as high as a thousand personnel. So with feelings of goodwill for each other as there were only the three of them for the next two weeks, Tara opened the orders on the small hand held computer which outlined their respective jobs. It was very much as described in their respective curriculum vitae. The only exception was that the two men had to obey the orders of the leader Tara Luapog. They settled into the routine of their shuttle and knew that they would be at their destination within 24 hours at their current light speed.

It was a very calming site as they arose to hear Tara say, "we are there, rise and shine lads".They looked at their screens and saw the sun, which was like all the others. The shuttle was equipped with sensors of all variety and types so it began the automatic process of logging information as to distance, radiation type present, making photos of almost every thing in its path to a radius of almost a light year away. As the tons of information sped in front of their screens, they quickly adapted to the salient parts necessary to each of their respective portfolios. It was not long before they had vision contact. They have been on the research ship for over three years but it was always exciting when they went into a new space area and saw planets for the first time. It was always the feeling of being first to see new territory.

In front of them was a sun which was being dated by the shuttle computers, measuring its spectral flora, radiation and all other aspects many of which was pre programmed for others to evaluate. What was fascinating to them was the planet circulating around the sun once every twenty four hours. It was similar to that of the earth in more ways as they got nearer and slowed to begin observations. So far the scanners revealed a densely treed planet with no obvious large bodies of water but the atmospheric mixture of gases showed an earth-like combination of twenty percent oxygen, some hydrogen (1%) and nitrogen almost 70%. There was carbon dioxide and other inert gases taking up the remaining 19 %. Humidity was approximately 60% and there some cloud formation, which were small and not long lasting. All this was good news for it was not necessary to wear the bulky and cumbersome space suits with portable breathing apparatus. Both Tara and Len double checked the entire instrument to make sure they were all functioning correctly. Les began the planning of his experiments into looking at the microscopic life forms of both plant and animal variety. Biological scans tend to look at the large presence of carbon based forms so it was always risky when microbial forms are investigated carefully and this could only be done after landing.

With their respective responsibilities outlined and after satisfactory answers to enquires, the three crewmen were ready to land and have a look around. There were communicators and space scooters, which would cover great distances. It was up to Les to go out first and to check the air, radiation and of course the microbial world. Since it was necessary for everyone to be cross trained, his task was to verify what the others had already found out using the technology on the shuttle. Len took over the tasks of making sure all the hand held analysers, communication devices, the scooters were functioning properly and were linked directly into the shuttle computer system.

There was also a back up system which allowed information gathered by the shuttle's continuous monitoring system to frequently download the accumulated information to the parent ship which was several light years away. With all the safety precautions checked out, Les left the shuttle which Tara had landed in the middle of a clearing of the lush green forest. This was strange to find such a spot since it appeared that the total planet surface was covered with an almost impenetrable rain forest similar to that of the planet earth—a long time ago. At least that was the picture which came immediately to their minds. When Tara pointed out the clearing to them it was difficult for them to see it, at first since it was a small turf covered savannah. As the leader in charge Tara made the decision to land and there were; only silent murmurs of positive approval. It may be because there was a silent excitement of just wanting to land. This feeling appears to all workers who spend most of their lives on these exploration space ships. The mere site of any land in the form of planets, large silently gliding comets and old burnt out stars were always a welcomed site and there was the anxiety of just wanting to feel a form of terra firma under one's feet.

Les quickly affirmed that the atmosphere was indeed acceptable to humans. The radiation was almost non-existent and all he could pick up on his micro monitor was bits of dust particles and some pollen. The information sent back to the two in the shuttle was verified by the larger back up system, which was placed on continual monitoring to the exclusion of only maintaining life support. A quick screen to check for toxicity of the pollen revealed a mild collection of nutritionally trace factors with no toxins to carbon based life. After the monitoring of the life support environment, Les raised his eyes for the first time to see himself, surrounded by some of the largest trees he could have ever imagined. The grass felt lush and soft even through his mesh of plastic and metal covered feet. He was able to move so quickly in spite of his clothing and indeed he could feel the slight warmth of the sun through his space suit. It appeared as if his own space suit support system had shut down and as though he was free in of artificial protective clothing. Towards this end he reported back that they had found another earth planet. The information forwarded back to him that it was alright to take the next step which was to try breathing in the planet's air. He shut down his own air supply and through a system of filters fresh air passed into his lungs and he felt a purity and ease in breathing, as his lungs filled with the natural air, which felt fresh and wholesome. He turned it off and returned to his own air supply system. It was almost like a jolt for it appeared that he was re breathing a stale source of air which he was. His body returned to the response of the artificial but he felt a longing to open up to the atmosphere again but he waited for the return of the approval system checks from Tara and Len on the shuttle.

It seems like ages before they responded when in actual fact it was just five or more minutes before he had approval to remove his head gear breathe regularly for another 30 minutes but to return his head gear at any sign that was alien to him. He then was free to move closer to the woods while remaining in sight of the crew. As he got closer to the trees, there were small flowers on the turf but one had to focus down without the head gear. His eyes remained sharp and he also found a freedom of movement brought on by the fact the his head could move around freely while his eyes scanned everything around him. Maintaining eyes on his hand held monitors, he bent down to feel the grass with his bare hands and there was a softness, which almost caressed his skin. He just thought that this is to be expected since he had only been in contact with space equipment for the past five years. The trees and food plants on the parent ship were only handled by the space gardeners and no one else was allowed to go into the garden. It was considered a security area since it was responsible for over 80 percent of their life support system providing food, oxygen and moisture to the whole vessel. Here he was feeling all this vegetation around him with no competition from fellow humans. He also understood that he was also playing the "guinea pig" for the others on the shuttle, who monitoring even his psychological responses so there was a levity which he had to respond to but this easy because of his scientific training. Failure to respond from the tried and proven policies of space flight could get one into a great deal of trouble, not only for the individual but for his colleagues and indeed may jeopardise the whole mission, which was extremely costly. He had attended enough mission debriefings to see the effects of those individuals on sour missions. Non-the-less, this freedom he was feeling became an urge to strip off his space suit and to run around and shout but he resisted all these primal feelings to go through the steps outlined to him. He replaced his space head gear and returned to the shuttle's cleansing chamber. In this small room he placed his gear into several drawers, which appeared in the order he removed each item of clothing they then shut automatically for screening, cleansing and re-packing.

His naked body was then exposed to a surrounding shower of soft water which was warmed to his body temperature. He remembered when he went through these exercises how his body was always sweaty and it was pleasing. Since this was his first real life experience all he could feel was a the tiny droplets hitting his body. He was not sweaty after his three hours outside and if anything he felt energetic and almost happy. He could not wait to have a debriefing with his commander—Tara. In an hour he was doing just that. Tara was businesslike in her task of evaluating his answers and the overall opinion was that there was noting toxic to human life outside. Les would have to sleep in the isolation chamber for tonight in the nude and from time to time he would be checked by the others. and by other automated equipment as his life signs will be compared to his history. It may seem that this was excessive precautions taken but it was really routine which had to be followed.

Les slept as the proverbial baby and there were no effects due to his exposure. Rather than completing more tests Tara made the decision with the others, that there tasks be broken down into the following for each to have more time with their specialities. Les will go look and record his findings on the flora and fauna. Len would look at the mineral make up of the planet and make plans on the location of mineral deposits, while Tara will try and look for water either on the surface or in underground streams. She also wanted to check for animal life especially avian life form, since she recorded trees with nuts and seeds apart from the large conifers which were in the majority of the forests. With all that food source around there must be some form of animal life. This little observation was noted and was shared with all so it was also part of their task to look for the same. If any form of animal life were seen it was necessary to place out a contact call via the portable intercoms to which they were all attached. All contact would also be stored on the shuttle so it will also act as a contact communication source in case their signals were blocked from each other either by a physical structure, such as a mountain, valley or cave. It was suggested that they all use the repository of the computer link on the shuttle at the end of each work day. Rations were packed, some emergency medical supplies and the usual solar cells etc. Each crew member had light packs to carry and they also had their scooters which folded into a rucksack type easy enough to carry. With a shake of hands Tara set out with a determined set to her jaw since she had to cover the whole planet which was approximately the size of earth. Len set out to tackle a North South circumference, while Les travelled in an East West direction.

The rest of this story covers only the exploits of Leslie Ram, *the Stellar Micro-biologist who was given the task of checking out the microscopic forms of both animal and plant life. It is here that a strange selection process appears to have taken place for he immediately felt at home with this planet. In fact he said later on that he felt as though he belonged to the place. He also explained to the debriefing committee that there was something that he felt which was not picked up by any of their scans or their psychological inquiries. He felt first of all that they were all under some type of observation but which he felt intuitively was benign.*

He had to explain that since there was no obvious signs of animal life form as shown by their distant scans and by the probe which they had discharged and was hovering high above the planet in an orbit that allowed the shuttle to have an eye over the twenty four hour cycle of twelve hour day and night from their central location, he did not feel it necessary to record any of his thoughts on the subject. Indeed he almost felt that it would be the wrong thing to record and so he put it all down to being the first to leave the ship and to the absolute loneliness of the area, which had a calming effect on him and mellowed his spirit.

For the first time he was aware of the total absence of the continual humming of the shuttle engines and also that of the parent ship. His hearing had to cope with a mild ringing sound due to the complete absence of mechanical sounds. His feeling of being observed was enhanced as soon as he left the shuttle to begin his mission. Before he entered the forest of trees, he stopped and looked as his colleagues just as they disappeared from sight, neither of whom turned to look back or to wave farewell.

PART 2.

It was almost with some anticipation and more than an excitement that Les entered the glade in front of the shuttle. When he turned around to look back at the shuttle and to set the co ordinates for the position of his locator the craft looked so lonely and small to him. He smiled to himself and began to walk and look at the trees around him. Their heights were phenomenal, three hundred feet some twice that size. His recorders soon revealed a temperate type forest with lots of evergreens and few deciduous but what had caught his attention was the size of their leaves, which measured two to three metres across on trees similar to the umbrella trees. The pine and fir trees were straight and had girths of two to three metres at their base but he soon saw some even larger ones as he continued his stroll through this majestic garden of Eden. He also noted that the ground was soft to his tread because of a continuous carpet of soft fir and pine needles. There was the occasional small bush like scrub at the base of these shaded trees but they too appeared to be lush with a dark green leaves and a soft main stem. His analyser showed that the chlorophyll was similar to that of the programmed control, with a slight accentuation in the amount of red type, which was not obvious as he looked at the few deciduous trees around.. He smiled as he breathed in deeply and thought to himself that this place must be the most colourful when the autumn comes along—if indeed there was an autumn.

Leslie stood under the canopy of the monster size trees and made a video recording of all that was around him. He stopped and went over to look closely at the trunk of the trees, which was smooth, free of the normal longitudinal bark scorings common to the pine and spruce trees. It was as though they had the clean smooth feel of the Australian Gum trees. He also noted that some of the same trees also had different coloured bark, some with the accepted brown colour while others had a ghost blue-white colour. Then as his video was recording his observations he felt more than ever that there were eyes looking at him but these were not terrifying observations but quietly observing eyes. He spun around quickly to look between the trees, then he looked up at the cavernous canopy and realised that his mind was probably playing tricks on him None of his analysers showed activity of animal or humanoid forms present. He left his analyser on permanent search in case he might miss a signal.

It was strange that he could still see the sunlight dancing in between the trees in spite of the thick foliage of the branches and the canopy. The quietness of the forest was eerie since he could only hear his blood pumping through the carotid arteries near to his eardrum. There has been a small medical problem which Leslie had and it was a genetic fault. His parents and school personnel did not feel necessary to it surgically fixed. Even when at rest Leslie's blood pressure would be elevated to the abnormal level for men of his age. Leslie did not tell anyone but as he got older he realised that he just had an abnormally high blood pressure when at rest. The medical staff did place a small monitor under his right rib cage with a small dose cartridge which would deliver a beta blocker if his BP went to higher levels not contiguous with his personal range. The microchip had the history of his medical file, which was continually checked as a back ground. As a result he had his own personal case history on him with his normal values with which to compare.

As he continued to walk through this soft carpet of pine, fir and spruce needles, he did not see any twigs, or fallen leaves and he did not get close enough to touch the trees. It appeared as though these could have been a crop of equally spaced trees which were kept by an army of personnel for nothing appeared to be out of order. He looked at his watch and realised that he had been walking and recording his surroundings for almost three hours and it was nutrition time but he did not feel like eating. His mouth was not even dry and his breathing was slow and relaxed he felt under his armpit for any dampness and it felt dry. He thought that maybe his sweat was been taken up by the air. What did not fit in was his lack of water for he did not feel thirsty. However, through his training he withdrew his flask of liquid drink and took a swig. Normally he would have held the flask to his lips and have a long drink allowing the sweetish fluid to fill the back of his throat before he removed it from his lips. Indeed he would have three to four such drinks if he was on the ship before he replaced the flask. As it was the one swig was all he had and as if in a daze he replaced the stopper and slid the flask into his shoulder pack.

He continued to walk forward but he drifted and had to blink his eyes several times to clear his vision, he felt as though he was staggering after an evening of drinking too much wine. He settled himself and began to place one foot in front of the other. It was still bright light and he knew that he had approximately four more hours of daylight. He looked around him and felt a bit woozy again then he saw an opening in the trees ahead and so he headed in that direction to catch the sight of the sun. His staggering appeared to have left him but he had a feeling of euphoria again similar to having a few glasses of wine and he began to smile to himself maybe Tara was playing a joke by replacing the nutrient solution with some wine. He took out the bottle and held his analyser next to it and sure enough it read nutrient solution. There was indication of alcohol present.

Ah!, he laughed then it must be the air, too much natural oxygen in lungs accustomed only to manufactured breathing air of the parent ship of which he was a worker for the past five years. That is what is making me heady he laughed loudly to himself and he was startled when the sound of his laughter echoed back at twice the decibels as was released. Ha! there must be a wall or obstacle nearby which is acting like an echo chamber. He picked up the pace making for the sunlight opening which he saw just ahead of him but after awhile he let out a loud "Helloooo", only to wait for almost 10 seconds and have it ricochet back at least fifty times louder. It hurt his ears and he placed his hands over the pinna and ran into the opening which was only a small patch of grass covered area not more than a hundred metres square. He stopped and looked up at the sun above, which was beginning to slant towards the western sky. His head settled and he drew in a deep breath and as if by magic his senses were alert. He looked high into the canopy of the tree nearest him and he thought that his eyes were playing tricks for he thought that there was a green head looking down at him with large brown eyes with a green face and hair—revealing a smile on it's branched shaped face. It was similar to looking at the clouds in a blue sky, where one could see faces of monsters or giants and other things. He looked down and across the verge of the grass at the red bark on the trees similar to the Sequoia, but these were not like those recorded on Earth two thousand years ago. He went over to the trees and as he packed away his recorders and other gadgets he put out a hand to touch the smooth bark and to his utter surprise, it was as though he had touched another human skin.

It was soft and warm and appeared to allow him to keep his hand on its trunk as he stroked it for it was comforting to him as well.

Oh my goodness! What type of tree are you, he thought to himself. It is not something that he had ever experienced and he thought that he would collect some samples the next day and do a quick DNA analysis for the records. When he removed his hands, a mist of small pollen like dust appeared to drop out of the branches. Leslie looked up and saw the microscopic mist of pollen grains dropping aimlessly on him and around him and then he felt for the first time a small cool breeze brush at his naked face. Leslie did not tie up the fact that his stroking the bark of the tree and the pollen grains as well as, the wind as being connected in any way. Again he had a quick glance at his watch and looked up at the clear blue sky which was changing to a dark blue as the sun began to slope away and thought that this was just as good a place to stay as any. So he began to unpack his small tent and to make preparations for sleep for he was feeling quite relaxed. He extracted a damp wipe for his face, armpits and groin area. He also thought that it was time to urinate but he did not feel the urge for any toilet relief. His body needed to acclimatise itself to a terrain existence, he thought to himself.

Like his training ritual he set up his communicator antennae and laid out his bed pack for the night. He stored the wet wipe into his small garbage container .and lay his scooter pack on the ground unopened. He placed his tent near to the tree which he had stroked and thought that he would use the slight hump at the root as an elevation for his pillow. Again Leslie looked at his rations but did not feel like any food at all. He thought that he would scout around to look for some source of water as the silence did not betray any sound of water fall or streams or rivers as been close to where he was. These giant trees needed a lot of moisture to produce all this organic material

There must be huge underground rivers or aquifers or the roots of these trees must burrow very deep indeed to draw up moisture necessary for the formation of all this cytoplasm in the leaves and the flowers and fruit—cones which appear at the end of the pine and spruce branches. There was little or no humidity in the atmosphere to nurture this gargantuan forest.

As Leslie settled down to his light chores which was part of an automatic behaviour as a result of a training ritual which he has had to do for as long as he could remember, he thought how lucky they were to have stumbled onto this biblical "Garden of Eden". These very large great trees, which appear to form a cathedral ceiling over four to five hundred metres high, with the unusual bark appear to be so healthy and clean, where no crevices for insects to hide and feed are available. That was the other notable fact the total lack of insects, so these plants must be all fertilised by wind. But even the wind was limited to a sub sensitive level just enough to keep his skin cool and relaxed. Again he looked at the trees and mentally noted the presence of a tree similar to the cedar, birches which had a pure white smooth bark appeared as though they were white washed with a bright white paint and the slight ripple or hum from a poplar tree were all that he could superficially record. As far as he could detect there were little suspended organic material and no microbes were detected in the air. If there is a lot of organic material suspended in the atmosphere then there tended to be even more microbes also suspended, since they ride the wind on "the flying carpets" of dust and other organic material.

Les intended to take samples of dirt, organic soil material, take specimens from as many trees as possible and to take his time doing the DNA typing and cataloguing in the nest few days. He felt that he should make preparations for the night. He knew from their earlier monitoring that the temperature would not change much in the night and he was sure that with the low humidity there would be little risk of inclement weather. He settled down surrounding himself with monitors, communication links on alert and decided to just lay down under the azure blue sky and dream a bit. A quick check of his surrounded paraphernalia brought a sense of incongruity and shock to him for the first time his little collection of devices looked so limited and insignificant. However, he let the thought pass away just as quickly as it came to him. He did feel the urge to remove his foot wear and heavy trousers and upper shirt. He laid them out in orderly mosaic on the floor of his tent. He placed another ground sheet on the ground outside his tent and when he lay on it, there was a feeling of softness as though he was lying on a mattress of cotton. He smiled to himself and said loudly as though he was talking to fellow campers, "well to night I shall camp out doors, since I have never done this before it will be for my personal diary".

He touched the two transparent patches on the ground sheet and a soft light glowed and as it got darker, his light looked soft and comforting. His whole body began to feel a cool glow for his skin had not been exposed to anything other than to the artificial environment of their space ships. As the light disappeared, he was aware of a sweet odour just in the air and he walked up to his pillow tree and sure enough there was an stronger odour coming from "his" tree. It was invigorating and he reached out to stroke the strong smooth bark again. To his surprise the whole tree appeared to shudder to his minuscule stroking He laughed and try to push it harder but the feeling on his naked hand was like pushing the muscle of his wrestling friend when he worked out. He stopped turned around and leaned against the trunk, slowly sliding down to a sitting position. Again there was a slight shower of pollen and a cool breeze which moved the upper leaved and blew against his face and bare legs. It was soothing and he felt the need to just rest but he knew that he had a silly smile on his face. He reached out and turned off the communicator next to his ground sheet for he could feel its throb. He thought I shall contact the others in the morning for I need a good rest tonight. He had covered over 25 kilometres today very easily and his recorders and monitors were documenting his every move. A quick and automatic look at his time locator, showed it to early evening and he still did not feel the need for either water or food. As he lay down and looked up at the now deep twilight, unusual clusters of stars began to show in the distance.

This was also comforting since he was always surrounded by night time and stars for most of his working life. That strange and delightful breeze again appeared to stay close to his body rendering a delightful languor which brought on a pleasant drowsiness. As sleep came on him he reached out for his defender laser weapon and dragged it close to his chest. He smiled and thought of how stupid this action was but his conditioned training just made this a reflex action. Les laid on his back and had a last look at the covering branches of his protective tree and from that position he noticed the large swellings of cone-like structures hanging at the end of each branch. From this vantage they seem to appear larger but it just could that with the darkness now in the canopy everything did appear to have a larger attachment shadow. With this thought he was fast asleep.

Les felt his eyes open first before he moved. He was aware that he was quite alert but did not move his hand felt the security of the laser comforting in his hand. He continued to breathe regularly as if he was still asleep. It was still night but it was a bright night and this in itself was odd since there were no other circulating moons which would have reflected the light of the single sun and the stars were several million light years away to have little or no effect in providing any light. From this foetal position, he looked around at his surroundings and all appeared to be the same, but there was a continuous breeze which was still providing a soft kiss to the skin only now it was continuous. The sweet smell of the evening was replaced by a distinct lavender one just as pleasant to the senses. His monitors were still on as was his bed sheet light. He slowly shifted his weight and stretched out rolling onto his back, keeping his eyes slitted. This gave the impression of total relaxation. He looked down towards his feet and through the V shape of his feet which was pointed towards the open grassy patch, which now appeared yellow golden in this bright twilight. He thought that it must be the reflection of his monitor lights but they were so dim and could not have given such a bright colour reflection.

CONTACT

Leslie found that his hearing was acute with that peculiar slight ringing which was as a result of the total absence of sound. However, something did wake him up and he was trying to remember what it was. As he lay on his back looking through slit eyes, he glanced up at the trees above and he could still see the canopy even the colour which was darker but still definable. However, he noted the cones at the end of each branch appeared much larger, actually a lot larger and he thought that it must be a trick of the darkness.

He slowly sat up stretched and looked up at the patch of stars in the still dark night. He cautiously rose to a standing position and as he turned around away from the forest to the grassy verge he stopped transfixed for he thought that there was something out of place. He looked hard at the edge furthest away from him and thought that there were small thin trees which were not there earlier. He moved in that direction to examine closer but as he neared the spot, a wind blew around him and the trees rustled. He thought that the small tree was an apparition which appeared to walk away from him or so he thought.

He turned around quickly to his stack of gear and picked up a portable light to shine in the direction of the small tree or at what he had imagined he had seen. It was not there as the yellow beam of light just reflected off the yellow grass. He moved forward again to check out the spot at the edge of the grass verge and there were no small trees but he could now discern a path in the grass so he began to follow it. Looking down to make sure that he was on the path, he cautiously proceeded to search for any obstacles in the path. As he raised up the light to peer ahead he thought he saw a shadow ahead. It was bipedal but very thin and it was moving from one shadow spot to the other away from him.

He shouted " Hello wait!" But the apparition moved rapidly away in the dark.

Then there was the loud echo of his voice booming back to him. It sent shivers along the back of his neck. He stopped and thought was this fear, that he was feeling for this was alien to him.

As he peered into the darkness moving his light from side to side there was nothing he could see. He fixed the light on a clump of grasses which he had no seen the previous day but now he was in new territory. He moved up to it and had a scan around and could only see shadows. This is useless looking in the dark and as he turned around to retrace. His steps putting it all down to an active imagination, he caught a movement out of the corner of his eye and there was movement right next to him. He flashed his light in the direction suddenly and saw a humanoid form leap up to its height of near enough two metres tall, thin brown but what astounded him was the size of its eyes. They were large round white corneas with large brown irises. It looked at him and moved with remarkable speed as though skimming above the surface of the ground. He focussed his light at the departing humanoid form and began to give chase and not looking at the path, which opened into a grass plain.

Leslie was panting a bit by now in the excitement and kept calling "Wait, Hello, don't run away. Hello I am friendly"

He was fast losing ground to the departing figure and he felt for his laser, which he withdrew while on the run and decided to fire above the head of the fast moving figure. It discharged with a loud hiss and showed a flare, where he could see the lank form bend down close to the ground and was scooting low to the ground. His sounds along with the discharge echoed back with such a velocity that he felt himself slide to the ground and rolled over as though pushed from behind. He let out a yelp as he felt his ankle twist under his weight. He knew that he broken his ankle for he had never felt pain like this before. He tried to sit up and when he shone the light he could see the angle of his leg and he immediately knew that it was bad. The pain was excruciating, his laser gun had fallen out of his hand. " Well that was a lovely way to meet folks in a new planet. I have also dropped my guard and not followed orders and training "so this is how failed missions occur", he said loudly.

Leslie began to feel sorry for him self as the pain of his broken ankle began to take all his attention. Every move to straighten his leg and to sit up in a comfortable position brought on sharp pains. He had no foot cover, a small pair of pants and a summer shirt reminiscent of a vacation summer wear. His laser was lost all he had, were his light and his body monitor. He was so involved looking at his ankle and pulling himself up into a sitting position, that he did not see the figure standing next to him. He turned around and shone the light into the face of a thin, humanoid figure that had no artificial vestment covering his torso. It's eyes were large, its head square to rounded. Its arms were spindly ending in three long finger-like appendages. It looked back at Leslie sitting on the ground and reached down to gently push the light away from it's face. Leslie shouted "who are you? Can you speak to me?" The figure ignored his talking and reached for his ankle before he could say much more for he felt a pleasant sound purring in his head. He looked at the gentle tri finger with no nails holding his dangling ankle and realised that it knew he was hurt and was trying to help him

Leslie again heard the purring sound in his head then sounds appeared to come into his mind—words, yes words. "Ah! You are telepathic". The brown head bobbed up and down and a finger was placed over its mouth. Leslie caught on, he must be making too much noise so he focussed his thoughts into the first question " Who are you?"

The purring sound came again " you will know all soon. Please stay quiet while I heal your broken appendage"

Before he could inquire as to how it would be done, two soft fingers were placed on his temples and he felt himself relax. He closed his eyes but could only feel his legs straighten out and he was gently pushed into a prostrate position. He found that he could not open his eyes but he was also relaxed and his pain had disappeared.

SEE NO EVIL

Leslie awoke as if from a deep sleep and either by his training or from a practised habit, his eyes opened first before he moved. He quickly recalled his chase and meeting the strange bi ped then he furtively reached down to feel his ankle and as he carefully flexed it there did not appear to be any problem. Did I dream this whole episode? He was on his ground sheet but his position was not against the tree with the warm bark but in the middle of the dense forest under the hugh canopy. He relaxed from his foetal sleeping position and rolled onto his back.. He then sat up and looked around and about him. As he surveyed his position, there was a pleasant buzzing in his head and words came to him, "Halloo! are you feeling better?"

He stood up and whirled around and could see nothing but the trunks of the trees with the dappled sunlight playing about the high branches.

He relaxed and closed his eyes, "Yes, I am. Where are you?"

"Would you like to see me?", came the reply.

"Yes, I really would and thanks for healing my foot," he replied. He was getting the hang of speaking his thoughts by this very pleasant telepathic form.

" Is your name Leslie Ram," asked the inquisitive buzz in his head.

"Why yes!, that is what I am called," he replied. Leslie noted that the buzz was no longer the lead into the conversation.

"What is your name," he quickly added. "And where are you?" Les asked as he kept turning and looking around.

"I am called Proto, hee, hee," came the very pleasant reply. Les could not believe that he heard a giggle in his head.

"Do you always have so many questions in your head all the time," asked Proto."Hee, hee, hee"

Les began to laugh to himself as he continued to move around and look in all the passages through the trees. " I apologise for my inquisitive behaviour and curiosity but I am on a mission to look at your planet," as he bent down to pick up both an analyser and hand held scanner. They were both dead and non functioning. He laid them down and for the first time he felt helpless.

"Your things do not respond?,"asked the voice in his head. "Hee, hee"

"Yes they appear to be non functioning. I do not understand why since I checked them out last evening and they were fine" replied Les trying to keep the dialogue going.

" Hee, Hee, I did that, Hee," replied Proto.

"Oh! You did that," laughed Les nervously. "Why did you damage my equipment," he cautiously inquired.

"They are not damaged," replied Proto. "But your thing made a lot of noise, so we made them quiet, Hee, hee." he continued.

" What thing?" then, Leslie remembered firing off his laser gun over the head of Proto in his chase. " Proto, I did not mean to hurt you I just wanted you to stop and meet with me. I am truly sorry and please accept my apology". Leslie was truly apologetic.

There was a silence then a slow buzz came into his head again but no sound. Les raised his head and asked "Proto are you still there?" please accept my apology.

"I really did not mean to hurt you or anyone else. I just wanted to make contact since I thought that there were only the trees present on this planet, so your appearance startled me. I am truly sorry for my hasty action".

" My scanner did not detect your presence, Proto", continued Leslie. He had a feeling that he was losing contact and whirled around again looking around him.

" I know that you meant no harm to Proto and his family and I also know that your family is also safe with us," replied Proto.

" Have you contacted my other friends' proto? Are they all right?" asked Leslie with some concern. There was a long pause before the reply came from Proto.

" In answer to you question, we have not made contact with your family. Secondly, they appear to be "all right" and have shown great interest in the ecosystem of our home. In your words, they are OK Hee, hee".

Proto continued preventing Leslie from asking another question, " We thought that it was best to make contact with only you since you have shown warmth to our brethren by stroking them and showing affection to them".

Leslie had no idea of what he had done to get such a response from Proto and thought better than to ask what it was. Besides he was getting quite accustomed to this form of mental communication, which he found to be exhilarating.

"Proto where are you I cannot see you and I am looking around for a focus from where your thoughts are coming. Is there a problem that you are hiding from me? Why did you choose to contact only me and not my colleagues,,, Oh! I mean my family?" Was the earnest inquiry from Leslie?

There was a long pause before a reply came " Les ..lie, you have too many thoughts floating in your mind. We will answer all your questions and what you wish to know......only do not use your vocal..... apparatus for it startles.... my, our...family." came Proto's response.

To Leslie this response appeared laboured as if Proto was receiving instructions from a third party. He could also feel a background buzz in the back of his mind but he could not concentrate to decipher any significant thought. Maybe this was the equivalent of whispering in telepathy. He could however, feel himself mastering this form of communication and for some unknown reason to him, it was like he was at junior school again and learning something new.

He could feel an excitement of achievement and he knew that he would pass. It was a strange and pleasant feeling of youth learning quickly and becoming confident and wants to move ahead more quickly. This was how it was when he was in junior school and had a mind like a sponge and when everyday was exciting for there was something new to learn and master. It appears that Proto through his telepathy subliminal coaching of Les, had dug deep into his sub conscious and chosen to awake the same youthful learning ability with it's corresponding endorphin stimulation This in turn lead to this excitement that he was feeling for the first time in quite sometime. There was the total lack of fear and apprehension at what he was experiencing.

And he loved every minute that he had telep—communicating with Proto. He tried several times to think of the logical protocol to follow when meeting a new species but it appeared that all his training had vanished and he had to find out as much as possible. He felt for his personal attached recorder, which was attached to his inside shirt and pressed onto his chest. He had a quick glance at this monitor and saw the dim light on so he felt that all will be recorded and so he did not have to worry about following any set protocol. These thoughts raced through his mind and he wondered if they were being interpreted by his unseen contact.

He called out mentally, " Proto are you still there?" "Yes Les... lie right behind you". Leslie turned around with a start only to see the full sight of his contact. He was astonished and startled. In broad daylight, Proto was as tall as he was which was near enough six feet but he had little bulk. Narrow shoulders, skin brown and smooth, his most prominent feature was the box-like head with those huge brown eyes which were so expressive. His feet also ended in three toes which did not have any nails. They were clubbed toes with a flat sole. He had no sex organs between his legs. His mouth was a very small slit and where his nose should be were two small holes on a very small promontory. He had no ears with a pinna, just two small holes at the side of his huge head, relative to the rest of his body. His eyes moved up from time to time to the top of his cornea when he was communicating with Les.

"Oh! You startled me, Proto. Can you make yourself invisible? Were you behind me all the time," asked the excited Les.

"Too many questions too fast. Sorry Les...lie, for startling you. No. and No.. Hee...hee", Proto's eyes went up as though he was laughing.

Les laughed and kept a smile on his face then continued " Oh Proto !, I am so excited to meet you especially when I or we thought that there was no animal life much less humanoid form on the planet just these beautiful, magnificent trees. Our scanners must be malfunctioning for we would have prepared differently to meet with your people".

"In fact we would not have landed on the planet since it is our people's policy not to contact alien life forms for fear of being misinterpreted as being invaders", continued the excited Leslie.

"Les...lie, slow down. We were with you always. Your scan... ner did not mal..function. We did not wish to be seen so we stayed in our ..hive ..eh..home", responded Proto.

"Shh.. Let me continue Les..lie. Look at my ..our family they are also excited to meet you. Would you like to meet our family, Les..lie?."

Leslie beamed at this brown face with the laughing eyes. "Oh Proto, I would love to meet your family and to see your...hive, if you will lead the way".

"Les..lie there is no way to go look at the trees, our hive," and he pointed to the trunks of the trees.

Leslie was startled for from every tree bodies separated from the trunk of the trees like plastercene and before his eyes each tree was surrounded by so many of Proto-like forms that soon the forest was full of these bodies forming a circle of several individuals deep. There was also a sweet smell of lavender and spice filling the air around Prot and Leslie.. Then his head began to buzz, as Proto raised his three fingered skinny arm—all heads were immediately bowed and only one voice was telepathically transmitted.

" It is good to meet you ..Les..lie. Welcome to our hive and our family. We will show you all you wish to know".

Les looked at Proto who kept looking at Leslie through out this latter communication, with his eyes looking up to the top of his head then down in a most expressive way. They were kind eyes.

Proto looked directly at him and said "Les..lie, it is better if only one communicates with you. If the whole family communicates at the same time—ah mm, Hee ..hee your head would be hurt. You cannot take this stress right now, maybe after some time..."

"Proto the trees, are they your home ah hive?" asked the startled Les.

"Hee...hee no Les..lie, we are the trees and the trees are us" replied Proto." I will show you how we are one in one, but later".

"You need to rest," said Proto and from the crowd a little whistle arose like that of a twit sparrow, soft and melodious. 'From the top of the trees, a light dust of pollen descended on all of them and they all opened their little slit of mouths and inhaled this dust. Leslie looked up and opened his mouth and stuck out his tongue to trap some of this pollen.

This was observed by the mass of beings and then the buzz began in his head first like a laugh then like an overwhelming roar which made him dizzy and as he looked around him at all the little slits with pink insides all staring at him, he felt faint and turned to Proto whose eyes opened even wider appeared to be concerned and he raised his hand. The family immediately bent their heads and the sound of the buzzing stopped immediately.

"We are sorry Les..lie, the family thought that you looked funny sticking out the lip in your mouth and they all wanted to...laugh, like you. It was too much it will not happen again. You must rest".

"As Les turned around he was amazed at how quickly all the life forms attached and literally melted into the trees. In less than a minute there was only Proto and himself.

Les looked at the pleasant face of his host Proto and asked "Proto what is the name of your people or race who lives in the tree?"

Again those laughing eyes, "we are called Proto and this the Birthplace," Proto simply replied.

"You rest now and we will show you how we live in the Birthplace"

Leslie was beginning to feel quite relaxed and indeed he felt as though he could crash on the soft floor of needles and just go to sleep. Instead he went to his ground sheet near one of the trees walking with Proto, who was pointing him towards it and then Proto said "Les..lie, you will sleep at my hive" as he pointed to the tree where his tent and ground sheet was laid out. Les thought that Proto would just melt into his head 'pillow' tree and smile at the thought. He had hardly sat down when he turned to the nearby Proto, yawned looked at him and said " It does not look like night time as yet but I am very tired and sleepy. Thank you for all you have done today. You are very lovely folks" He rolled onto his sheet and was fast asleep. Proto looked at him shifted his eyes up then melted into the tree.

HEAR NO EVIL

Leslie could not remember any of his dreams as he opened his eyes through slitted lids. He cautiously tried to recall all that he thought he had seen yesterday or was it all just a dream. .He looked from his fetal position at the forest opposite from him and all he could see were trees and the dappled sunlight filtering through the upper branches. He rolled over onto his back and was shocked to see Proto sitting at his back with those large expressive eyes, he was jolted but smiled and sat up immediately. Proto stood up and began to walk away, Leslie followed and he found that he was light on his feet and very energetic. "Sorry Proto, I must have over slept. Were you waiting long for me to arise?"asked Les with a bright smile.

"Proto also moved his smiling eyes and said "Proto did not wait for you to awake, Les..lie"." I have brought you to the Birthplace, so that all will be explained to you", he continued.

" Ha Proto!, you have brought me or you will take me to the Birthplace" replied Les with his beaming smile. He was pleased that all he could remember did happen and he had met with this new species.

" No Proto brought you to the Birthplace and he pointed to the back of Les, who turned around to see the most fantastic site before him. He was never here last evening and he turned enquiring eyes back to Proto. Before he could ask the obvious question, Proto placed one of his digit to his small slit of a mouth. Les realised that he would be told everything especially how they transported him and his little cluster of space paraphernalia without waking him. While it would have torn at his mind as to how they did he just was so full of enthusiasm and goodwill that he turned and followed Proto to the site of one of the greatest trees that anyone could have imagined. They were looking at the largest Sequoia with a width that blanketed his vision so he thought he was staring at a huge red wooden trunk, which obstructed their path with no end in sight.. He looked up and the canopy of the tree, with massive branches extending for hundreds of feet in the air and it covered such a massive area that there were no other trees which could be seen anywhere around. This one tree was a forest to itself. He stepped back to look upwards and could not see the top because of the branches which were letting the sunshine to lighten up the whole mass.

His neck was straining as he ran first to the right and turned to Proto with questioning eyes then he raced along the root to the left. He just could not bring the whole monstrous size tree into any perspective. He returned to where Proto was standing and he heard a sharp buzz which startled him as his head sharply turned with a reflex towards Proto, whose head was bowed. He reached over to touch Proto for the first time and he felt a warm smooth skin give under his touch. Proto raised up his head and his eyes were smiling and moving up and down in his hugh big head as though they not under control. Les quickly moved his hand and Proto's eyes began to settle down in his face.

"Sorry Proto, were you praying to the mother tree .. Ah Birthplace", Les was confused.

Proto began to mimic Les giggle " Do not distress yourself, Les..lie, you Hee...hee.. tickled me

when you touched me. It made me excited for your touch is very...very ..stimulating to us. It was told to us the first time you touched our hive where you slept the first night. So we all know what your touch is like. Later I shall pass your touch to all the family." thank you Les..lie.

I must now try to answer some of your questions. Close your eyes and let me explain".

Proto moved closer to the root of the giant red wood and they sat on the root ridge. Les sat down and immediately closed his eyes.

A pleasant buzz began in the front of his head then went to the mid of his brain. It then changed into a sweet"lullaby like" song :—

"Leslie" came the soft voice. "The trees and us Proto are one and the same. Look at my branches and you will see the large round fruits hanging at the end of my branches. These are the new Proto which will be fertilised this evening. We are trees but we are the Prot also. When you touch the trunk of the tree, you touch us the Proto. Your hands are warm and it is pleasing to us. If you did not touch the bark

of the tree or stroked it we would never have shown ourselves to you. But we searched your mind when you were asleep and we found that you did not bear us harm. We wanted to make contact since you wished to "take samples" from us. That would have destroyed some of our family. Your friends also want samples so we have given them some of our departed Proto. I will ask that you follow what Proto ask you to do for you will see the reason for our existence as well as your existence. Your questions will be answered—have patience"

"Proto hold Leslie's appendage and show him our role in the universe". Leslie keep your eyes shut and all will be projected into your mind—trust us."

Leslie nodded a positive or agreeable assent and then wondered if they understood what a nod meant. He smiled to himself and he relaxed totally. Through his slitted eyelids, he held out his hands to Proto, whose finger barely touched his. They then both began to rise up the slope of the tree and he noted Proto's digit on the other hand just barely touching the trunk of the great red Sequoia. It was if they were in an old fashion elevator described in the old text books of the twenty second century of his home planet earth. They both rose up the shear trunk of the great red and settled several hundred feet above the ground on a branch which had the width for ten of their shuttle craft to park comfortable next to each other. The finger digit contact with Proto separated as they settled on their feet. Proto pointed to the edge of the smaller sub branches and then to the giant leaves and finally to the large globular round fruiting bodies each about the size of two soccer balls. They were brown and looked soft as they bobbed slightly. They both stood comfortably where they could see the rest of the forest in the distance. Les could also see a large savannah grass covered plain out through the branches. He could also see the sunshine bright as ever and even the swaying of the large green to yellow golden grass. Th si was different from what he had been seeing for the last few days.

There was a creaking sound as if the whole tree was shuddering but only just slightly. A wind came up it was gentle and cool to the skin. He was still inspecting the height of the tree and the massive branches which could have supported the rail system used in the mother ship to move personnel and supplies around. It was strange that he made such an analogy to the mother ship for he was watching a tree, which was a huge forest in its own rite but was almost as big indeed even bigger than the mother ship. This mother ship carried over one thousand men, women with supplies of food, water and parts for the shuttles and probes enough to remain in space for over ten years. Granted when the opportunity presented itself to take on supplies then the mother ship availed itself to do so but this was a rare occurrence.

In the midst of his mental rambling he felt a touch on his arm and Proto told him to sit down on the branch. Just as they both had sat down, there was another stronger breeze which appears to persist and from this vantage point, Les could see and hear the leaves tinkling or rustling above and around them He could also hear the hard rubbing of the branches as they were pitched against each other but this only occurred at the ends of the forks of the giant red tree, which hardly showed any effect of this wind. He did see the fruiting globes swinging at the ends of the ultimate branches. Then Proto pointed out beyond the tree at a mass of small white umbrella-like seedlings blowing in the wind headed for the Sequoia. Proto appeared to be excited while Les could not quite understand the reason as it just appeared that some tree had just discharged it's flowers on their umbrella like parachute apparatus so that they could fall else where and germinate. Earth Botany was not quite what he had expected but it was rather close. As they both watched intently at the horde of white umbrellas approach, two things were apparent fist they moving positively towards their tree and secondly this was not random distribution, for it appears as if the Sequoia was actually setting up the breeze or wind to bring these botanical bodies towards its branches.

It was not long before the upper branches mainly at the end with the leaves and globule like fruit were having these umbrella forms attached to each and everyone. As soon as the umbrella form was attached to the round brown fruit it was adsorbed onto and into the fruiting body. Another amazing observation was that there were no spare globule or left over umbrella seeds. Every one of the umbrella forms were used. Proto touched Les' arm and they both stood up as a huge earthquake like shudder rocked the giant tree. It only lasted for a brief few seconds but threw them both on their backsides. The big brown eyes of Proto danced as though he was truly happy. He reached out to touch digit to finger and Les did as he was told and closed his eyes. He could feel them elevate and then begin to descend and it was not long before they were on the ground Proto beckoned him to follow for he had a determined look about him which was not observed before. As they went along the back side of the tree which was on the opposite side to where they had began, Les could see the grassy plains in the distance away from the massive trunk of the tree.

Proto lead them away from the tree towards the field of swaying grasses. For the first time Les felt he had to extend himself physically to keep up with the fast moving or gliding Proto who was intent in moving forward with some urgency. This was not the time to ask any questions as Les knew that he was receiving answers to questions as he went along. After about thirty minutes of a most harried walk, they came to the verge of the grassy plains and Les was taken back at the height of the grass which was indeed golden but the reeds were five to six feet tall. Proto turned around and pointed back at the tree. At this distance the top branches of the tree were still extended just beyond them. Les turned in the direction of the pointed digit just in time to see a greatly enhanced size of the globules or fruiting body. The fruits were expanding into large circular bodies. Then a magnificent site took place as these huge suspended fruiting bodies transformed the huge tree into a large decorated Christmas tree with these suspended bodies dominating the size of the upper branches. Then the wind as if by some defined signal, Les was beginning to be aware, began to skim across the grass with more of a force than he had ever felt before. It just could be that he was in the open for the first time and could feel its force and they had to anchor themselves as it was coming from their back across the grassy plains swaying the grass reeds and making a swishing sound. They felt as the force of the wind passed by and around them to cascade up the hugh tree and almost at a signal, the fruiting bodies which were now over four feet in diameter began to fall to the ground.

Les would have imagined that they would have broken, 'like a ripe melons' as they hit the ground. On the contrary the huge brown bladders hit the soft needle covered carpeted ground which was everywhere, they just laid there not even bouncing or rolling. It was if these 'boulder' like shapes were being caught by the carpeted ground. He observed that as they hit the ground there were no reverberations or shock as some of these fell just in front of where they were standing. He went forward to touch one which was just six feet away from him, Proto made no effort to prevent him. He could see the soft smooth brown surface and he touched they were warm and soft. Like the bark of the tree which he had touched the very first day he went into the forest, the sensation was the same. But in the sunshine these soft to the touch bodies began to harden into almost granite like hardness. Les found this speeded up process similar to the formation of spores in botany and in microbes. This process occurred when there were adverse conditions such as the absence of water or extreme conditions, when "microscopic forms of life sporulates" to protect themselves. This was all part of his basic training where he dealt with the microscopic forms of life not with huge trees.

The analogy was the same with one exception, the planet and environment was still lush with some concealed water, sunlight and all the trees and vegetation appeared to be healthier than ever. He turned to see that Proto was keenly observing his actions with those large laughing eyes.

Before he could phrase a thought to ask what he had in mind, Proto placed a single digit to his slit of a mouth and Les heard the following:

"Les..lie, you do understand much about other forms of life. Proto and his family use this method to extend our family. Inside these eggs are small Proto which are developing into big Proto and then into trees when they are ready. This crop of Proto will not stay with us for they have a new job to do. The soft shell hardens quickly to protect the young Proto. We are happy for there are a lot more Proto formed more than we have ever had in my life time which in your time is over one hundred and fifty

years. These baby Proto, in their eggs will be collected by us and he pointed behind Les who turned around to see a mass of Proto descend into the fields from under the great tree and began to roll these 'eggs' towards the grassy plains, which was in their direction. Proto again interrupted Les' thought and said let us look from above and get out of the way. The whole process was being carried out with absolutely no noise or confusion. He turned to touch the extended digit of Proto and closed his eyes, he felt the gentle elevation and ascendance above the ground. His legs were dangling but for some unknown reason he felt safe, as though he would not fall. Proto said 'Les..lie, open your eyes and look down.' Just by the touching of Les' hands they were suspended over fifty feet above the ground. Les could see as Proto showed him this field which was very vast and which hid hundreds if not thousands of these boulders strewn through out the plains and these newly formed ones were added by the mass of Proto below who were rolling them into the grass and returning back into the forest. Les watched fascinated by the spectacle below him. He felt them begin to descend just outside the grassy plains.

When they were back on the ground, without any communication, Proto turned and set a rapid pace for Les to follow him back into the forest. It was quite a walk and from time to time, Les looked at the Proto who were also walking rapidly into the forest. Some were pale cream coloured others were white to grey in colour, while there were a few yellow others red and a few really black ones. Some had different coloured eyes ranging from different shades of brown to green and blue while others had almost red corneas. For the first time in daylight Les saw the population of this planet. As this moving crowd of Proto entered the forest they seemed to just disappear. He could see a few attach themselves to trees but they just vanished until only Proto and he were standing alone under the 'mother tree'. Les found himself understanding these life forms and he also found that all he had was just wonder for what he had just witnessed and a strange affection for these beings who were turning out to be far superior to his species. His scientific mind just kicked in and thought that this was just a different form of evolution, which after all just fitted into his training in biology. He was becoming comfortable with this explanation to himself. He looked up at the huge canopy of the red wood tree which even more vast with the absence of the fruiting bodies. Proto had remained very quiet on the return trip almost pensive.

They stopped at the base of the tree and there laid out on the ground was his tent and ground sheet. He was amazed to see all his space possessions being carried around and laid out each time exactly as he had done so meticulously the first night. His sense of humour kicked in and he thought that the Proto were almost "taking the rise out of his ritual". However if it made him feel comfortable and happy let the space visitor have his blanket and toys with him

as he prepared for sleep. Proto told Les to look up and to extend his inner lip—his tongue.

Les had learned by now that the floating 'pollen grains' which he adsorbed were the only nutrition he had since meeting the Proto and he was also aware that he did not need to use the toilet or to drink water wherever it was. He looked at his rations but they remained untouched.

Even his communicator and monitoring devices were up and supposedly running. He did not seem to care whether they were or not for some strange reason—it was not important at this time.

Anyhow after licking at the falling pollen grains, which dropped from the top of the tree he was told by Proto to rest on his sheet. Les did feel as though he was tired and his eyes began to feel heavy. He wondered if the pollen was a drug or some narcotic, which brought on his sleepiness but they were on the move for a long time. He had lost all sense of time.

"Les..lie, the 'pollen' is food and it is good for Proto and you. It does not bring on sleep. By your time you have been awake for twelve hours of your day time. Proto must rest like you but we do not keep your time for rest and work. So you must ret for I must show you the night when we meet again. Proto must go to his family but he will always be close to you.. Stop thinking so much Les..lie"

By the time Proto had finished his speech Les found himself laying into his usual fetal sleeping position and before he could answer he could feel himself nod off.

METEORITES—THE PERFECT TRANSPORT SYSTEM

Les work up suddenly, to the call of some strange noise or call, which emanated from his dream. He could remember very little of his dreams which always seemed to be pleasant. He did his usual slit eyes routine and did not move until he scanned his surroundings. It looked as though it was still night time and he had no idea how long he had been asleep. He looked up and saw that he was lying on his sheet under the hugh canopy of the great red Sequoia tree but he could see quite clearly through the trees so there was some light around as he was contemplating his solitude he felt very rested then he felt a slight buzz which was so fleeting that he could have just ignored it but he knew that he was been tuned into. He closed his eyes and reached out in his mind calling mentally to Proto, asking "Proto are you there?". A voice close to him said why do you distrust Proto, Les..lie, came the reply?."

"Proto why do you ask such a question, I do not distrust you," replied Les.

" Then why do you awake and look around you before you open your eyes fully. It looks as though you feel that you will be hurt by some being" Proto continued.

Les was getting so used to telepathy so he just smiled to himself and said "Proto how could you know how I awaken myself?" he slyly replied knowing that he was found out.

"I know, Les..lie, because I have watched you every time you have to be awaken" was the deliberate response.

"At this Les sat up straight and stood up looking around him rapidly. There right above him on a very tall branch was Proto sitting looking down at him with his bright big brown eyes flicking in a smiling way at him.

" Proto how long have you been here? Did you wake me with

that buzz?" came the rapid confused questions as from someone who had prematurely awaken.

"Shhh...", Proto, placed his mid digit to his slit mouth and his expressive eyes danced even more like the false eyes of the children dolls of the twentieth century, he had seen in the museum back on earth as a young lad. "Too many questions, I have been here all night. I thought that as it was close to night time again I wanted you to see the transporters in the sky. So yes I gave you a ;little nudge"

Les looked up at the smiling eyes of the figure, which remained perched over him suspended on the huge limb of the red tree. Proto looked so small at that great height. He smiled back and then Proto raised his spindly arm and pointed to him with the three fingers lined up tightly alongside each other. "Close your eyes, Les..lie".

Les did as he was told maintaining a fixed smile on his face. He felt his body sway and he knew that he was rising and he opened his eyes through slits only to see the ground being left under him as he rode up in an invisible elevator and in a few seconds he was sitting next to Proto, who folded his tiny arms. His eyes were even more expressive which gave the impression of a smiling person. Proto did not appear to have the muscles in his face even though his head was very large compared to the rest of his body. But this form of communication which is peculiar to humans was definitely present and could be felt by Les.

"Proto how do you move me so quickly and easily? Where do you get the power to lift and elevate up and down the trees?" inquired Les.

"Les..lie, you must be part of the whole life force. The mother tree gives us power to move to protect and to assist her with keeping the young Proto safe in the fields. Just as she made the wind to bring on fertilization or pollination so new Proto would be formed, she gives us the power to move around quickly and it is better to move through the air rather than walk. When Proto enter into the trees we are all connected and we meet our family immediately" was the simple reply. Our mother tree controls all our movements, provides all food shelter and distributes the Proto as they are needed to work and to assist her with her plans—like I am helping her with you. Les..lie, you are my project !".

A pang of caution or warning passed through Les' mind. If he did not feel so protected and relaxed he would have become very suspicious and almost as reflex he asked Proto as they were both looking away in the distance through the huge branches, "What do you mean Proto, by saying that I am your project?".

Proto looked at him directly and for once the brown colour of his eyes were just slightly shimmering in the middle of his large white cornea and not dancing about, " I asked to be the one to show you who we were and to introduce Proto to your enquiries for we were all watching you. You touched my hive first and we liked it when you touched it. All Proto also felt your touch. We know that you have a life task and so we must help you to do that task since it concerns us. I asked to be the one to do the task for the hive. It was then granted by the mother tree that I should have the project—therefore you are my project"..

Prot continued giving more information—"Mother Tree causes the darkness to come, the pollen to feed us and allow us to become trees that hold all together. She also watches the Universe to see the different quadrants of the universe and when it is time to move our home or Planet and Sun from this area of the universe she will move them to another part by calling for help to others in the Universe" Proto kept his eyes looking into the night sky and Les was fascinated looking at this new species which was telling him a child bed time story. But all was said with none of the joy of story telling or of fiction. Les knew that this new species which he just managed to meet was telling the truth to him as a matter of fact.

"Tonight you will see our Proto Translocator as it comes into the quadrant but first you and I will go down to the golden grass fields where we saw the new Proto added to the old unborn. However, I must show you some of the lifeless fertilization, very sad thing before we go down to the fields. In order to show it I must ask that you close your eyes as we travel for it will be hard on your physique, Les..lie", he concluded. Les, found that while he understood much of the "religious life" of Proto he felt that this being was relating the folk lore of his community. Being diplomatic he decided that he will not indulge in any discussion of religious or biological philosophy. Indeed he felt that he quite understood what the huge biological or rather botanical forms, were doing over the complete surface planet, is what he had already known to happen in basic Botany.

It was advanced in that somehow the trees hid the zoological life forms within their insides. He was willing to believe what Proto had said that both the zoological and botanical forms of life on this very unusual planet may be inextricable bound together but then that also would be feasible. His biology knowledge was from his terran planet, Earth and it was an accepted fact that animals, birds and insects all work to the cycle of the flowering and fruiting of the plants. There were carnivores, which lived on the flesh of herbivores, so indirectly they also were dependent on the botanical forms of life.

For a fleeting moment Les realised that he was carrying out the information search of part of his mission. He looked over at Proto who was staring quietly into the night sky with unblinking eyes. He felt a great fondness for this creature which had asked to be his guide and who had taught him so much. He was about to make telepathic contact with Proto and called out but for some unknown reason he could not form thoughts in his head so he reached over to touch Proto to get his attention and for the first time in a long time tried to use his voice and a horrid croak came out. His eyes for once must have got to the size of Proto for he was struck that he was unable to use his voice. Proto turned and looked at him with a slight upward movement of his brown eyes and spoke out " Did you enjoy being your self, Les..lie?".

Les felt the return of mental communication and with a shock asked, "Proto why did you break mental contact with me?"

The odd ungainly movement of the brown colour of his eyes returned when they appeared to be like a "doll like movement" and to be humorous. Proto replied matter of factly " It is necessary for you to have some privacy and not be part of our hive. When it is time for you to rejoin your family you will not have a problem with leaving us".

Les then wondered about how much control he really had of his thoughts of his planned duties and came to the conclusion that regardless of what he had to do on this mission and what his instructions were he was in fact doing the correct thing by being an ambassador to this odd and fascinating group of life forms. In all his studies of life forms found by earth scout and explorer space vessels, there were little humanoid forms ever encountered. At least those that were found were not intelligent forms capable of communication by any of the known forms to date to earth people. If only his instruments were recording all these wonderful conversations then surely ambassadors will follow up on his pioneer work.

With this thought Les turned to Proto with his biggest smile and said

> *"Your thoughtfulness is to be commended. You have the ability to read all my thoughts and even anticipate my questions before they are formed in my mind and you have both the physical and spiritual power of all your natural surroundings at your command but you have chosen instead to give me an education about who you are and to share you knowledge with me so that I can bring it back to our peoples. Such behaviour is known to be the highest form of civilised behaviour. Thank you, Proto and the mother tree and the rest of your hive for your welcome to this space traveller"*

Les was pleased with this last speech to his alien friend for he was speaking as an ambassador for all earth people. The history of earth's population involved with space exploration is filled with wonderful speeches given by those pioneers, who did the first act or found the first important relic, or made other findings, which fitted into the grand plan designed by much more important and cleverer folks than those actually doing the job. Les thought that he was just an ordinary man doing the science which he loved but in the broader expanse of space. He thought of himself as a kind and understanding man. He also felt that his attributes of not feeling too strongly about most things based on his private philosophy that everyone is entitled to his/her opinion allowed most of the more assertive people to convince others of whatever they are saying. In his case by his quiet demeanour and non combative attitude as well as his attention to the individual making a forceful point gave confidence to the protagonist. This of course made him sort of popular since he was considered to be a "nice bloke" to have around, in actual fact he was just thought be inoffensive. Many knew that he was quite clever at whatever science he was doing but no one really knew other that his closest superiors. He was rarely given the opportunity to talk about his work to anyone since he was always the one listening.

His thoughtful rambling was made to some extent to justify why he was the chosen one. This was an unusual position for Les to be in but then he thought that it had all began by being chosen to come on this mission to begin with. After all his discipline, dealing with the microbes in space, was really one of the most innocuous of all the disciplines. In fact to use the idiom of an earlier time on earth's planet, it was not a "very sexy" subject and only merited any attention when there was an infectious problem. Few of the really brilliant graduates of the Academy ever showed any interest in the subject, other than to make a good grade in the early part of their training so they could go forward on the really "sexy" professions, such as Astrophysics or Cosmo-extrabiology, which essentially dealt with the use of technology to manipulate DNA in a space environment. The main reason was that it was possible to get results in a faster time frame than would be possible, if such experiments were done on earth or in the presence of any gravitational atmosphere. As a result, there were rich rewards and more patents filed in that discipline than any of the other sciences..

In his world he was driven by the rewards of financial security and movement up the administrative ladder, within the Space Exploration Agency. This was one of, if not the most powerful and important Corporation on Earth. This was the goal of many of the students at the Academy, who felt the need to repay their parents in prestige, who supported them through out their academic training. Essentially, Microbiologists were only needed to solve the problem as to why an infectious problem began in the first place. This role evolved later on because scientists could use the ability of microbes to experiment with genetically thus solving many human infectious problems. Much of this was accomplished over two hundreds years ago on Earth. It was then thought that there would be a wonderful opportunity to develop the discipline out in space, where 'new microbes' could be exploited to continue development which was beneficial to earthlings. While this was exciting to begin with, the enthusiasm and support soon petered out because the biochemists developed automated systems which detected the products of microbial respiration hence the need for pure Microbiologists also diminished.

Les yawned then felt Proto touch his arm. "Les..lie, it is time to communicate with Proto. We must go higher up to see the undeveloped Proto and await the passing of the meteors in the sky—it is The Coming.". Les felt the need to ask what "The Coming meant but he knew that all would be explained. So he asked Proto, "How often does' The Coming' appear to the Proto?".

Proto was standing and turned to look at Les, with a serious, intent direct eye to eye contact fixed on Les's question and after a time, he slowly responded, " The last time was over one thousand years ago in your time. Proto and his hive were not there at that time but his earlier family, who were chosen, is still on the golden plains."

" While Proto live for a long time our mother tree know that we must rest, so some Proto volunteer after five to six hundred years to become seeds which form new Proto. Others live to be over two to three thousand years old." Proto extended his digit to Les, who automatically held out his hand to clasp the three digits and closed his eyes. The sensation was imperceptible but by now he could feel the slight movement upwards. He tried to slit his eyes and found that he could and glancing at Proto, who had his neck and head looking upwards, he noticed Proto's other hand was brushing the main trunk but only lightly and it was obvious that the power or force for this movement came from this beautiful, massive red tree. The upper canopy of this mother tree appeared to be younger and healthier as they rose upwards. Les scanned these upper branches, which still appeared to be young and growing and to be swaying in the breeze. They arrived at another lateral branch which allowed visibility at its end to reveal the night sky. It was a dark intense blue rather than a black sky and he could see many star formations but all were unknown to him. By some unknown light he could see a number of small meteors, more like large rocks passing away in the distance. It was if Les was looking through the port hole of the mother space ship which had brought him and the crew to explore this segment of space.

Again Proto touched his arm and communicated, "Les..lie, you will enter the mother tree to see the unborn undeveloped Proto. Hold my digits close to your chest and walk with me to the centre where the branch where we are standing touches the main trunk of the mother tree." Les did as he was asked to do and like two dancers facing each other they did a "crab-like" walk towards the middle of the tree and the trunk of the mother tree had a hugh knot facing them. Proto touched the middle of the knot, which immediately opened and Les found that he was no longer touching Proto's digits but that he was standing in a huge living room type of setting. There was a pale light which emanated from the walls and the opening through which they had just entered closed immediately. Proto was on his knees and his head was bent in some sort of supplication. Les followed automatically and also bowed his head but he went further and placed both the palms of his hands together as though praying. Some of the earth people still do so in some of the quiet corners of Earth. This action by Les, brought a small shiver to the whole tree, which was like a small earth quake commonly felt on earth. Les kept his eyes closed and slightly shifted his weight on his knees to compensate for the movement of the tree which was short lived.

There was a slight ringing in his ears, which was very pleasant then a thin female like voice sand out, "Les..lie you have impeccable manners. Proto was right to ask for you as a project. You have learned much and yes to your question, we do have some imperfections. Feel with your mind as I open up the next chamber for you to see. Les felt an intense happiness as the voice sang out in his mind. He could see another bed chamber as if it was from an old historical earth movie. There was a yellow glow and in it were several of the 'fruit like oval marble like forms' about the size of three to four feet in diameter. He could feel them as hard. He could also see Proto reach out and touch one of them but with the odd digit. There was a bright flash as it immediately split evenly into two halves. A pink glow emanated from inside. He mentally saw himself move to look at the halves and he saw a small Proto lying as though fast asleep inside but coiled in a fetal position. It looked like the inside of a cradle. Then Proto pointed to the feet but they were not separated but appeared joined together like a tear shaped leaf. Then the singing voice say, "this Proto will be absorbed to be food for Me the Mother Tree. A newly formed Proto will be made some time in the future."

Les was astonished at what he had seen and he could still feel his hands clasped in this praying position. He knew that he had been paid one of the best compliments ever from one race or species can ever give to another. A slight breeze caressed his face and almost imperceptibly he found himself standing on the outside branch through which Proto and he had just entered. Proto was looking at him with those dancing brown eyes. He reached out and embraced this thin little lithe figure and felt his arms meeting together at the back. He then realised how physically fragile his friend Proto really was. Proto appeared to be taken by the surprise hug from Les and his eyes moved almost frantically but Les knew that Proto was overwhelmingly happy for this was forced into Les' mind.

Suddenly, there was an extreme brightness penetrating the branches of the canopy of the entire tree and the surrounding area beyond the cover of the tree. The golden grass shone brighter and yellower than ever, indeed the whole sight looked like the painting of one of the wheat fields which he had seen in one of the art gallery museums back on earth. Proto pointed upwards towards the night sky which was also as bright as daylight. Like a ball of yellow and white light came a meteor high up above with a long tail dragging behind but shedding an uncanny light around the whole land area. It arched in the sky some many million miles out in space but its light intensity was too great relative to the small sight in the distance. Just as quickly it disappeared and there was an even more intense darkness. All the bedtime children rambling of Proto were explained in an instant to Les and he could feel an excitement in the air. His guide and protector looked at him and extended his three digits for Les to hold onto as he also automatically closed his eyes. He felt a lifting of his body and he did not feel the urge to open his eyes. There was a constant breeze passing his whole body and it was some time before he felt the light touch of the ground under his feet. Proto's digits did not remove immediately and Les did not open his eyes immediately for he knew that something extraordinary was about to happen.

After what appeared to be about five minutes, in reality it was just about thirty seconds, of his time, he felt the slow melting away of Proto's digits. Les found that they were standing at the edge of the large grassy plains in twilight. They had covered a distance of over ten to fifteen kilometres in just a few minutes. .He was completely taken back by the tremendous activity which was taking place and all very silently. In the time he was with Proto, he was aware of a number of other Proto around. He did see quite a few when the fruiting spores were being rolled into the grassy plains but now they were crowded out by hundreds of moving figures all of whom were Proto-like forms. Proto touched him and they were elevated to about the same height as the day before approximately fifty feet when he the harvesting task done by a collective farming community, very reminiscent of the early nineteen or twentieth century farming practise back on earth, with a difference the farming of salient life forms

From this elevated vantage point Les, could see for the first time the great area of this grass field with its yellow to gold surreal reflected light. He also saw the hundred or thousands of Proto moving towards the perimeter of the field. "Les..lie, we are in the hundreds of thousands of Proto, near enough to a million of your citizens," volunteered Proto. Les turned to look at Proto who was looking at him intently and obviously read or anticipated his question as to their numbers on the planet. All these living animal bi pedal forms of life and none of the sensors picked up any evidence of life forms—similar tp that of a primate species. Then an almost hopeless thought crossed his mind, just how effective is the technology of us earthlings. Not one evidence of any living animal form of life while there are literally a million or several millions all secretly watching them land and bring their helpless technology with them. This was an incongruity which had to be explained.

Before he could ask why so many Proto were around at this time of night and what they were doing. Proto lowered them back to the ground. Again he gave a pre-emptive answer in his simple telepathic monotone, "Les..lie, I shall have to leave you for awhile. I will come back to you after I have contributed to the hive. You will be placed into the nearest branch of the mother tree to see what few of us Proto have ever seen other than those who are over one thousand years old or more. There are very few since most Proto prefer to give them selves up to form new Proto.

Again Les felt as though Proto was showing the ability to read his thoughts as they are formed but at times Les thought that he was capable of reading those thoughts before Les had formulated them. Proto reached out for his hand and as a reflex, Les closed his eyes and within seconds he was sitting on a branch which was as wide as fifteen feet and he was just sitting crossed legged on it's surface. When he looked straight ahead he could see the massive expanse of the savannah plain several hundred miles square all filled with the continuous swaying of the large golden grass leaves. Now there was the continual bobbing of heads with many appearing like tiny stick figures. with square heads. Proto kept looking at the scene anxiously and Les got the impression that he wanted to join that mass out in the plain. Before he could give his approval, Proto broke into his thoughts and said " Thanks, Les..lie. I shall be back as soon as we have finished our task. The Proto are ready to be released for the Mother Tree has been collecting the unborn for many thousand of years". Les watched as Proto walked away from him and straight into the main trunk of the Mother tree and simply disappeared. He turned his eyes at the scene below and in front of him. The silence was deafening and his mind appeared to be empty of any thoughts. He then began to think of the mundane and how could so many sentient beings collect themselves in the field below without betraying any sound. It was as if they were all responding to telepathic instructions but he was not able to connect with any Proto. Ha ! He thought to himself, they are using another wave length or band which is leaving me out of the loop and he laughed to himself It was interesting to note that there was some diversity in the colour of the Proto skin and in their eye colour. Why Les thought of this seemingly useless piece of information could not be explained. In his reverie and in the silence Les noted that there was a change in the activity for all the Proto were lined up around the perimeter of the field of golden grass. The wind which was causing the grass fronds to wave had stopped.

Then as if by some uncanny form of military instruction, all the Proto bowed their box-like heads and it was an odd site. Les again felt a little shudder taking place on the big Sequoia or Mother Tree but it was almost imperceptible.

Almost immediately a wind erupted on the grassy plain and there was a swishing sound as the grass blades swung against each other. Soon this wind developed into a localised storm which appeared very odd from his perch high in the Sequoia'.There was still no effect on the Mother Tree but Les now heard the noise of the wind rustling in the grass leading up to the huge red tree. While the noise was still very low it was noticeable and rising. Dust from the round began to rise into the air and from his perch Les could see and hear the powerful force of the wind on the plains as bent the tall golden grasses to the ground. The incongruous part, was while all this atmospheric upheaval was building up, the Proto remained silent on the perimeter of the large field with their heads still bent.. Then the "penny dropped" for Les, who now realised with some shock and surprise that the wind was being caused by the collective Hive of Proto who were combining their will and mental strength to cause the formation of an old fashion tornado funnel. This whole process was developing right in front of him and for the first time in a long time Les could feel the force and intensity increase to a terrifying level. Although he felt safe in his perch, even in the Mother Tree the power could be felt on the ground supporting this magnificent tree so even it began to tremble slightly. He stood up as if to get a better view but he was having the best view. It was just that he was caught up with the excitement at looking at a change in weather taking place around him but he was in a zone of utter calm. This pastoral scene with its picturesque forest of magnificent forest where he has been living and enjoying every moment of his time there, was showing the signs of a catastrophe about to happen. From the plain a humming sound began to grow louder. Les thought that the sound was coming from the line of Proto surrounding the plain but he could follow the notes, which appear to be coming from the upper branches of his tree. The humming changed key and sounded like a lullaby soft lilting and cooing. It soon became louder than the sound of the stormy wind blowing around and across the grass lands.

Les felt a peaceful calm overtake him and he settled down into a sitting position facing the spectacle in front of him. He then noted a movement across the grassy plains which he thought at first was the wind blowing across the surface of the now flattened grasses. He continued to look across the fields and these wisps of movement built up like a torrent of rivulets all moving into the centre of the plain. As the crescendo of the lullaby increased the rivulets of little rapid moving forms was revealed to be the round hardened globes which were strewn on the plain of golden grasses. He thought that he had seen a few hundreds maybe at most a few thousands. What he was witnessing was a torrent of these hardened egg or spores containing foetal Proto all heading or being pushed by the force of a 'hurricane-like' low lying wind into the centre of the field. There had to be many hundreds of thousands moving at the speed of over three hundred kilometres per hour. As the first mass of these spore-like forms reached the centre, almost instantly the heads of the Proto on the circumference of the field began to rise slowly and the mass of spores also began to form a pillar. Because of their now pale brown to whitish colour it looked like an old fashioned Grecian Doric Column. The as more were added to the poll in the centre location the mass began to tower until it looked like it was going to get to his level which was over four hundred feet high. Les was mesmerised by the sight as the number of spores were added so furiously and with such large numbers that the level of the tower rapidly passed his level and shot up higher than the Mother Tree. The golden grasses on the plains began to lose their shimmer and the field was darkening except for the glow given off by the wind directed spore tower. The sound of the wind was jarring to Les' ear drums which was unaccustomed to and such erratic noises for such a long time. He placed his hands over his ears but now there was the intense lullaby which was bringing a calm around the column. The column of eggs was moving with a centrifugal force of such power that the individual round spores could not be detected.

Les was looking at this show of absolute power and control and when he could move his eyes from the magnificent tower, he could see the Proto clearly with their heads fully tilted towards the night sky. For the first time, Les felt the great tree breathing like a huge pump and his branch began to shiver. Suddenly with a loud ear splitting scream from the heavens, an intense light filled the whole field including the continuous covered canopy. Les tried to look upwards but the intensity of the light was so bright he turned his eyes towards the ground and he could see the base of the tower of Proto containing spores begin to shimmer like a golden pillar with the surrounding field golden and bright like the brightest daylight.

All this was followed by a phenomenally increasing level of sound which caused him to squeeze his hands to his ears, even tighter, while looking away from the bright light above. Les thought that the mother space ship was about to crash. Just as he thought that his ear drums would burst he saw the pillar of golden spinning spores lift off the ground and shoot upwards out of the surface of the planet and as he watched in awe, it shot off into space with a speed unlike anything he had ever heard or witnessed in his whole life. He could not help but continue to look at this now departing bright tower of spores, when a rapidly moving comet with a bright tail came into view and into a collision course with the massive tower of spores. As the two forces met there was a blink in the combined light intensity but both seemed to merge into each other with the combined comet and pillar of Proto containing spores, heading out of this quadrant of space and into outer space. All this was too much for Les, who closed his eyes and slid onto the floor of the branch where he was watching the spectacle, on the huge Mother Tree. He lost consciousness.

SPEAK NO EVIL.

Les awoke from his sleeping or "fainting spell" unaware of how long he was not conscious. He looked around him only to see a concerned Proto sitting and staring down at him. They were on his bed roll on the ground at the edge of the forest where he had spent the first night. As he looked around him he saw the carefully laid out monitoring and camp surrounding equipment just as he had done that first night when he had entered the remarkable forest. He quickly recalled the events before he had spoken for then he realised how close and protected he was by his alien friend of the past two or three weeks. The smooth bark of his pillow tree was at his back. He sat up and found that his head was quite clear. Indeed he had a special feeling of overwhelming happiness and of goodwill to every one and thing around him. He looked especially at the concerned face of Proto, whose face and small features he had sub consciously learned to interpret despite the enigmatic appearance of his almost dour demeanour. He smiled broadly and said, " Hello Prot my little magician friend. How long have I laid here? as he stood up and looked around and down at Proto.

Proto asked quietly again the telepathic communication was so easy for them both to use,"Are you alright , Les..lie? You have been asleep for a very long time and I was worried that you became too stressed by our 're seeding of the universe ritual'. Mother Tree said that you appeared to be enjoying yourself but when I returned back to you I found that you were in a deep sleep and I was told not to awake but to let you recover on your own, Les..lie"

"Well, how long have I been asleep, Proto?', he inquired reluctantly knowing that it must have been for a long time. "Four of your twenty four hundred hours", came the droll reply. "Four days!, exclaimed Les "You mean that I have been out of it for four days.

Wow!"."I feel fine I mean wonderful. You and your hive put on a wonderful display. I have never seen or heard of any such thing in my life before. I just could not believe that the mental power of your combined hive was so great as to send all your brethren to join that comet. I just do not understand why after accumulating so many unborn Proto you just blasted them out into space"

Proto listened then quietly asked, " Do you not understand how we have used the 'comet' to take our new Proto throughout the Universe?" We call the comet the Proto Translocator for it carries the unborn Proto throughout the universe until it finds a planet which has all the right conditions the it will release the Proto like small meteorites onto the surface. Within a number of years new Proto will be formed and will be just like us. A Mother Tree will develop and she will give life to all that is needed in the new planet. The cycle will develop and another Proto Translocator will be called upon to carry another Hive away into the cosmos. That is the mission of the Proto." Proto remained silent as Les looked intently at him. "Proto I must ask this of you and apologise in advance but, Are you Proto planning to conquer the Universe?". Les knew that this was a very insolent question to ask of his friend but he knew that he would get an honest reply. "But of course, Les..lie. But I would not say conquer. We have no flight machines like you and your species. We do not have a military body which plans to take over other civilizations"

"Les..lie, we create new conditions for civilizations to develop. We make the new planets habitable for new forms of life to develop as the planet conditions require them. We are the Proto. From us Proto—Les..lie, all life develops. We are the first—we are the Proto".

He continued, "Our secret to you is that YOU, Les..lie, were also developed from Proto many long centuries ago.". Our Mother Tree said that this was the first time that a life form has returned and it was exciting for her to be the one to welcome back an evolved species from one of the Proto several millions of your years ago. You, Earthlings are the offspring of an ancient Proto."

"The Proto will never show ourselves, again to any of its future life forms in any part of the Universe, even in the expanses which are being created billions of your light years away. We shall be going there after you leave us"

Les found himself sitting near to Proto who was speaking in a casual manner on this most profound of subject. His mind was vivid and he was taking in the significance of what is being said to him. He knew for the first time he was being lectured to in the best possible manner and his insignificance in the cosmos caused his shoulders to sag under the weight of what was being said to him. On the other hand why was he the privileged one to find out the origin of Man. If what he just heard is true and he had no reason to disbelieve this being sitting in front of him looking intently at him with no movement of his brown eyes. Proto I do not understand how we could have evolved from you, we are so different physically and we do not have your tele-pathic power or your skill of kinetic self transportation or ability to levitate. We cannot enter into trees or become trees or anything else for that matter.

For the first time Les thought he heard a physical laughter sound coming from his slim fragile companion and looked up to see the shy dancing eyes appear as well there was a slight opening of the slit mouth but showing no teeth or anything else. "Les..lie, but you are made of the same substance as your surroundings on your planet Earth. In the early history of your evolution and in some of your "rac-es" the ability to levitate, and to 'thought travel' were common. Your species did lose some of that ability. Instinctively you have always pro-tected the trees. You have even farmed the trees, which were your life source. Why do you think that you did that?. Your science did work out how the evolved forms of the 'animal life forms' and plant life are interdependent. What you lost was the ability to become one with the plants. But it was not important for you to remain as Proto for you had to evolve differently since diversity was needed to maintain the life forms in your part of the cosmos or galaxy"

Les was pensive with an absolutely blank mind, he asked Proto "When will I meet my colleagues. I have lost all concepts of time and space". "You will meet them now, Les..lie. Please close your eyes and count to three as a digit moved and touched his hand". He laughed to himself and counted in his mind to three. He opened his eyes and there he was standing just out of site of the explorer at the edge of the forest. He heard laughter coming from the shuttle, which was showing some of the light from within. It was early .evening. He looked at the brown laughing eyes of Proto, who appeared to be happy. Les was happy and he placed a hand around the shoulder of Proto, whose eyes danced so rapidly and the slit mouth remained ajar for a long time. He however, felt a surge of power running through his body which caused him to shiver. The shin of Proto was so smooth and warm against his bare forearm. At the same time he found that he was grinning broadly. He knew automatically that he was the only one who had this experience and he knew that Proto would not show himself to the others. He also had a feeling that he accomplished a great deal and that his task was completed. Proto pointed to his shuttle then said, "You will only remember some of what you have seen. The rest will come to you bit by bit and the rest later when you are very old. I have a gift for you, Les..lie". Proto stooped down and picked up a white stone about the size of two of his thumbs lying side by side. He slipped it into his pocket. "He looked up to Proto and said "I must go now, Good bye my friend and tutor," as he held up one hand in a parting salutation. He turned his back and began down the shallow hill. Halfway down he turned around and he saw, Proto with his hands upwards. Before his eyes a large spruce tree took root. He looked back as a huge spruce tree rose up to over twenty feet tall. He knew that it was not there. He continued towards the laughter coming from the shuttle.

REUNION

"Hello there! Just in time for we have only just arrived" said the laughing Tara, whom he had never seen laugh so broadly or enthusiastically before. They both approached him with such great joy and welcoming and threw their arms around him. This familiarity was not present before, in fact it was not present among any of the crew at least, none of the crew that he knew. He loved this reunion. They were all trying to speak at the same time including him. They soon settled down.

Tara spoke first and said that she could find no water on the surface but believes from the lushness of the vegetation that there must be very deep aquifers under the rocks. She did collect some samples but they appeared to be withering away. She had collected some pollen but they were so small. She said that she enjoyed sticking out her tongue to collect them. Then they all said that they had done the same thing. It looks as though they were behaving just like students at University for they broke out into hilarious laughter. Les said that his trip was a total failure for he could not collect or detect any of the acceptable or well known minerals. There were traces of Na, K with minute traces of C and S. It was the most insignificant findings anyone could have stumbled amongst this planet of so much vegetation. His geologic findings did not reveal a hot centre and there were no volcanoes. Tara interrupted and said that she had found a combination of Carbon, Hydrogen, Oxygen and Nitrogen in such a combination that photosynthesis, under the broader light bands of ultra violet light and infra red part of the spectrum coming from the sun revealed that the chlorophyll of the tress were functioning at near enough one hundred percent efficiency.

She felt that the specialist botanists from the mother ship may want to have a more in depth look at the planet. However, she had collected some samples and had video recorded as much as was possible with her equipment. She did note that she had collected some leaves at evening before she turned in and she could not help but notice that they had reappeared the next morning.

Everyone appeared to be healthy and in good and positive spirits. They noted that they had hardly used any of their rations and when they collaborated with each other they just broke out laughing again. They all felt super healthy and they had no explanation to explain their obvious vigour and almost cavalier attitude to this their first mission. After a god night rest they woke up almost simultaneously and began preparations for departure. They had all their equipment and sleeping gear which they had taken with them. They had plugged themselves into their computers to download their findings. It also recorded their physical health and mental aptitude. If anything they all appeared to be healthier than when they had left the shuttle.

It was a smooth and almost dull return home with absolutely no problems other than the fact that they were in such an ebullient mood. As they approached the mother ship, they were contacted and shown a port along the side where they were to enter. The mother ship which they had not seen for such a long time. It lay like a huge suckling pig showing the port entrances which looked like her teats. They noticed the number of explorer shuttles which were docking and leaving their stations that the information collectors must have been over worked. They were working twenty four hours continuously.

Tara was the first to be debriefed as the Leader of the team. She also transferred all the data and video data from the shuttle computer which they controlled. There were computers on the shuttle which stored data involuntarily and operated independently of the crew. Tara had to explain the obvious lack of surface water in this lush planet. The odd occurrence was when Tara was told that their long range scans of the Mother Ship could not find either the sun or planet in that quadrant from which they had just explored for the past three to four weeks. This was none of her responsibilities and in a short while after telling her other two fellow crew members, they soon forgot all that they had experienced. The medical review showed that for some reason the genetic high blood pressure which was a permanent document on Les health record had to be changed. It no longer was detectable. So also were some of the transient illnesses on the other partners of this trip. Even old broken bones could not be detected.

NOLO CONTENDERE

Les went up to the observation deck of the mother ship to look out at the passing shuttles but also to scan the surrounding stars in this galaxy. As he was standing there by himself he tucked his hands into his pocket, which were normally empty. He felt a hard smooth form and pulled out the shiny white almost marble like pebble, which was given to him by Proto just before he went into the shuttle to join the others. He had kept much of his experiences away from the others. He looked at the oval form in his hand and felt it begin to glow and become warm. He cupped it in his closed hands to see the white glow intensify in the shallow darkness of his hands. He brought it up closer to his eyes and for a fleeting moment it became warm, then translucent. A small face with dancing, smiling eyes appeared, winked and disappeared. He looked as the pebble became a dull white form in his hands and stuck it back into his pocket.

The End

SPACE ACADEMY
(as written more than twenty years ago to entertain my two girl children)

BY

Darryl Leslie Gopaul

CONTENTS

THE FAMILY

It was early summer and like all the suburban families in the subdivision of Oakridge, everyone sleeps in on Saturday morning. It was no different for Don and Donna Mills. They were Laboratory Scientists and they were "On Call" for the laboratories shift this weekend, so they enjoyed a "lay in' as was said in their old home country of England, at least until the telephone rang for their services.

Don and Donna came to Canada more than five years ago and in that time they had re qualified in their new country to get jobs. They had moved to a new city to live and it was no coincidence that the name of the city was London Ontario, which was located in the South West corner of the province. As well, they had brought their first house and had the time to begin a family which eventually was made of two daughters. Both Donna and Don had qualified in the UK in London but there was no future in looking for any promotion, since they would be waiting for 'dead men shoes' as their colleagues had said to them. So as soon as their professional journal arrived at their graduation, they decided to take advantage of job opportunities abroad. They were lucky in their choice for they were accepted as immigrants and there were job offers. They began to pack in preparation for travel to Canada. Since there was a shortage of Laboratory Scientists, who were qualified especially in their fields, they got the choice of very good jobs. They could still recall how quickly their papers were processed and how rapidly they had given in their notices to their employers who were not pleased at them both leaving after having trained them for the past five years. Within four weeks they had got rid of all their belongings and packed new clothing and quietly left for Toronto.

They have often discussed how lucky they were to have taken such a chance and how fortunate they were to have met such wonderful folks who rapidly became their friends. In such a relatively short time Don had stopped work for three years to get his Canadian undergraduate degree and Donna had taken the time to produce a thesis, which gave her an advanced technical diploma. Don wanted to get the university degree since he felt that it would become necessary in the future for he could see that there were major changes coming in their scientific fields which would demand higher academic knowledge also it might just help in getting promotions. In fact they had both thought out their future plans very well for they had both achieved what they had originally wanted to do.

Then it was that fatal evening as Don used to call it when Donna said to him "well, should we begin to think of having a family or not? I am getting into my thirties and it is not healthy to begin having children in my thirties"

Don said that he had not thought too much a family, since he had come from a relatively large family while Donna was an only child. Both her parents had passed away when she was just turning twenty. First was her Mum and when she was twenty three her dad also succumbed to cancer. She had carried on with her studies and her internship until she had her first advanced diploma. She knew that Don was ambivalent about having any children, since he remembered his own childhood when there were none of the joys in belonging to a large family, as depicted in the movies of the fifties. He had come from a fairly well off family and he was given a boarding school education all paid for by his parents. Donna was the first of her family to attend a Grammar School and was the 'apple of the eye' to her working class cockney family. There is a bit of fogginess about her mum and dad. Dad was a carpenter but had gone through two world wars and some of the depression years. Mum had a job reading for the War Office as a young lass but that was during the first World War This was bit of family knowledge that had only just come to Donna's attention, when they visited her late aunt Bessie, who was in a home for old folks.

However, that was all a long time ago and as they retrained, got themselves equipped to take on full employment in their new home country, they were very happy. They noted that their new friends were also changing. After attending a University in Canada both Don and Donna just naturally found that they were becoming more liberal minded. There was the feeling that they were exposed to more than an education and to a more dynamic culture, to which they quickly and willingly adapted. The world in which they found themselves was new in so many ways so they quickly gave up much of the "old baggage" which they had brought with them from the old country. They embraced the new foods, the music and the pseudo-academic way of living. Their friends appeared to give them the benefit of their back ground, as though they were extra clever, since they had come from 'jolly old England'. They both began to become leaders in their respective jobs and over time had built a reputation of some 'upper class' practices. While harmless, they were not arrogant but rather discouraged others from taking life too seriously. It was fun to have the Mills family at parties and social functions. It was exciting and they found themselves thinking of new and modern concepts about life and so a new philosophy developed for they had become the 'avant garde' in their small circle of friends. Don's career had taken off and he was making quite a name for himself by building up a number of academic publications. He also became quite an accomplished lecturer in his field. Donna was also known for her quiet demeanour but meticulous work of a high quality. She was an accomplished scientist and made a different reputation for herself. However, whenever the Mills name came up at laboratory inspections they both were known by the bureaucrats from the Government.

So it was that after much discussion with their group of friends, which were made up of a wide range of ages. They cautiously made prudent enquiries from those who did not have any children and found out that if those folks had to do it all over again, they would have a family. They had both done quite a bit of travelling to the West Indies and to Europe and had settled down in their professions. There were not very much more that they really wanted to accomplish outside of their jobs. And like every thing that this immigrant family did they approached having a family just as cautiously. Donna came off the pill for the required amount of time specified by her obstetrician. Support came from Don, even when he had to put up with the complications of not just rolling over for sex but actually having to prepare to have intercourse by using condoms and creams et cetera. They had their laugh and within three years they had two lovely daughters separated by two years. They just could not swing the one boy one girl part to make it perfect. With no immediate family in the country, they began taking trips to show their offspring to Donna's cousins aunts and uncles in England. They knew that they were lucky to have such beautiful kids and of course, they had to take the children to Don's mother and father, who were also ecstatic. It appears that all was well.

After each pregnancy, Donna and Don were lucky to find a surrogate 'Grandma' as a baby sitter within the sub division. This was a remarkable person who had just moved into their area after she and her husband had sold off their farm in Western Ontario to retire in the suburbia of the city of London. They were successful in raising six children of their own and many of whom were working in the southwest area. This unusual baby sitter did everything they had said that they wanted her to do, for the children. When Don and Donna came home from work, both children were showered dressed up in their pretty clothing and were well fed. It was a dream, come true for this hard working couple. Don and Donna had read that the children should be exposed to music as small babies so they took out a selection of classical music and showed "Grandma" how to put on the player so she could play the music quietly as the babies had their after noon nap.

When the children were old enough to have stories read to them, there were lots of books around as well as stories on records. Indeed the black and white television, which sat on a small table in the corner of the room, was rarely on except for a sport game or for the news. The CBC Radio was almost their sole source of home entertainment along with their now vast collection of records, hundreds of novels and hard cover first publications of their favourite authors. Life was organized and in full bloom for the Mills family. They continued to attend the summer theatre, musicals and classical recitals with a now select number of friends. Because of the size of this country, it was to be expected that many of their colleagues and friends would move for better opportunities of employment or for family reasons.

A discussion as to how to educate their children came up one evening, when there was a lovely supper and much wine followed by the usual after supper brandy and liqueurs. They always had wonderful friends who brought up great topics of discussions, which were lively interesting but most of all informative. Here was a topic, which Don and Donna were aware that they had to deal with, in the next year or two since the older of their children Elizabeth, was going to be three years at her next birthday. Their second daughter was having her first birthday. The family only had advanced education in their new own country and did not know anything about the schooling system in Canada at the kindergarten, primary school or the high school level. What opinions that they did have, were not very good, since the bad news was often what was heard and not the successes.

Their friends were also at a loss to give worthwhile opinions since many were born outside the country and had to retrain, while others never took a Canadian diploma since they felt that their training in Europe was far superior to anything this country had to offer in the 1960's to 1970's. Both Don and Donna did not agree with this type of attitude or with such back handed comments for they had embraced their new country totally and did not intend to ever go back to Europe or any other part of the world to live for that matter. However, there were colleagues and friends who were born in Canada or came as very young children from other countries so they were brought up under the Canadian Education system and who were citizens *extra ordinaire*. Don just explained to Donna that the Canadian system was a modern one and had a wide range of choices. Some of the less progressive students chose the quick way out and many just became the low wage earners having non progressive positions. There are the others who because of upbringing or drive by the parents and family cause the children to work and be more academically ambitious at school. Those were the ones who did not avoid the difficult subjects and may have even sought out the challenges and as a result became the graduates of choice to be hired by the better companies, who also invested in their success.

It was after such an evening of wine food and healthy conversation that the debate over what to do about the children's initial schooling took place. The decision was made by both Don and Donna to begin the process and prepare the children to be sent to the Montessori Private School System, which was catching on in the city of London Ontario. The good thing about this was that the girls began school at just under three years of age for Elizabeth and Ellen also started but a little earlier. Don and Donna were very pleased with their progress and in those early days both children could read many of the children books by the time they were three years old and they also developed a passion for all things which required reading writing and sums or arithmetic. It was a treat to have them chat about their achievements at supper time and the encouragement from the parents just enhanced their progress. Both parents although they tried to down play the children's progress at social occasions still could not help but be proud about how their little girls were progressing.

This story begins at this stage as both parents became so enthusiastic about educating their daughters that they were willing to sacrifice almost anything to let their little offspring get the best education going.

AFTER A NIGHT OF FOOD, WINE AND COMPANY

"Donna, what time is it, luv?" Don asked as they slowly became awake. Donna also yawned making herself awake and reached over to pick Don's watch from the bedside table. She always transferred Don's watch every night from his bedside table to hers right next to her glass of water. This little idiosyncrasy had become a ritual for more than ten years. His watch was always twenty to thirty minutes late and it had been so for many months. Don said to himself that he must get his watch fixed but he just never got around to doing anything with his watch. They had both become accustomed to adjusting their routine to take in the extra minutes. "It is seven a.m., and it is Saturday so go back to sleep. You do not have to go into the hospital laboratory today and you are not 'On Call'.

"That's right" Don responded as he yawned again."Thought I heard the girls' voices, are they up as yet?' he asked sleepily

"NO. Turn over and I will give you a cuddle," she replied.

"OK" and turned his back to Donna. "What did we do last evening?" he yawned again. But Don did not feel like going back to sleep and so he lay quietly as Donna placed her arms around his chest and began to snore.

What a week he had, with the plans to open the new laboratory or rather refurbished quarters. It was the same space and location but the contractors had done a good job rebuilding the space into more modern quarters. It now included all the regulatory and mandated precautions for a safe work place, thanks to the unions and the Government Regulations. The health of the working staff, which included the professional medical technologists, was now given a priority since they were always dealing with potentially infectious specimens from sick patients. But all did not go well over the last few weeks for he knew changes were made by the Old Medical Director, who took over from him while he was on vacation. Of course, it was Murphy's Law if anything had to go wrong it would be at the time he was away and the old Brit thought that he knew everything and so made decisions to alter some parts of the plans. For Don, this was a nightmare since he had to have administrative support for any changes to realign any of the contractual alterations.

He also thought that it was a jolly good thing that he had taken the time to check out his lab space for he found a Mirror and soap dispenser on the wall but there was no sink or water outlet on the wall. He thought to himself, "what does these workmen think about" . He became arrogant, thinking of course his assumption to begin with was wrong and that was that the workers were capable of independent thought. These early meanderings of thought revealed that his work of the past week was still on his mind. But his thoughts became more passive as he made himself awake. Crickey Man!, One would think as the guy was putting up the mirror and a soap dish he might just mention to the foreman that this was odd and ask "shouldn't a sink go with this assembly.?" This work crew worked as though they were robots. The plans did call for a Wall Cabinet and he wondered maybe the chap could not read. He might have been one of those new immigrant workers, who could not read. But this was nonsense since the trades were full of immigrant workers, who were trained in their respective country. They may not be able to read but they certainly knew their craft more so than the young 'Turks' who leave school prematurely and feel that they can make big bucks in the building industry, which appears to take them on without any interview.

He did not really pick on the immigrants since he was very conscious that he was an immigrant and has been in Canada for more than fourteen years. He came to this conclusion as he rolled over onto his back fully awake and he could hear Donna breathing regularly next to him. She had gone back to sleep. My goodness he thought to himself fourteen years and they never thought once of leaving to go elsewhere in Canada. There were job offerings and he remembered when a colleague called to ask him if he wanted to take her position in Vancouver, actually on the island. At that time he was having a bit of a rough time with the old Brit in charge of Laboratory Medicine. He went off for the interview and who did he happen to meet but a younger Brit from the North Country, who felt that he was in the colonies and his job was that of the "Raj in her Majesty's Service." When he thought of the salary and the offer of this man with a thick Lancashire accent, who also offered to pay his moving expenses, it was a plum position. But his main reason for moving from Ontario was the persecution by another older Brit. He would be jumping from the frying pan into the fire. No thank you and after discussion with Donna, who had already made up her mind not to leave Ontario anyway, even before he had told her but she never mentioned it to him in any of their discussions. Anyway after he told her of the results of the interview and of the offer, she asked if he wanted to go and in truth he said that it was so far away from everything and everyone they knew. "Great" was her reply and said "then we are staying" He remembered her contented smile. The children had begun their schooling and the west is still too backward for they do not have the Montessori school system out there as yet. It was too much to give up for the amount of salary increase he was offered. Well Don sent back a rejection reply, which provoked a really terse and aggressive response from the Lancashire Medical Director which justified his decision.

He smiled as he lay on the bed staring up at the ceiling and was fully awake. He could never understand why these little 'Lord Fauntleroy's' who had built up their little empires just could not enjoy the privilege of their position but rather got the ire of everyone against them, including their medical colleagues. They intimidated their Lab staff and were often found shouting at them with very little feelings for what damage they were doing to the individuals. It is for that reason many of these little tyrants hired the Chief Technical Scientists from the old country—Ah! They were better trained was the philosophy and their job was to train the locals. But Don had met some of these fellow Brits and many were badly organised, some lazy while others were here to make enough money to return home. There is no doubt that quite a few had been responsible for the growth of the profession by becoming teachers, administrators of the College system and many ran the provincial societies which were the professional bodies. In some ways this also became the "British Mafia Group," which many of the home-grown workers felt was unfair but were not able to enter the system until after quite a number of years.

This country was very good to them, Don comforted himself with all the inside 'politicking' he had learned how to 'bob and weave' through the system without offending too many. Of course there were always a few who would sort you out anyway but thankfully they were few. He was in his forty-second year and at times he thought that he was lucky to be that age, especially as he was free of any chronic illness. His daughters were doing well and appeared to be well mannered and actually were a treat to take anywhere. He was cognoscent, however, that nothing was really given to them for they had literally worked their respective 'buts off' as the colloquial expression go, for all they had. Donna was a good Scientific Worker and she still had a lot to offer and as she moved from full time to part time when the children were young, it was only temporary. It was not long before she again moved into a full time position. Such generosity of job movement would not have been possible if she had continued to work in the hospital system but she was allowed to have this type of arrangement because she worked in the private sector. Of course, as we both entered into our forties we began to think of taking things easier at work. Donna did what she had to do because the family needed to have the extra income. She did not particularly like cleaning the house and doing the laundry so Don had made arrangements to have a house cleaner come in once a week to do a thorough once over the house and to do one major wash. Donna grew to like this luxury, which was a topic of conversation with some of the other wives. Don had given up gardening as a form of exercise and a potential hobby because it became a necessity. His fixation to have things in order placed an added strain on this domestic task and it took on the same proportions as his strenuous job. Luckily as he was going through this ambivalence to all things domestic, he was approached by one of the older European porters of the hospital, one by the name of Felix. He had seen this tally porter come into the lab on many occasions and he was always cordial to him smiling and at times taking the time to show Felix what was under the microscope. Felix asked if he could come and look after the garden since he had reached the magic age of sixty-five and he was asked to retire. Don had an interesting relationship with this man, since he had as a hobby the collecting of Trilobites from a site which only he knew. So he would clean and polish these specimens and bring them in to be examined under the plate microscope. Don was interested but only in an academic way but he learned a lot from this man, who was so intense about his hobby as he was about his other hobby wood carving.

With all these domestic rearrangements taking place, both persons had to work to pay for all of these luxuries, considered by some but now a necessity to them and their emerging life style.The possibility of moving to other greener pastures had passed his way and the thought was always there but as they crossed over the magic forty birthdays, the attraction began to lose some of it's lustre. Besides moving from one institution to another to do the same job was not worth it and he had found that to change careers now was too difficult, since he was a well-known Microbiologist and his reputation was growing. No way could he go to another profession and do as well. At least that was what he had thought since he had always wanted to be a 'laboratory man', who were known to be very practical people and this transferred to almost everything that they did. If one did not intern from young and over a respectable period of time one could not possibly be any good at anything that one did, certainly one could not call oneself a professional.

"Donna, I swear I can hear the girls' voices in the family room," he said to the now tossing figure next to him. "Don't tell me that they are up so early watching television?"

"Why do you not settle down and have another sleep, you are just hearing things," came the sleepy reply.

"I cannot sleep any more" he replied. What did I do yesterday after work? he thought to himself. Ah! Yes he remembered how the fellow chiefs came together in the Interns Lounge on the Friday after work and told jokes and had a beer or two. It was a wonderful practice which became a ritual and actually did some good for the lab chaps met the clinical chiefs in a social situation where many difficulties were explained and where individuals had an opportunity to share their problems and solutions. Writing this fact twenty years later, it is now against the law to drink in many hospitals and the Interns Lounge is a thing of the past and a source of reminiscing to the older chaps. He recalled as he lay in bed that they were laughing their heads off at the old Brit Director who insisted that he have hard wood benches, which he would have the technical staff rub linseed oil over its surface every day after work. My repartees of having the technical staff doing it twice on Saturdays brought renewed gales of laughter.

There was lots of fun about the use of Formica and granite tops for benches as the whole lab had been brought up to modern standards.

" I do not believe in these new synthetic materials m'boy for they have sharp edges, which is a risk to the young ladies for they will get their nylons torn and there is the risk that the young men will have their balls hooked off," the old Brit broke off in loud laughter "Ho…ho..Ho.. Ho," was his response.

I could not leave well alone and interrupted him with "Oh! That's all right then since all your staff, are females, you could add a line in your inventory 'Nylons' and have them replaced as they are torn". He would not concede and replied quite soberly; " for now that may be OK but when I leave the new head may hire males"

That was the maximum of long range planning considerations given by this very obstinate man who kept us waiting for twelve years to have this lab rebuilt.

The architects were having a really rough time for they wanted to do what was right for the institution but the task of modernizing the premises were still in the hands of 'old time professionals'. These were the same people who had kept the place from improving and actually brought on the terrible conditions which the Ministry of Health demanded of the Health Centre that they be changed.

The old Brit had caused a stoppage of work by his belligerence and stubbornness about re-creating the past. The other directors tried to be diplomatic by explaining that it was really quite safe to use these new products. The Brit stood up to his six feet six inches and said, "that may be quite acceptable within your discipline but definitely not in mine. "

As the Friday night 'transfusion' occasion in the interns lounge was coming to an end, I saw one of the female technologist arrive, so I offered to buy her a beer. She refused and beckoned me towards her and whispered that my wife had just called to remind me to bring home some red wine for supper. I had completely forgotten and re-turned to say "sorry guys; I gotta go we are having guests over for supper tonight". Needless to say, that there were lots of 'guy deroga-tory comments' as I left them. I did collect the wine and went home.

Needless to say, that I was not present to assist with the meal so before my breadth could be smelt with the fumes of beer, I offered to set the table right away from the missus in the kitchen. When I went into the kitchen Don looked over Donna's shoulder and asked what was for desert. She proudly showed him a large trifle. He asked if she had put sherry but remembered that the evening before she had taken the sherry from the bar cart in the sun room and remarked that he should replace a new bottle for she was going to use all of what was left.

Our guests always brought a bottle of wine and recently they were in the habit of bringing two bottles of wine, one white and one red. It was a great evening and it explained why we were still sleepy at seven thirty in the morning, since we were in the habit of getting up at five forty five. It was the usual winning meal of roast beef, scotches to begin with several glasses of wine with the main meal. The sherry trifle was also a hit and the brandies and liqueurs with coffee had its effect this morning. The previous week of trials and tribulations and difficult people had all been forgotten.

Don knew that his head was stable while he was lying down but it would not be so when he got up too early. He also felt that if he turned onto his side his brains would pour out of his ear or so it felt, as a result he continued to become drowsy and to doze off again. He thought that he could hear the giggles of the girls who tended to sleep in as well on Saturdays. It was Donna's turn to become awake suddenly "That's strange I can hear the girls laughter quite distinctly but it is so early", "It is very comforting to hear their happiness through their laughter', she said to Don. She did feel quite happy with the sounds coming from the area of the family room. Don asked, "what are they so happy about?"

Donna replied " I do not know but their laughter is quite comforting, it is almost as though I can share their happiness. Can you not feel it, Don?".

"Oh ! What are you on about now, woman?," he jokingly asked.

" Listen", she said ". Don lay back on his pillow and relaxed closing his eyes. A glow of total relaxation appeared to flow over both of them and he put it all down to the booze, which was still present in their system. The girls' giggling appear to become louder and in some way it appeared to come from their bed head board suddenly, so loud and immediate that they both sat up suddenly with a start. It was if the girls were in the room giggling so loudly but it was just the two of them. Then just as quickly the sound disappeared to a gurgle in the next room which was the family room. They looked at each other and jumped out of the bed and rushed into the corridor leading from their bed room past the girl's rooms, which showed empty beds with their usual strewn blankets on the floor. This was the usual morning disarray and they continued .towards the family room. Don looked at the clock in the corridor and noted that it was only ten minutes past seven and said to the rapidly walking Donna, "Really these kids are watching telly too early", as he stooped to pick up some of their stuffed toys which were laying on the floor. It was then that he heard "Don come in here immediately", for Donna was in the family room ahead of him. "In a minute I am picking up their toys" replied Don. He then heard a shriek

"Don!".

He rushed into the room to find Donna standing in the doorway as thought she was paralysed for she was staring through the picture window of the family room. He looked up and followed her eyes at what she was looking at through the small covered patio attached to the family room. There were the two girls still in their pjs floating in the air. The patio appeared to be enclosed by a glass bubble.

They had the biggest smiles and were focussed in front of them and away from the house. They looked like gold fishes in a glass bowl. As both Don and Donna automatically moved towards the large picture window they could see a third figure standing in front of the floating girls. It was a slim figure with a silver blue fitted jump suit. The figure was giving the girls some instructions and they were laughing and intently focussed on the person. Both Don and Donna rushed outside and began to bang on the bubble but in spite of the transparent nature of the bubble the girls did not look at them immediately but slowly turned around and looked at them and waved at them but continued with what ever game was being played. Quite distraught both parents began to shout and bang on the bubble but still there was no response from either the third figure or the girls.

STRANGERS AT DAWN

Don and Donna rushed out of the sun room still in their night wear, around the containment bubble and could find no entrance. Don said "maybe there is an entrance from above I will climb on the rail and have a look". Donna stopped shouting immediately and appeared to be concentrating on the adult figure in the middle of the bubble staring or directing the girls. As she stopped moving and just looked at the figure in the silver suit, Don came and stood next to her. Suddenly a voice came from behind them from the entrance of the French doors out of which they had just ran out of the house "there is no opening came a soft voice."

They turned around quickly to see a second figure clad like the individual who was in with the girls standing in the doorway. The figure had no obvious face since the clothing appeared to cover the whole body but there were eye openings which looked like the 'cut out' of a Halloween mask. The eyes appeared to be large and brown but they were gentle and appeared to be smiling. Where the nose would have been was a slight elevation of the mask and no obvious outer nares.

"Who the hell are you?" shouted Donna. "Get my children out of that dome thing, now," she shouted.

"Settle down Donna, the girls do not seem to be in any harm, are they?" The voice was not that of Don but of the second being standing in front of them. It continued with it's soft and lilting tone "the children are safe". Both Don and Donna stood closer to each other and to the second clad figure, who was standing in front of them and they felt almost paralysed to make any sudden moves. It was a much shorter man-like figure. It was then Don realised that the 'Being' in front of them did not have a mouth. They were hearing inside their heads which was unusual not unpleasant and it was non-threatening.

Don tried to speak but found he was whispering, "how are you speaking? " He formed the question in his head and asked the figure.

"My name is Toros. You are taking part in telepathic communication. Do not use your vocal cords. Just think of what you want to say to us and we shall reply in your mind. It is easier. Yes we are from out of your galaxy", came the quiet explanation before they could ask. "Are you aliens?" asked Donna with a tremor on her lips. "Maybe you are the aliens but 'yes' to your question" came the quiet reply again in their heads, a bit of ironic humour. "I want my children back" sobbed Donna.

"The bubble is sound proof from the outside so the children cannot hear you and they cannot hear the communication, which we are having. It has enough of the atmosphere so they can breathe easily...without difficulty. "The Instructor" has a need for a different mixture of breathing gases that is why the "bubble is present, " came the quiet reply which, continued "Of course, you can have your children back. Calm yourself! We are not vandals or robbers and do not intend to hurt anyone especially not the children" "They are priceless beings in this universe" came the calming thoughts of speech into their heads.

"How do the children come out?' asked the shaken Donna. Don was holding onto her arm and was very close to the "Being" who was non-threatening and he felt quite calm. He was more curious than frightened. "Yes, how can one enter into the bubble?" he heard himself mentally form the question.

"There are several entrances or openings, which are made but only by the individuals from the inside" came the soft reply. Don could feel Donna trembling although, he appeared to be a quieter person he could sense that she was becoming distraught. "Beckon to your younger daughter to come to you. Donna went towards the bubble which now felt like a soft plastic.

As if by some unseen instruction, Ellen turned her head towards them smiling. Donna beckoned with her hand to come. Ellen turned completely around and floated towards them with a huge smile and walked through the wall of the bubble and her mother's arms."Hello

Mummy, Daddy". And with open arms she raised up her face for us to kiss her."Isn't it neat?. We just woke up rushed outside and walked into the magic balloon", she laughingly said to us. Donna hugged her closely towards her chest and raised her up like a baby. "Are you OK baby? asked, the still distressed but calmer Donna. "Oh! Yes Mum. When we woke up the magic bubble seemed to call us, Mum. The Instructor has showed us how to speak without using our mouths. Is it ever neat", she continued.

" I have to go back inside now. Bye," and before we could hold her she slid out of Donna's arms and re entered the balloon. Both Don and Donna tried to follow but felt the pressure of the transparent wall force them back.." How can we get in?" They turned to ask in a panic of Toros. By this time they did not seem capable of controlling their voices.

Again the quiet soothing voice in their heads appeared to respond before they could form any question and appeared to anticipate their question. "Close your eyes, Don and Donna". They did as they were told instantly.."You will have to become accustomed to the weightless atmosphere within the balloon. Just imagine that you are on a roller coaster and hold onto each other.". They felt as though they had lifted off the ground. Don held onto Donna tightly who had a damaged ear and her balance was not as good as his. Again the buzzing sound in their ear "now walk forward with your eyes closed" came the simple instruction. They just did as they were told and for some unknown reason they both appeared to become very relaxed. Don felt as though he was about to smile in fact he was actually smiling.

As though by some magic wand they were floating about two feet off the ground but they were in the balloon. "Hi Dad!" shouted Elizabeth. "Meet our friend the Instructor" as Elizabeth moved immediately between both of them hugging their waists, looking and smiling up at them for she had lowered herself to their height. Don and Donna just held onto her for contact to begin with but also for stabilizing themselves. They turned around to meet the first "Being" whom they had first seen in the bubble. Don was still in his pyjamas and Donna in her nighties and they felt a bit incongruous but Don stuck out his hand and heard himself say within his head "How do you do?" came the rhetoric question. Donna still holding onto Elizabeth automatically stuck out her hand. Both their hands were held by a very slim small hand of the one called the Instructor. "How do you do Sir, Madam" came the very formal soft lilting voice in their heads. They could see Toros standing outside the bubble looking away with his back towards them.

Don found himself asking the Instructor." How are we standing off the ground?. Is there no gravity in here" inquired Don. Both Don and Donna had frozen grins on their faces. "How can we float up straight? Is this what is called weightlessness" Don questions were in full flow.

"There is very little gravity in here; just enough for you to control your position" came the simple explanation from the Instructor, who continued " can I continue my chat with the children, Sir, Madam?" was the soft inquiry.

They both heard themselves say simultaneously "certainly and they moved towards the wall of the balloon and they were extruded with a slight jerk and found themselves standing outside the balloon next to Toros, who had turned around and reached out to stabilize their return to the firm ground, for they would have certainly fallen down on the ground. Donna found that she was holding down her nighties close to her self as if to preserve and to protect some modesty. It was almost humorous for they were both looking very dishevelled. Don turned towards Toros and formed the next statement "Donna does not stand heights too well. Her ear was damaged when she was young" he seemed to stutter out as if to form some sort of explanation. It had nothing to do with this scene in their backyard. It was still an early summer morning and no one in their neighbourhood would be up. " Yes, I can see that her cochlea is damaged maybe from the intervention by your 'surgery' not by the childhood infection" came the reply from Toros.

They were all facing the balloon with the girls still looking intently at the Instructor and still floating around but closer to the ground. Elizabeth curls were rising up over her head and Ellen's straight hair just had it's ends curled up as by a small breeze. They were in their children's pyjamas which had the Disney characters printed all over them. They looked so pretty, as they always do when they awoke in the morning. Both Don and Donna felt as though they were both thinking about the same things at the same time and appeared to be agreeing with each other. They were actually communicating silently with each other but tele-pathetically.

Don turned to the silent slight figure which he had begun to surreptitiously inspect closely and asked "where are you from? You are not from Earth" came his rhetoric statement. "We do not have any known living other beings in our galaxy" continued the now inquisitive Don. Donna appeared to be listening to the conversation, while keeping her eyes on the girls and the Instructor in the bubble. She looked quickly around at Don who was facing Toros and nodded in agreement with Don's questions.

"Yes", came a thoughtful pause from Toros. " We are from a distant galaxy several light years away, that is by your earth measurement", Toros 'matter of factly" communicated.."We are called the Omni and I am known as The Guide. My companion is called The Instructor.".

Toros stopped communicating and appeared to be thoughtful He slipped his hands into a slit on the top part of his full tunic as though reaching into his breast pocket but his suit was fitted so tightly to his body non the less, a slit was present and his gloved hand slipped into it. He withdrew two flat silver plates and reached over to Donna placing one on each side of Donna's face. She still had that sort of grin mask on her face. It was if she was uncomfortable and there was some fright which all combined to show acute nervousness. She did not move as Toros, The Guide placed the plates on both sides of her face to cover her ears. She just closed her eyes after about thirty seconds to a minute. Don was watching this little act quite dispassionately, then, the Guide removed his hands with the plates and tuck them back into the slit in his vest suit. Donna opened her eyes and with a big smile said loudly in speech "Oh my gosh! What a sensation! I feel a bit giddy. I think we should go inside and sit down". She was smiling and Don held onto her arm and said "Are you all right you look a bit flushed, love".

"Oh I feel great", she smiled and the strain which was on her face just a few minutes ago was replaced with a calmer face and the radiant disposition which was the norm for her. "What did you do?" Don turned around to face Toros who appeared to be looking intently at Donna.

Toros replied "Donna, you will be all right in a few minutes. You will feel a tingle in your head as the nerves which were damaged in your ear are rejoined together. Your mastoid bone will also grow back in a few weeks.

"What are saying!" Don said startled, joyous but confused. Donna was also staring with a great big smile on her face. "If what you say is true that would be utterly amazing since our surgeons and physicians said that some surgery could reconstruct the ear drum but that there would always be scarring on the mastoid bone of the inner ear. The nerves were damaged and there was little our medicine could do at this time."

Don looked at Donna again and back to Toros, who because of the covering on his face showed no change in his demeanour. Don stretched out his hand to Toros, who looked down at it and placed his fingers which was also gloved and held Don's finger tips. It was not a hand shake and Don realised that Toros probably did not know this type of greeting but obviously had some sort of version of it. In this instance it was holding onto his finger tips. Don's inquisitive brain was stimulated and so was the calmer Donna as both their scientific minds kicked in and the outcome was pure medical and scientific curiosity. "How did you know all that about Donna's ear problems by just looking at her?. How did those plates work? Why did you feel it was necessary to heal her? What are the side effects of your plates?" the roll of questions just appeared to come into both Don and Donna's minds.

"Slowly", responded Toros. They became quiet and calmer suddenly. Both Don and Donna were glancing at the girls from time to time. They had stopped jumping around and appeared to be in some sort of communication with the Instructor looking intently as they do with their teachers at school. The couple now focussed on Toros as they stood next to each other looking over Toros shoulder at the bubble behind him.

Toros looked at them and responded "These 'Shells' are charged and interphased directly to my nervous system Hence when it is exposed to another nervous system, it reads and translates, then relates to me all the information of the foreign body."

"It is up to me if I wish to make a joining with the foreign body. I then transmit my demands through my nervous system to make the damaged tissue whole or repaired. The shells or Plates use my nervous system to get the specifications" stated the soft tones in their heads or minds as Toros replied to their questions. They could not describe how they were communicating but they were aware that they were also cross communicating with each other and for some unknown reason a relaxed atmosphere was forming and much of their apprehension was being dissipated and replaced with a calmer feeling.

"Can I see your 'Shells', Toros. Can I touch them?" asked the now curious Don. "Yes you can see the "Shells" and yes you can touch them."

"But, Don they will only work for me Not every Omni have these with them. The 'Shells' are only given to a few. If another Omni or alien were to take them or misplace them, so that some other being were to find them. They will not respond but will self destruct quietly", replied Toros.

Toros replaced his hands into his vest and brought out the Shells but he held on to one end of them so that Don could feel them and turn them over but he never gave up total control to Don, who understood why this was so. Don looked up at the figure next to him and said "Toros we see gadgets like these on science fiction films portraying the future as visitors from another planet."

He continued " Look here Toros, I still want to know who you are?, why are you here? won't you be seen by the neighbours? why...".

He was interrupted by the raised hand of Toros who when Don was silent said "Sorry Sir, let us take your wife's suggestion and sit down in your garden. I will try to explain as much as possible.. Right now you both have a need for sustenance or nourishment. He took out of his upper inside pocket from the same slit where he kept the Shells two small oval pills. Swallow these with some water."

"What are these?, asked the suspicious Don. The Guide explains that the pills contain all the growth and nourishment factors that the human bodies require for health living except for water. He continued that they will not feel the need for engulfing large amounts of animal and plant tissues for the next earth week or longer. "What are the side effects on us ?" asked Donna. "How do you know that our bodies can tolerate your concentrated food matter in this pill?"she continued. "After a pause the Guide looked at both of them "maybe I did not explain it thoroughly to you both. We have used the same source of food from your planet to make this concentrate so that it suits your earthly bodies. Both the Instructor and I have a different extract". He continued quite seriously but where his mouth should have been there was not even a slit. They could hear and were both thinking of what they wanted to say but they could hear what each other was thinking or about to ask. "The other Omni, who have visited your planet before, were the first to use your vegetation to make the pill to match your physiological requirements and we were issued this stock for you."

Don caught onto this last statement and asked "Excuse me but you mean that you have been observing us earthlings for a long time".

"Yes", said The Guide "That is our job. But first let me answer your initial question. On our planet many years ago, we have dispensed with your type of food and have mastered the science of concentrating the important elements of life along with the accompanying slow release of nutrients as the body may require. This became necessary five centuries ago when we began to travel across galaxies. Our bodies do not harbour the 'uni-cellular organisms' which you require to break down your heavy dietary food source. In fact we have harboured our uni cellular microbes to work for us and they are not distributed through out the environment of our world. We must protect ourselves from your microbes meticulously lest we contaminate our transporter and other Omni. I will explain all of this since you are both scientists and are engaged with the fundamentals of this type of Biology"

As though by some silent command Donna got up and went into the house and returned with two glasses of water. Both Don and Donna looked at each other smiled, raised their glasses as though doing a toast popped the pills into their mouths and drank the whole glass of water. When they looked into the 'bubble' the girls were looking at the Instructor intently with the bright smiles on their young faces. The Guide did not drink and Don went over and brought over two patio chairs. They were still dressed in their pyjamas and were facing the visitor called Toros or The Guide whose back was against the bubble. This allowed both Don and Donna to keep an eye on the girls and to observe the Instructor. They could not hear or tune in on what the girls were doing inside the bubble but it all appeared as though they were quite safe and enjoying themselves. They both faced the Guide in front of them with the same intentness as the girls. They felt relaxed and felt no fear, rather there was an intense curiosity as their scientific minds took over. Before they could form any questions in their minds, Toros said to them "listen to our reason for being here and all of your questions will be answered. "

He began as though he was about to tell them nurseries rhyme " your neighbours and surrounding folks will remain asleep longer today. We are all surrounded by a fog which we have caused to happen. They will not be hurt in fact they will have the best sleep that they have ever had since they will be in a sleep deeper than they have ever been and this will make them very rested." At this stage they saw the Instructor take out a sort of game board and showed it to the girls then all three sat on the base of the sphere and began to concentrate. It looked harmless enough for Donna got up went over to peer at them as they were still concentrating and no one looked up at her, when she went and leaned on the bubble. She returned to her seat The Guide raised his hand and they began to focus on him "You were chosen by our pioneer Omni as are other families on your planet, (excuse me) Earth, who are having a similar visit by another Guide and Instructor" Don picked up an as if by a reflex action and interrupted asking "What do you mean by 'chosen.' and by whom,? he asked forcefully. "Sh hh, Don" said Donna in an unusually calm whisper. "Let us hear him out. He will explain everything to us and then we will ask all of your questions"

Don looked over at his wife and then to Toros. Toros continued "Thank you Donna. To answer your question Sir, actually you chose yourselves. For we have heard that you have reservations about the educational systems and you have had some discussions with your friends as to how to better educate your children. It is for that reason that we are here. We know that you are the correct persons to offer our services to since you have already accepted so many unknowns such as 'that you are communicating now to 'off worlders or aliens' , 'the bubble', 'the food source' 'this form of communication' 'the Shells' and all of this has been done without primitive anger or suspicion....not much anyway".

If ever there was a hint of humour this last statement and pause appeared to be it. Both Don and Donna looked at each other and smiled but soon became attentive again. "You asked for a better education for your children and we heard you. On our planet many centuries ago when we began to travel we collected much knowledge and information of other life forms. We have never intervened or tampered with their civilizations or their evolution. Earth has been one such planet which has evolved more rapidly than expected and we believed that there were some other 'Beings' in the galaxy who might have intervened and speeded up your evolution. This made us uncomfortable but after a search of several hundreds of your years we have not been able to find any other life form, which would be capable of doing such a thing. As a result the decision was taken by our Planetary Leadership that we should be a source of some assistance to other civilizations since we did not meet any civilizations as advanced as ours. Our decision to participate at a Cosmic level, was that we should take some of the young populace, educate them and reintroduce them back to their societies, so that they would become the leaders of their world. The intent was they would be able to assist their own population in an organised manner. In fact to advance in Science while keeping an ethical perspective for the population. The future generations of Earth will soon travel outside of this little universe which surrounds you and there must be thoughtful respect for what you will meet."

Toros continued "Our peoples loved this new idea of sharing education and so we have become the Tutors of the Universe under the guidance of an organization of which we are part of a section known as the 'Space Academy'."

"At present we have recently returned four such trained individuals back to your planet who hold positions of high authority which will be useful to your population as you take the great leap to explore outside your Universe. You should also know that throughout the past four hundred years of your planet you have had the assistance of such individuals. They have been responsible for keeping the Earth's population safe from self destruction." At the risk of interrupting this alien being in front of them, Don asked "who are these individuals? What steps have you taken to insure that they do not become tyrants on Earth? How do you know that you can trust them to do the correct thing? Again to Don's surprise it was Donna who said "please Don he is explaining all to us calm yourself"

Don and Donna sat quietly and calmly and they could see the calm brown eyes of their visitor called the Guide.

"Do you mean to say that you have been observing us as some great laboratory experiment and have interfered in our existence with out our permission, knowledge or respect for our opinion" asked the alert Don. He was shushed again by Donna, who settled him down as though by some unseen force which must have had a calming effect on him. Donna got up and moved like a cat towards the bubble and again looked at the children for some unknown reason she thought she knew where this was leading to and her maternal instincts came into play. Don looked at her and asked her to come back and sit down. She saw that the girls were engrossed in whatever board game they were playing and were obviously quite happy.

"It is our task to look for replacement students from Earth and at this time the Instructor is evaluating your children to see their suitability as the next to enrol in the Space Academy" related the quiet voice of Toros.

"Come on Toros ! Human beings do not voluntarily give up their off spring. If you have really studied our species you would know that we are not like that. We as a race and species, by and large are inextricably bound to our children, bonded by a powerful emotion, which has nothing to do with intellect" said the terse Don.

"We are aware of all that you have said and this is the first time that we are using this technique of temporary adoption by bringing the parents into the process. We have in the past used the lost child and later found child system. In some cases we have had parents act as adoptive parents who have voluntarily allowed their adopted children to seek out their birth parents so that the family could be re united later. It has taken us a long time to understand your 'emotional parental' attachment. We have not found such an attachment in any of our other races who have voluntarily given up their progeny for the advancement of their community but Earth people are different. Your literature used to be a source of wonder to us for you have written a great deal about the 'love attachment'. However about two thousand years ago, some of our scholars began to follow your continued addressing of this emotion and its impact on your civilization, has been almost essential to your development and growth. As a result we have tailor-made our educational support to include this emotion and our philosophy has changed so that we choose the families whose children would be the best candidates to be adopted and educated.

We would like to take your children to be part of this endeavour if they pass the Instructor's review" concluded Toros.

Don was up from his seat with his fist in the air "how dare you be so arrogant and insolent to believe any Earth person would give up their children voluntarily. How dare you, Sir !". "Donna get the children out of that bubble thing!" He continued to take over with a sort of low key anger but his voice was failing or his thoughts were, for it lacked the conviction which would normally accompany such an emotional out burst. Donna interrupted his mental thoughts which, was a sudden onslaught by touching his shoulder causing Don to sit down and look towards her. When they had sat down again Donna said to Don but was looking at the Guide "Don we are being given an option of having our girls become leaders on Earth only if we believe this preposterous story. She looked directly at Toros and asked "How do we know that all you have said is true.? she used an assertive tone in her questioning.

"I could let you enter my "memory store" so you could check out all that I have told you," came the serious reply. "You can stop the Instructor now, Mr Toros!" came the vicious response from Donna. "I think that you just want us humans to experiment with and you would like us to be volunteers in your weird game to capture our in-nocent kids. It is not on and if you dare to touch our children it will be over my dead body." concluded the now angry Donna.

At this stage like a blast of anger and aggressive resentment came with such a jolt to their minds as Toros sat up straight then moved to his feet but began to levitate.. A very loud voice entered their minds but was addressing Donna, " Be quiet! Madam". It was such a com-manding tone that they both began to sit down. Don could feel the anger and strong emotion building up in Donna's mind as she turned and stared at the two girls in the glass tank which they continued to call the bubble. Then the quiet lilting voice again interrupted her head and they both turned to face Toros, who quietly said "To answer your questions, no one could see us now and if we wished we could have taken the children from you. We did wake up your children and we also woke you both up so that we could explain all that we have spoken about. It will be difficult for you to lose your children for this short period of time but we promise to be around to assist you both with the temporary loss and to assist you to adjust for the time that they will be away"

Both Don and Donna could feel a fury building up in them since the whole thing looked like a 'fait acompli' and Don rose to his feet to try and rip the masked face from the Guide called Toros but he felt a choking sensation which kept this strong animal response in check and they both sat down again. Don looked at Donna whose hands were clasped around the rails of the plastic garden chair. They felt as though they were immobile and some force was keeping them both in check. Then a mass of information came into their heads, "We know how difficult this is for you. We understand how you will suffer to begin with the temporary loss or separation. We are not barbarians and we are not unfeeling 'robots'. We have been exposed to emotions and feelings such as you but have brought it under control you are incorrect about how you understand the 'scientific fiction' plays where all aliens have no emotions and are barbarians. Your writers are quite incorrect about how they imagine visitors from other galaxies. It is true that we do not all reproduce in a viviparous way like you do. We gave that up to be born in nurseries for we remove any genetic faults before the young are born."

Toros continues to explain "We donate our genetic material for birth in vitro. Individuality is maintained. We do not have the genetic illness and deformity which, continue in your species. We also have allowed a higher form of understanding without the fault of too much emotion to persist and to blossom. There is no disease in our culture and all genetic related impurities have been removed a long time ago from our species. The last illness in our population occurred over three of your light years ago. Genetic vigour is maintained in much the same way as yours that is by mixing the genes which cause enhancement from our pool or race. We do not intend to use your daughters for any medical manipulation."

That last comment seemed to have lightened the emotional load on both Don and Donna. They seemed to visibly relax. Toros continued "We do keep an emotional involvement in our progenitor or 'parents' Before we biologically die, cells are taken away stored and later on used to form new individuals of ourselves, so we have an op-portunity to see our replacement taking place. We also have the op-portunity to interact or as you say 'play' with the clones of ourselves. Surely that is the ultimate in understanding between two beings. Both our mental and emotional forces are reunited in the young offspring, which keep our experiences and knowledge as they continue to advance in the new generation. Again your children will not be used as 'guinea pigs'. They are taken to be educated in our advanced learning centre, where they will be exposed to a wealth of knowledge which you do not have as yet. They will bring back that knowledge to cause a quantum increase in your growth as a species."

Don interrupted "but you will only be equipping them to survive on a planet similar to yours and I do not see how that will help Earth. They will behave and be treated like 'odd-balls when they return to this society". Don sort of blurted out this last statement but felt as though a force was holding him down. He then realised that this force which had interrupted him was coming from his wife even though she had a relaxed appearance on her face.

Toros calmly replied "I can assure you that the re-introduction into Earth's society and governing body will be done within days of their return"

Donna was determined and persisted "what will we do about their school here and how shall we explain to the authorities? What shall we tell our friends? What.........?".Her questions were coming with a trembling voice and a panic tone was being assumed.

Again the calm and soft voice of the Guide came to them "you will have to cope with those little details but we shall be of some assistance to you if its needed"

Don interrupted "Donna you are assuming that the kids are going with these foreign beings, are you ..?.". He felt a combined force of both the Guide and his wife stop him cold and then he heard a quiet voice in his head and it was Donna

"Don, I do not think that we have any choice, luv. We did ask for help to cope with the type of education over here since we were brought up elsewhere. This alien being is offering the ultimate education and a future for our children. Anyway if they wanted the children they could have taken them without us knowing. I believe that they are trying to live up to a different standard.".

"You do not have much of a choice" came the soft voice of Toros, the Guide.

He continued, "this will be our fourth and last foray to Earth on behalf of the Academy. That is our quota. Both the Instructor and I will retire to our world to raise our own clones and to document our experiences for the past five hundred of your years into our archives"

"How will our daughters return? And who will be their Guide?" came a frantic reply from both Don and Donna almost simultaneously.

"Oh! We will have to complete this assignment which includes the safe return of your daughters. Our task is to relate to the inhabitants of other planets, to seek out the student candidates, evaluate the students and their family, transport, protect, guide and direct our charges, which become the most precious cargo that anyone can have as an assignment. On Graduation from the Academy, where there will be thousands of Aliens (your term)/ citizens from a multiple of Galaxies across the great Cosmos, all are returned to their respective planets. Upon integration and assimilation into their communities we, the Guides and Instructors return to complete our records to the Faculty of Cosmic Studies. We are then desensitized of some mental and physical abilities because the security of the students and confidentiality which are promised by the Academy to the students must be maintained. The Academy quietly monitors the growth and development of their Alumni to see if they are assisting in the growth and welfare of their home planets and their peoples. We the employees of the Academy will not remember our students or build any long term attachment since this could be damaging to the essence of the Mission, which our people hold sacred to themselves and the philosophy which is tied to their destiny"

Don felt a surge of enthusiasm as though a curtain had broken down for suddenly he felt he understood what these aliens were doing was worthwhile and he turned around totally in his petty opposition to this golden opportunity for his daughters. "That is fine we will come along with you." " He felt the total support coming from Donna, who was also standing next to him and when he glanced in her direction he could see that she was in total agreement with him."I am prepared to leave the planet with you as is my wife, " for he could feel Donna's hands in his as she excitedly squeezed his hands. The

Guide averted his brown eyes from them and moved backwards from them by a few steps and after a brief silence the soft tones entered their heads " I am sorry but you will not be welcomed only the children must come alone. If you are present that will be an obstacle and distraction for the Tutors will not have the total attention of your children."

Then before they could shout or make any opposition, the gentle voice continued " your physical being will also be the source of distress to the other students. It will also be difficult to prevent your built in prejudices from contaminating the other faculty and alumni. This will defeat the purpose of our primary objective necessary for Intergalactic Co operation & Understanding.

Don found himself mentally shouting "who are you to judge our open mindedness are!" Almost at the same time both him and Donna sat down and sheepishly looked at their visitor.. There was no force holding or keeping them in a sitting position. Both stood up, one on each side of the Guide and looked into the bubble and quietly watched the girls and the Instructor, who had a small white box open in it's hands. The girls were engrossed at the apparatus which looked like a bedside clock radio. The difference was the acute intense impression on the faces of the girls. As they were observing the trio at work in the bubble, Don became aware of the sweet song of the Red Cardinal coming from the nearby locust tree, which could be seen on the other side of the glass dome. As he was trying to have a view of the birds location, they were brought out of their temporary reverie by the sound of the soft voice of the Guide "Here, Don, Donna touch this and as they turned to look at him, his outstretched hand had a small silver cube" They both looked at the object and simultaneously asked "What is it ? What does it do?"

THE PACIFIER

They both automatically reached out to touch the silver glistening cube. "It is called a *"Pacifier"*, which is the nearest form of translation of it's capabilities, in your language." They both touched the little square which could just about fill a normal palm. As if by some magic both girls looked up simultaneously, from their intense concentration and walked over to them. Then with the most gorgeous smiles, they stepped through the bubble and walked over to them and threw their arms around their hips. They bent over to receive their hugs. Don bent over to lift up Elizabeth as Donna picked up Ellen. They snuggled up to them and kisses were exchanged by both parents and daughters.

Don and Donna sat down with the girls on their laps on the plastic garden chairs and looked up to see both the Instructor and Guide looking down at them. Suddenly, before any words or thoughts could be exchanged a buzzing sound in their heads brought this sub-urban family to attention as they turned to look at the pair of aliens standing before them. "The Pacifier connects your emotional and neurological systems to that of the children for you are the most powerful emotional source at this time of their lives. They will always respond to that 'Call or Touch' of their parents in any part of the Universe. Your touch will surpass time and space for they will always respond to your call or touch."

Both Don and Donna if they responded to either give an opinion or ask a question found that one stood aside, as the other lead the way but they both wanted the same information. This was just a natural combination of their need to know for they had become fully compatible both emotionally and intellectually with each other

They were both jolted into some reality as the voice in their head was that of Elizabeth's "Mom, Dad we know that it will be difficult for you to let us go but Ellen and I want to go with these people" The parents were shocked as they looked into the sincere eyes of Elizabeth, who was still hugging her dad and looking earnestly at both of them. Donna bent over to kiss her cheeks and said "Darling do you know what you are saying. Do you really want to go with these strangers into outer space and leave your Mum and Dad?"

"No Mum, we will come back. You and dad have always said to our friends that you always wanted the best for us. We have been chosen from the children population of the whole Earth to have this opportunity. It is the best learning opportunity for us and we are really lucky to be picked, do you not think so?" Spoke the quiet and 'oh so sensible' little voice who was not moving her lips but looking directly at both of them with eyes that were speaking. We have just taken a test like we do in school" continued the quiet voice of Elizabeth.

Ellen little voice interrupted, " It was like a game, Mum but it was fun as well as a test."

For the first time they heard a different intonation in the telepathic voice and it was from the Instructor " Sir, Madam, it is my task to evaluate at site, the students who are chosen for the Academy. We are just in time to take these children away for already there is some neurological deterioration of the hypothalamus and limbic regions." Turning to the Guide, the Instructor related, "We must inform the Academy search committee that they should make the selection for this species at an earlier age. Mental liquidity is impaired at a very early age by the emotional developmental responses. Already there is some physiological changes in the older of the two children, which our physicians must attend too immediately. She is also in need of a stimulus to the immune system for she is prone to many of these earthly microbial infections. Many of these must be addressed as soon as we enter outer space. It will not take long to cure these imperfections and stimulate her immune system before our arrival at the Academy. The wonderful news is that they both Interphased easily with the *Educator*," as she pointed to the small box.

The Instructor looked at both Don and Donna and pointed to the little box, which looked like a bedside alarm clock and said "this works like your little computer." Don's curiosity perked up as did Donna's and he found himself asking, " do you mean to say that the children can have reciprocal exchanges with that box". "It is a little more complicated than a mechanical box or your computer used in your home. It contains all the technical advances of your planet to date. It also has the demographics of atmosphere, minerals, biochemical engineering as well as the biological and psychological knowledge of your world. It can instruct children to do the most complicated physical things, such as how to make one of your rocket projectiles. It will show them how they can get the resources, and then give the instructions as to how it showed be assembled and used from their homes."

"I do not think that this is such a good thing," said Don and he could feel Donna's agreement. "It is just an example" came the quiet reply of the Guide."They will not use your primitive method of assemblage of raw materials, but with training of their mental faculties when in full power, would take the materials needed from the atmosphere of any planet or asteroid if the products are available then begin the development of anything they wish. The 'bubble' as you call it is a product of your atmosphere and it was made by this 'box'."

"Your world is evolving rapidly and at times, a bit too quickly for many mistakes are made, which is wasteful because of lack of emotional and psychological immaturity as well as lack of true planning capability. It is such a waste of energy and it will be even more disastrous for you are about to exploit and use the power of DNA. You need both the philosophers, ethicists, your intellectuals and you do have them, as well as your specialists in the humanities. Of course there is still the basic need in your society for the exchange of wealth, so your fund managers must also work together, at least until everyone is equal or have equal opportunity. It is essential that the society as a group work as a team to consider all aspects of the research results. The need and choice of how it may wish to implement the knowledge while accomplishing benefits for your peoples. Your leaders are heading for a grave catastrophe with this powerful new resource and tool, if social changes are not manifested soon."

"We cannot sit idly, while you work with such resources, so we must assist you by seeding your population with suitable skilled individuals, who would be able to contribute to your pool of expertise. The future of every new generation lies with the offspring or progeny. You have not begun to use this vital part of your future until they are too old. The psychological, neurological and overall brain development, are not allowed to be focussed with the knowledge requirements necessary to develop the population. It is a distressing waste of the human resource. Your primitive use of the in vivo birth technique is still left to chance even though you have the evidence of the successful use of in vitro fertilization. Again the products are in your hands but you need to have a proper philosophy to make the best use of all available knowledge and resource."

Donna interrupted and asked quietly as we were being lectured to " how long has our family been under your observation?" "You began the process when your husband wrote an article many years ago on how humans should breed the best of the species. It was written as you say in your language 'facetiously.' Don interrupted loudly verbally, which caught both the aliens and Donna off guard. "I wrote that article for our fledgling newsletter to get the by and large apathetic members of our society to sit up and notice. It was not intended to make any more an impression but rather to get a 'rise' or laugh from the membership".

" Non-the-less your short essay did have a very important message which caught our attention and we thought that it was worthwhile following such individuals as yourself. You were heard on many occasions saying to your friends and colleagues that you wanted the best education for your children." responded the Guide. . "I object to this breach of our privacy and family life. Regardless of your supposedly noble intentions our children will not go with you" was the very emotional response from Don, who had a hard set to his jaw. "But we have been looking in on your family for the past twenty years" answered the Instructor. "We would not have come to this home if we were not sure of your willingness and co-operation"

"Well, you are wrong Sir or Madam whatever you are. You are a little too glib with your explanations and answers to our questions. You have shown us some of your technical toys and have not furnished us with any worthwhile evidence of such an Academy or any individual on earth or elsewhere who has gone through the system and are currently contributing to our Earthly development. Our children will not be guinea-pigs to your plans and we shall tell all to our press of your invasion of our human rights" answered the now very angry Don. "Our presence will never get out for you will not remember any of our conversations if we do not wish you to" stated Toros in a mono tone voice heard in their heads.

"Sir I ask that you settle down, please. There is one other family who has agreed to have their children come with the Omni. Your children will not meet them at any time not even at the Academy."

The Instructor then continued slowly as Don sat down for he felt the pressure from Donna to listen. "Sir, your apprehension of your Government Leaders to exploit these skilled children is a real danger that is why we have built in safety checks, which assure that they are never detected. Can you really afford not to have your children be among the leaders of your planet in the future?"

At this stage the Guide took his chance and said, "Sir, we have hundreds of Earth-years of experience doing this job and your apprehensions are the same as have been expressed by your predecessors. We know that we have had the answers to all of the questions which may account for our supposedly 'Glib' explanations."

There was silence as Don placed his right arm around the shoulders of Donna who was hugging the children tightly as they both faced the Guide and the Instructor. They were afraid to think as they both felt naked in front of these polite but persistent Aliens, who were capable of reading their minds.

Don and Donna thought simultaneously "Give us some time to think over your proposition" they asked.of their visitors. "We are sorry" said the Instructor, " we do not have any time for you to mull things over. The children will come with us today. We would rather have your understanding and compliance for we felt certain, because of your professions that you would agree. That is why we woke you both up for we could just as easily have taken the children but our new instructions based on a change in policy, were to include the decisions of the parents."

"Under such conditions with the loss of your children you would have had to go through the trauma of the worst kind with your law enforcement officers, as well as with your friends and neighbours. Showing ourselves to you, gives you the opportunity to prepare plans to remove such complications."

"May I speak to my wife and children without you being present or listening and we will use our vocal communication not your telepathic method?" Don politely asked the Guide, who appeared to be the one in charge. The Interpreter appears to be a female if there were male and female in the Omni. The eyes of the Guide shone through the face mask and one would have thought that they were smiling. It bowed from the waist Japanese style and said "you have our word that we will not listen". They both turned away and re entered the bubble almost instantly. Donna turned around holding the hands of the children close to her and they all entered the house. The whole family of four sat on the large sofa very closely together. Donna was the first to break the silence

"Don what are we to do?" the tears were streaming down her cheeks but there were no sobbing sounds as she clutched the girls tighter to her."Sh..hh..hh, let us think this whole incongruous plan over," Don said. He was interrupted by Elizabeth, who said "Mum, Dad may I speak?" "Sure luv," Donna replied. "Well all of this does concern Ellen and me. We really have no choice but to go with the Omni since they have specific plans which they have been working on before either Ellen or I were born. If they wished, we could just vanish and never see you again.". She turned to look at her father "Dad, do not try running out the front door and into the car. I can hear what you are thinking" Don was shocked and said "But they said that they would not listen!". Dad they are not listening but I can focus like they thought Ellen and me to do, so we can talk to each other without moving our lips, isn't that right Ellen?"

Ellen who was the slender and tiny one held onto her mother's hands and had said little until now,. "Yes Liz, and I can also use the telepathic way of reading minds. I learned quicker than Liz. Mum, I do not understand why you and dad are so unhappy with us going to school. You said that if you had the money you would send us to Switzerland to a boarding school. Is not going with the Omni like going to a boarding school in Switzerland? I do not like the idea of going away from home but if Lizzie is with me I will be alright and we will look after each other. Mum, you know it is the right thing to do but you are just sorry to let us leave. It is Dad who has to change his mind and you must make that decision now for we want to go that school, in space"

With that little speech, she slowly removed her hands from her Mum's and moved over to the rail of the couch and placed her hands around her dad's shoulder. "You left your home in the islands many years ago and your Mum, our Grandma was very hurt but she knew that you were doing the right thing. We will be doing the right thing."

"Children, Liz, Ellen this not like taking a boat trip on earth! This is going with some very strange aliens into outer space. You might be used, or be experimented on, you may never see us again and worst we will never know what is going on with you. We will not be present when you have your first "girl period" or know when you are hurt and be able to kiss it better. We will not be there to kiss you to sleep and watch you grow into teenagers and then into young ladies and listen when you have your first date or your first kiss" came a strangled sob from Don.

"Dad listen to yourself it is all about how you and Mum feel. You have always wanted the best for Liz and I and it has all dropped into your or our hands. I can feel that the Omni are very honest and truly intend to educate us so that we shall be better than anyone else when we return and we will come back. As for watching after us Dad, Liz asked how we can contact you for we want to know that you are not unhappy when we have gone and we will be able to use the *Pacifier*. It is better than a phone for you can feel our presence and our feelings at anytime by just touching it. We will be in contact with you continuously and when you close your eyes you will be able to see us in your mind so you will be able to see us grow. You will not imagine us growing but you will actually have a clear vision of our body as it develops. The Pacifier will not work if it is in any one else's hands or if we were to die."

Young Ellen placed their parents into quite a position for they were startled by her lucid interpretation of the situation. Don could not help but laugh and hug his younger daughter "I have often said that you should be a lawyer and you better use that gift in what ever field you decide to study". "Dad, why would you want to call the police, do you really think that you can contact anyone. The Omni said that everyone around our neighbourhood is asleep and there is no electronic devices that are working. The clock has stopped and the light on the VCR is blinking at twelve" said the assertive Elizabeth. She continued "You wanted to discuss this situation and time is running out. We want to go, right Ellen?"

"Of course, but our parents have to give their permission, or we will not go voluntarily. I believe that the Omni will take us if not today some time in the future. We must make a decision" said a bright and smiling Ellen. The children had taken the decision from both Don and Donna's hands. The parents were feeling a bit better about letting the girls go but Don wanted more assurances so he said he will have a private talk with the Guide, but Donna said that she wanted to be present. At this the girls jumped up and hugged their parents as though they were being allowed to go to a mid night theatre show at an under age. "Great", Ellen said that she will collect her 'Lammie' and Elizabeth went to collect her 'Kawal'. Both of these were stuffed toys which the girls have had from the time they were babies and even at their age they kept these toys under their pillows at night. They even took them on holidays and there are a host of stories about these stuffed toys being misplaced on holidays and how they were found.

Before the girls went downstairs Elizabeth turned to face them " You know we will be good students and we already have tuned into the *'Educator'* which has taught us a great deal such as why there are no other living forms in our galaxy, how planets revolve and Mum, you know how you always wanted to know what Mars. Well it was like if I had travelled there in my mind and I know what it is like—I actually saw the planet. We will be able to talk to you by using thought waves as both Ellen and I can do now, right Ellen?"

"We sure can and we can also listen to what you and dad are thinking, if we wanted to, of course." replied Ellen. Elizabeth looked at her dad and said "Dad maybe it will be better if you work with the Omni for they can assist you with many of your Microbiological problems and so can you Mum. They do not do sciences like we do on Earth but it will be nice to go to this new school for we shall meet all types of different beings who do not look like us."

"We were told that many do look like humans but some are quite weird, sorry "different looking" At this Donna came back to some sort of physical reality and shouted "Stop it Elizabeth ! You are afraid of science fiction films like 'Star Wars' and now you feel that you will like to meet these new beings in real life? Anyway you both talk as though we have given our permission. We have not said anything as yet". At this outburst Don perked up and shouted "Elizabeth, are you being communicated with by telepathy from the Omni outside?"

"No Dad, they promised not to intrude or use their telepathy link to listen or interrupt. They are truly honest beings Dad". Don then carried on "Explain how you are using such adult phrases and are able to tell us what is on Mars and trying to make me deal with the Omni. Explain that to me?" He stood up to look at his young daughter who was standing at the end of the corridor leading to the bedrooms. "I really cannot explain how I am behaving but we definitely learned a great deal from the Instructor and the Educator. I know that I am speaking differently but I am only trying to make you and Mum comfortable with our leaving. With regard to permission, do you really have a choice?"

As if speaking to himself, Don quietly said "Are you not going to miss us?" Elizabeth came back into the main family room "Dad of course we are going to miss you, how can you ask that. But we shall be in touch with you from the time we leave so that we will not be lonely. Ellen and I will look after each other and we will comfort each other for we will not be separate, they have promised to keep us together. We will be safe where we are going but it is also very exciting"

"How do you know?" asked the sombre Don. "Oh! I asked the Educator but it has assured us that you will love us even more through the Pacifier and with practice we could be communicating with you almost daily I was told. Distance has no measure when compared with thought travel or communication."

"Do you really believe all this science fiction nonsense Elizabeth? What about your friends? What about your music lessons? Are you not going to miss your birthday parties?"

asked the very distraught Donna. "Not really Mum, let me show you. You remember how I wanted a method of remembering the pieces of music, well I asked the Educator and he showed me how to read and remember what I read permanently. I told it that you liked Beethoven". She went over to the piano and closed her eyes and began on 'Furelize'. They just could not believe what they were hearing. They saw a form of concentration and physical co ordination which they have only seen in professional artists but here was their daughter Elizabeth doing the same thing in their family room dressed in her Pjs. Don stood up and went towards the French doors, stopped and looked out to where he could see the Aliens, the Omni standing in the bubble with their back towards the house.

"OK how did you do that Elizabeth? You have been trying to play that piece for so many weeks. What has happened?" asked the suspicious father. "I can now visualize the whole piece of music by using my alpha waves or something like that, actually the Educator said that I can place myself into a 'hyp nindo state' and recall any piece of music once I have read the music What is interesting is that my fingers will keep up with the interpretation made by my alpha waves".

"Elizabeth that is utter rubbish! You have been hypnotised and have performed on cue for us" said the angry Donna. "Mum, how can you accept what you have just said but not what I have explained to you?" asked the spunky daughter. At this Don interrupted them and asked his daughter "what else can you now do since you have met the Omni, Elizabeth?

"Since both Ellen and I have been formed from both of you, we can assimilate all of your knowledge by going through the 'hyp nindo' exercises using telepathy. This can only be done with assistance from the *Educator*"

As if worn out by the situation Donna asked "Elizabeth, tell us about the Pacifier". " I believe that the Pacifier is connected to our brain waves linking our emotions to your emotional and brain waves.

When touched by either you or us—It signals our sympathetic nervous systems and we will always respond to the call regardless of the occasion or of the distance and time differences. I also believe it can allow us to communicate regardless of where we are in the universe. It is an extremely powerful tool designed for our human race and under extreme stress can be used in a process called 'trans materialization'." said the now tired youngster. "We must leave you soon and she went towards her parents and circled their necks with her small arms and held them for a while. Elizabeth and Ellen hurried through to the corridor to collect their toys from their bed rooms and to change.

Don and Donna went outside and found the two aliens standing outside the bubble which appeared to be vanishing before their eyes. The Guide was the first to address them "it is time for us to go. What is your decision? Don and Donna stood next to each other with their hands around each other's waist and said "Teach us how to use the Pacifier. We are also charging you and the rest of the Omni civilization to protect our daughters at the risk of your own lives"

'When they touched the object called the Pacifier, there was such a warm and comforting feeling and they closed their eyes. They felt themselves being hugged and opened their eyes to see their daughters hugging them. They were happy as they walked over next to the Omni and immediately the bubble formed behind them. All four entered. Both parents heard Tanya say here are a few more facts Dad and Mum—The Guide has just told Laura that the Einstein Theory of Relativity is only partially correct. We shall be travelling faster than the speed of light along magnetic paths formed by concentrated stars" she related as the bubble began to rise. "Do you mean 'black holes'". "Yes" came the strong thought into both their minds. The bubble just vaporized high in the sky and the mist lifted.

CONCLUSION

It has been over twenty years since our girls left us with the strange aliens called the Omni. We moved immediately from our address and went to another Province. We both got new jobs and we just told our friends and neighbours that the girls were in Switzerland attending boarding and finishing school. We also used the Pacifier sometimes several times a day in the beginning and the use was increased many times over that time. However as with all departures, when we lowered the use, then the girls increased their usage. We thought that this phenomenon was due mainly to make sure that we the parents were doing well, not sick or in need of protection from the Earth's authorities.

Donna's physician could not believe how her ear was so totally healed without a scar or any evidence of there being any damage, which was still present in her case history files. Don enjoyed almost perfect health even as he aged and his happy disposition was unfathomable. He did not ask for any help in his scientific research as he was improving and as is usual after years of research many facts drop into a pattern, which explains itself to the researcher. Hence, the belief that scientists should never really retire for their value comes after they have stored so much information, which only their brain and their experience can analyze and bring to some degree of fruition. But in Don's case, it was something to do with altruism and wanting to do all the work by himself.

Don was now sixty two years old and has taken an early retirement. Donna is only just sixty and she continues to work. They made a promise not to mention their children to their new colleagues and they soon let their old friends drift away since not many kept up the correspondence.

They had become a very private family of two, with children attending a European Boarding School. The girls had preferred to live abroad and theoretically loved their life style in Europe so they never returned to visit their home. This story was greatly enhanced by the frequent trips that the couple took to Europe, when they returned with the latest photos of their daughters. The children were always dressed in their school uniforms, some were traditional while others were really different—thanks to the power of the Pacifier and it's ability to 'Trans-materialise' The couple had got used to the regular mental communication becoming quite proficient and gaining a high degree of proficiency with reading each others thoughts as well as using telepathy between themselves.

Donna wants to retire when she is sixty two for that is when the girls will return, they will be twenty eight and twenty six years old and it is also the year of their graduation from the Space Academy.

THE END

ENCOUNTER
INTO
THE NEXT DIMENSION

"WHEN HARRIET MET JULIUS"

INDEX

INTRODUCTION

Julius Kane was a mild mannered man of modest means. He went through University and graduated with a Bachelor of Science degree. It was by sheer accident that one of the last professors in the biology department, a Dr Chempton, who showed some interest in this very average student. However, Julius responded by expending a little more energy when he was asked to join a group of students going on to their Masters Degree. Dr Chempton was the professor in charge of the fresh water biology section of the university. Julius was asked to do his project on the microscopic water plants of a nearby lake.

To this day, thirty five years later, Julius often thought about Dr Chempton and why he was asked to join the Graduate Masters Program. His marks were average and he had shown little enthusiasm for attending university. To him this was another task which he had to do so he could get a job and continue his solitude. Now that he had thought about it only in his last year did his marks show some improvement actually of the six subjects done there was an equal number of As and Bs but when he thought about it he did have a C in physics. That subject left him even colder to academia since it dealt with lasers and very complicated mathematics of which he had no idea of where to begin learning the fundamentals. He felt that the Physics Prof, who had come up to Canada from the USA to evade the Vietnam Draft was too detached and presumed that everyone knew about his research so he spent little time on the basics. This professor was very young and on coming up to Canada, he had found a bunch of foggy students and just gave a passing grade to everyone lest he prevent a whole class from keeping in the Honours Biology program.

Julius then found that the Masters degree opened up another opportunity to complete his basic research and gain him a PhD. He often thought about this little University which only had been in existence for ten years when compared to the really quality universities in the Province and the rest of North America. In the Grad Club he had overheard a visiting professor from the UK talking about his position and his need to move on since staying at this university would affect his career if he continued at this "red brick institution" and it would be difficult for the Governors of the University to shed this image and reputation. He did not like the tone of this disparaging comment which he had judged to be so but he did not know what it meant. He thought that he would ask his English tutor what the term "red brick' and it's connotation with regards to this university. He thought it might have meant that this university was not up to the standard of the so called better ones in the province.

Over the years he had the opportunity to meet many of these visiting professors and he did not like them at all, since they came off as being opinionated and their home university was always the best. He found that he was building up a cynicism but then he had stayed at one university, which he was lucky to get into when he did. He had several negative returns to his applications which he had sent out after completing High School. Many just wrote that he had not sent in his application on time, while others replied that his marks were not as good as the 'wonderful' marks of the graduates of that year who had all been accepted. Anyway he had persevered and after thirty years, he was about to retire from the one institution who had admitted him as an undergraduate, gave him the opportunity to do graduate work and had awarded him both post graduate degrees.

In the midst of his pleasure of being handed his doctorate degree, Dr Chemton whispered to him in passing, that there was a position available in the Biology department which could lead to a full time teaching position. After two years of port doctoral research to Chempton, he had learned the rudiments of making notes of the courses from the standard text books and he was allowed to give a few lectures when his mentor Chemton was not around. The position became available and he applied for it and was on the faculty as an Assistant Professor. Life had just become complete for Julius Kane for he was an only child and when his parents died in a car accident at a very early age, he was brought up by his grandmother who paid for him to stay at student lodgings. He visited her at the peak holidays but there was no fun since the old woman had made it quite clear that she preferred to be alone. He did have more than a generous income but he never felt the need to over spend or surround himself with any luxury. Over his university years he spent frugally since he thought that his income would dry up when his grandma died. He was never told of the inheritance left by his parents and he had never been told how to spend or budget other than when he was leaving to return to the campus, his grandma would say to him that she had very little money and he should make his income last as long as possible. On occasions she would send a little extra but there was a note which said how it was to be spent. In one of the last notes received, he was told to get himself a black suit so he could use it when he had to teach. When he eventually began to get a regular income from his position with the university he just banked all the allowance, which his grandma had been sending to him.

He was very surprised when he was told that his grandma had died almost to the day after she had heard of his success in receiving a PhD degree. He was called by the bank manager who was the executor of the Will and that was the second surprise for there was quite a bit of money as well as the property left by the old dowager, which he agreed should be sold. He asked the bank manager to invest all the income so that in twenty five years he would have enough to live on. The bank manager said that he already had enough to live on now, if he really wanted to stop work. Julius began to have a distrust of these men at the bank and he looked at the Manager unsmilingly and asked quite tersely whether he did not wish to invest his inheritance. The bank manager jumped up and realized that there was no humour in this very wealthy customer and for the first time he had a pang of fear at the possibility of losing such a young wealthy customer. He became ingratiating saying that it would be the banks pleasure, to take over the investment planning of his financial estate. "Just send me an account every month"said the unsmiling face of Julius Kane.

He had no feelings about the loss of his grandma, who was the only relation he had ever known and that was because he had spent almost all of his teen age years attending schools and living at student lodgings. He did not have any friends since his demeanour as well as, his pudgy physical appearance and wearing 'coke bottle bottom' glasses did not enhance him and encourage others to be friendly so he became a loner, which evolved into being a recluse. He had on occasion had some of the younger female students smile and gave him the respect of being an academic. He had some transient pleasure in knowing that but he had never pursued that pleasure any further. Neither did his transient pleasure show in any way on his face.

The faculty members, while appearing to be very civil to him did not go out of their way to make his acquaintance or to be friendly. Equally, if on the rare occasion he was asked to attend some social function he would often make some excuse as to why he could not attend. When that did not work and he had to make an appearance, he would leave as soon as the opportunity presented itself. Social gatherings held great fear for him and he was always uncomfortable, which just increased his social isolation.

However, Julius was not to be left alone once he had completed his thesis. As long as he could remember he had been hanging around the labs mainly by himself, but there was a very efficient and quiet female laboratory demonstrator, who was also shy, not very attractive but also wore pebble glasses. This was Harriet a very competent lab worker but a bit introverted who was an only child of old parents. When she did speak of her parents she said that she was a surprise to her mother who was over forty years old when she became pregnant. Her father was two years older than her mother and he was a carpenter who found work on a transient basis for he refused to join any trade union. The building contractors were bound to the unions and if one wanted regular work then one had to pay union dues. As a result he got little work and it was not regular so it was necessary for his wife to continue working as a secretary to a diagnostic laboratory. Maybe it was her mother who encouraged Harriet to take on this type of work. As a result, they remained as an average middle class family with a very modest income. In spite of their limited income,

Harriet got to a Community College, where she received a Diploma in Laboratory Sciences. She got the first job that she had applied for which was at the University, where the opportunity to meet and work alongside a young Professor by the name of Julius Kane.

Julius was a bit vague as to how he managed to meet Harriet, who was also putting in a large amount of time in the lab and so it was that they went to have coffee together on a regular basis. They said little to each other but were really happy to be in each other's company. Then it happened in the second summer of Harriet's employment, when most of the Faculty and students were away on vacation, that Harriet casually asked Julius if he wanted to go for coffee and he got up smiled and said "Let us go.". As it happened the kitchen staff was also away and the cafeteria was closed for repairs for two weeks. Harriet said that she just had to have a coffee so she volunteered to drive them to the small mall just outside the campus grounds. Julius thought that this was a great idea and he followed her to her car which was parked in the almost totally deserted staff parking lot. When they got to the mall's parking lot, to his and Harriet's surprise Julius jumped out of the car went around to her door opened it and smiled as she came out. Julius had bought himself a new Japanese Toyota Camry but after two years it had registered less than two hundred kilometers. He just walked to and from work and on occasion he used the car to travel across the city to pick up some chocolates which he had grown to love and it was really his only treat to himself. He lived in a small apartment within walking distance of the campus which had housed students for many years. He did not feel the need to change his home even when he had a full time faculty job.

Loneliness comes in all forms and there are a number of sayings passed through to me by my mother such as "Misery loves company", "Loneliness of the individual continually searches to find a mate" etc., all of which appear to have come together one summer and out of all of this attraction maybe love blossomed. The catastrophe of having both parents succumb in one year left a very lonely Harriet who was emotionally vulnerable. Julius sensing a soul spirit appear so close to him began to awake and the coffee breaks became his method of socializing and after all these years maybe it was a form of courting. Harriet must have felt the same way for she even used the initiative to take them both away from the campus for their summer ritual of having coffee together, so that they both could be alone with each other.

This continued even when the Campus became filled with students in the Fall and Winter months. She also felt that she could do more for Julius's practical classes. In some way Julius appears to have become more reliant on her doing so much for his practical classes and he gave her more scope to do all the planning for the students practical experience, which relieved him of the need to have any dealings with these students. When the students finally had to give their opinions on the quality of instruction being given by the science Profs., it came as a shock when Julius practical classes were given the most glowing of reports. Julius, who was not the most sensitive of men knew that all these little accolades were due to Harriet and while he was chuffed with the comments of his peers, he knew that it was due to Harriet who was always present for his labs and his students. He noticed that he always found a reason to chat with her and if for some reason he had to leave the class Harriet handled the students just as competently as any of the full time graduate students and other assistant professors, giving lots of support to the students who were going to be the budding scientists of the future.

It all began when Harriet got up early one morning to begin preparation to go to work, when the 'female monthly thing' caused her severe cramps and distress that in spite of her determination to go to work she just could not make it and had to call in sick. When Julius did not see her for their usual coffee sessions, he searched around with out asking any questions and it was only in the afternoon when the loyal Harriet, was not present that he went to ask the pool of technicians where she was and found out that she was not going to be in to work that day. They did not say to him that she was sick at home. He looked like a lost puppy continually looking into her room and going into her room as though expecting her to appear at any moment. All day he appeared to be distracted from his work and he was even more uncommunicative and obtuse in his dealing with others.

That evening he took out his car and after finding out where Harriet lived from one of the other technicians, he headed out for her home. He found the address where she had lived with her parents and where she had continued to live but he did not stop at the address, rather he drove around some more and went into a nearby mall. As the evening matured and it was becoming dark that he returned and saw a light come on in the front window of the house that he got up the nerve to park the car in front of the house and went up to the house.

He had in his hands some flowers and two coffees, one with milk and one sugar, which was for Harriet and one with cream and two sugars for him. He was in a bit of an excited sweat as he went up to the front door. He stared at the front door which had a rough beaded, ripple, opaque glass in two longitudinal strips thus not allowing anyone on the outside to see inside of the house. After some time he looked to the right side of the door and saw the lighted door bell button. In a mechanical movement he pressed the button once. He waited and after a short time a light came on in the hall way which, could be seen behind the slit of opaque glass. There was a shadow of someone coming towards the door. He found that his forehead was sweaty and his mouth dry. There were a number of locks being undone and door was opened slowly and was just ajar with the safety chain remaining attached. A worried and bespectacled figure of Harriet's pale face appeared in the narrow doorway. She looked at him unsmiling as her eyes became adjusted to the twilight outside then her eyes opened wide and with some shock.

Julius felt dryness in his mouth and heard himself blurt out "You were not in the lab today". Harriet looked at him and said that she was sick but she removed the chain stood aside and said to him,"Come in quickly Julius, I am still in a house coat." Julius walked in quickly and he found that he was very happy when he heard her call him by his first name. He looked at her and handed over the flowers and said "I thought that you may like a coffee since you did not have one this morning". For the first time, Harriet smiled and the paleness of her face appeared to flush showing a slight pink to her cheeks. She said "Give me your coat and hat, Julius". He turned around and he felt her reach to assist him in removing his coat. He already had his hat in his hand and had to switch hands as his overcoat was removed. Under his coat was his old sweater and his thin and wrinkled tie, Harriet took the coat and hat and opened the front hall closet to hang the coat and placed the hat on the top shelf.

The closet was tidy but there was another man's coat hanging as well as another felt hat on the same shelf. Julius looked inside the closet only briefly and as he was ushered into the front living room, he felt her hands on his shoulder gently nudging him forward. When he was in the middle of the tidy drawing room with it's sofa against the wall end lamps wearing pink lamp shades one on each end of the sofa, fronted by a small brown coffee table, which was semi surrounded by two corner individual arm chairs in opposite corners, he turned around suddenly so that Harriet almost bounced into him only the small card board tray holding the coffee across which lay a bunch of cut flowers separated them. He looked down at her tiny figure which appeared even smaller in the white dressing gown and house slippers, he felt taller and more confident as she looked up at him. He was very close to her when he said, 'when I did not see you today I searched all over the science floor for you and I did not go for our usual coffee break. I did not know what to do. So I waited for the afternoon labs to begin and you still were not there. I went and asked the other technicians where you were and they told me you were not going to be coming into work today. I did not have a coffee all day"

'It is alright Julius; I had to call the office. I always have a rough time with my monthly period and I can work most of the time but today I just could not move. I hate not being at work." she remarked She told him to sit on the sofa, which he did. She opened one of the coffees and it was the one he had bought for himself."Julius will you like me to pour this into a coffee mug or will you prefer to have it in this paper cup?" she asked quietly. He looked anxiously at the proffered coffee intently and nodded saying "No thank you I will have it now in the paper cup". Harriet said, "Sit there for a minute, I shall place these flowers into a vase with water and I will be right back". He looked up at her with his thick rimmed spectacles sitting on top of his pudgy cheeks. He could hear Harriet in the kitchen with the tap running then the sound of a tin being placed on the kitchen counter. It was not long before she returned with a small vase of flowers, as he had been sipping his coffee, which she placed in the middle of the coffee table. She sat next to him and opened her own coffee, then she brought out of her house coat pocket, a small tin of biscuits. She deftly opened the tin and offered him one of the Scottish short bread cookies. His eyes bulged as he reached into the tin to remove one of the tasty morsels. He sat back into the chair and they both became as silent as when they have their coffee on mornings. Julius sipped his coffee with a silent contentment on his face. Harriet was feeling a bit better for she had intended to go to work in the morning. She looked at Julius out of the corner of her eye and for the first time she saw his contentment and the pink glow on his cherubic cheeks

It was quite late before Julius decided to leave. The conversation was mainly lead by Harriet, who seeing his contentment decided to tell him about her mother and father who had passed away about a year ago. She told him that her parents were only children and that she was an only child as well, so she really had no family. He listened quietly and attentively as though he was in a trance just looking at her from time to time. The only emotion that showed on his face was one of sadness and his cheeks sagged a little as his thick lips became moist and protruded even more, when she explained her parents passing away. The whole tale took almost half of the evening. Harriet, after she told Julius about the little family history, found that she was feeling better. After a time when they had both finished their now cold coffees but still holding their cups, Julius suddenly said quite loudly said "I do not know my parents. I had a grandma who looked after me but she did not want me around and I knew that so I spent all my time at student lodgings, summer camps and residences. She died and left some inheritance to me. I did not love her. Actually, no one ever loved me and I do not know how to love anyone." He looked at Harriet with his huge bulging eyes and moist lips, making his face appear to be even larger because of his pebble glasses. Harriet looked at him in a stunned silence and she just touched his arm in an emotional reflex. There was sadness at this form of neglect which she could feel but she also saw a very lonely person. Harriet may have felt some of the loneliness of Julius but she had known her parents and at times they showed their affection to her by smiling at her achievements. When she came home from the lab on evenings they appeared pleased at her return but did not ask how her day went for they appeared to be just satisfied that she had survived another work day. While they did nothing to actively nurture her emotional growth they were there for her at least she felt so. Her emotional response was instinctive for she also knew that her parents just did not know how to nurture by the same intuition.

She suddenly felt an emotional twinge for Julius, who looked at her directly for a long time with this sad feature, that she asked him directly "What is it Julius?," "He sniffed a little looked away from her and said "Will you come back to work tomorrow? I do not know what to do when you are not there in the morning. I..." he stammered, looked back up to her "I miss you Harriet." He looked away from her at his sock covered feet and beads of sweat appeared on his forehead and on the sides of his nose. 'Yes, Julius I will be in tomorrow. I think that I am feeling better" she tried to sound casual in tone but she was feeling a bit choked in the back of her throat. "Oh! Thank you Harriet" came the unexpected and rapid reply in a louder tone of voice, which shocked Harriet who jumped in her seat.

"Julius, is something wrong? You are sweating and you look nervous" again she reached over to touch his arm. He placed his fat fingers on her hand to keep her from moving hers. Then slowly he slid sideways towards her. Harriet did not know what to do but she was overcome with a strong feeling of great sympathy towards this big man who had the face of an overgrown school boy. As his shoulders and face reached her small shoulder, he removed his spectacles and a loud sob was released. Harriet instinctively placed her arms around his head and broad shoulder as a mother would hold a teenage child. Then a shuddering and sobbing broke out from Julius which broke Harriet's heart. For the first time she felt strength in her frail frame which also reached out for a human touch. In a way the need in both these very lonely individuals became a form or basis of attraction to them. Julius felt the warmth of another human touch, his need could not be easily satisfied and his convulsive sobbing was a manifestation of this great loneliness which he had carried with him for so long. Such is the pathological need for social and physical contact of fellow human beings that lives are lost and only shadows of human forms walk among us in their loneliness and despair.

Sobbing uncontrollably, he buried his face into the house coat and the slight form of Harriet shoulder and her small arms for she could also feel his body wreck with a trembling and his body heat, which stimulated her to respond in an almost maternal way to hold this baby—man. "I thought that you had gone away and I would never see you again" he snorted into her coat as his hands held onto her sleeve. "I am so lonely, Harriet. Please do not leave me!" He blurted out in an emotional shudder. "You are my friend, Julius. I will not leave you. I just could not come in this morning". He was not listening and she continued "you are the only friend that I have and I missed having you around this morning but I was in so much pain that I fell asleep". Julius stopped sobbing after awhile but lay with his fat child-like face on the wet sleeve of Harriet's coat, where he could still feel the warmth of her nearness.

Slowly he began to sit up and was beginning to feel a bit embarrassed as he sat up erect on the sofa. Harriet slowly removed her arms from around his shoulder. She looked at him and a small smile crossed her face and when Julius looked at her he just thought how beautiful she was. He pulled out a handkerchief from his coat pocket and wiped his eyes, nose and cheeks while slowly glancing up at Harriet. "Maybe I must go now Harriet, it is almost eleven pm," and he made an attempt to sit forward on the sofa. Harriet was amazed at the time, which had absolutely flown by. She was normally in bed by nine p.m. "Oh! My goodness" she loudly remarked. "I will see you in the morning, Julius" and there was a sort of happiness in her voice and one of a renewed confidence. They both stood up and Harriet moved quickly around the coffee table towards the closet in the hallway. She opened it but she could feel Julius standing just behind her. He was looking into the closet as she removed his coat. She held it up and he turned around with his back towards her as she fitted it over his big shoulders. Then almost child like he turned around to face her as he began to button up. He continued to look past her at the hats on the top shelf. Harriet turned to remove his hat from the top shelf, where it was sitting. She quickly followed his eyes to where Julius was looking. Then she realized that he was looking at her father's hat next to his. "Oh! That is my father's hat. I have not got around to removing any of his clothing or any of my mothers belongings from the closets, Julius"

He looked down at Harriet and said "I am so happy that I came over, Harriet. I will go home now and I will see you in the morning". Harriet opened the door and he stepped out and walked towards his car at the end of the path. Harriet just held the door ajar long enough to see him off. He looked up at her and waved just before he entered his car and drove off. She closed the door smiled , turned the hall light off and set off for the kitchen to have a drink of milk before going to bed. She was happy as she turned off the lights in the kitchen and headed off to do her ablutions in the bathroom, before turning in for the night.

Three months later, Harriet had the same 'female' problem and just could not go to work. She called the office and gave her excuse for not coming in that day. She then tried to call Julius at his office but he was not there and he had no answering service. He never felt that he needed such luxuries since he was never in his office working for any period of time. It was a place just to leave his coat and his brief case. His relationship with Harriet since that night returned to the morning and after noon coffee breaks and their comforting silence. They had never brought up the topic of that evening and it did not seen to bother either of them Harriet thought about the possibility of them becoming a bit closer but when she turned up the next morning apart from a larger smile, Julius neither said nor did anything to enhance their relationship and she to all intent appeared to just leave things as they were. He never went back to her home and she never asked him back to her home again. Julius never asked anyone back to his apartment since there were many students, who were lodging there and he continued to just be a student tenant. The apartment met his comfort needs and it had become just a place to sleep, have his supper, a morning shower and the old landlady was pleased to have him around for he had been there for over fifteen years. The income was good and he never made any issue of complaining when she had to raise the rent. Such a good tenant was worthwhile keeping. When he was asked if she could do his laundry he readily agreed and went along with the increase of his rent, which now included his laundry and bed linen. The land lady had tried to find out more of this perpetual student but she never got any further than the fact that he was first an undergraduate student, and then a graduate student then he got a job at the University. He said nothing and he just took the fact for granted that she was like a paid grandma, whom he passively ignored and his only communication was the fact that she made supper and left it in the kitchen for him every evening, to which he had never complained. He returned to a room that was always tidy and had clean linen and laundry, not that he would have noticed anyway. There was a bit of a problem which she had to bring to Julius' attention, from time to time actually about three to four times in the past ten years and that was the wearing out of his underwear, his trousers, shirts and the black suit which he had for a number of years. She had it cleaned once for the summer and again for the winter but it had to be done the same day and that was always on the week end. He had to be told about these domestic inconveniences by this lady who had taken over the task of looking after this very sad boy now prematurely aging man. But he was still a boy to her and since she had no other family after the death of her husband she just looked after this unusual tenant, who asked for nothing extra, lived very quietly and was apparently working very hard at the University.

It was almost deja' vu of the incident which had occurred when Harriet did not come in to work because of the 'female monthly thing' three months previously. Again Julius turned up at Harriet's house in the evening a very bothered man and who was emotionally distraught. He entered into Harriet's house with the two coffees, flowers and was met by a pallid Harriet in a house coat which he did not seem to pay any attention to. He sat on the sofa after handing over his coat and hat to her. She hung the coat and parked the hat on the shelf next to her father's hat on the same shelf. Harriet placed the flowers into the vase then placed the adornment on the coffee table. She offered him a short bread cookie from the same tin and he willingly took one and sipped his coffee while she did the same. There was one difference and it came from Julius, who after finishing his coffee, looked over at Harriet and spoke loudly which seemed to shatter their silence. "Harriet, I do not like to miss you at work. I feel more lonely, than ever and I especially like to meet you on the Saturday mornings when we are by ourselves. I do not like Sundays for I try to sleep all day just waiting for you to come to work on Monday".He looked at his socked feet and continued, "Can you tell me how to arrange for us to be together all the time?". "Julius, are you asking me to live with you? asked the shocked Harriet. She did not believe the words which were coming out of her lips even as she was saying them.

"Harriet, I do not know anything about women other than what I have read and studied in my text books. I do not know how married people live. I do not believe in any religion since I do not and have never gone to any church and other than the fact that I bow my head at some of the University functions in prayer I do not understand why we do such rituals. I only know my science but in the context of doing some research, teaching a little and doing the labs for the second and third year students. I spend all of my time marking the labs, preparing lectures from text books and then correcting their tests on the week ends and over the holidays. I do not watch television or read anything other than the newspaper which is often left in the Faculty lounge."

This was the longest speech that Julius had ever had with anyone and that included his students, to whom he gave brief and almost glib answers to when he was forced to communicate with them or anyone else. The faculty continued to have very little contact with him and to totally ignore him. Since many of the faculty was also at least ten to fifteen years older than him, they continued to treat him as the kid on the block. He was in fact a 'persona non grata' in the eyes of the grad students and the staff on the whole. His unfortunate appearance of being over weight, his heavy glasses and his dated and worn out clothing were all walls surrounding him. The technical staff did notice that Harriet was looking after him in the labs and that she did have coffee with him, however they ate separately as the staff ate at the student cafeteria while the faculty ate at the faculty club.

Julius just found himself a corner with some of the student's lab work and ate by himself. In the days when Chemton used to come to the faculty club he would on occasion sit with Julius but there was never any real social conversation and their nods and singular speech always dealt with student work. Chemton appeared to have done his work with this strange lonely student who had become a man but who did not develop socially. He did not feel that the task of assisting this man any further in his development was his job and in time he began to go to his home at lunch time and avoiding the faculty lunch area. He took this liberty since he could pass on most of his duties to Julius, who never complained or questioned any of the added duties which he was asked to do by Dr Chemton and for whom he must have had a great deal of respect. To all intents and purposes Julius did not appear to miss his old mentor to which he had owed every bit of progress, which had happened to him since coming to this back water University.

Harriet was looking at Julius intently after his lengthy monologue. It was her turn for he had turned towards her and was looking for some reply. "Julius, we are alike in many ways. I look at television sometimes but not often. I read the newspapers every day for it comes to the house. My father had ordered it and I have never cancelled it since he died. I have no family or friends like you". She stopped and looked over at Julius whose lips were wet and protruding but his eyes looked like those of a very sad beagle. She just could not control herself anymore. She reached over in the same way as she had done three months ago and held his forearm. He immediately clamped his thick fingers over her slender ones. She could feel the warmth of his hands which were beginning to become moist.

She said "Julius; I will not live with you". His eyes almost instantly became moist. But she used her other hand to touch his lips saying "Sh.hh! I did not mean that I do not want to live with you. What I meant was that I did not want to live with you like the students do, y'know shack up together." "My parents would not have liked to see me do such a thing, you understand, don't you?" She inquired. While his eyes were moist they did not tear but his hand, which still covered hers were quite wet. Then as if she had a revelation she smiled at him and said very loudly, 'Julius, why do we not get married and live in this house. It is all that I have and it needs a lot of work. I do not have any money saved and I intended to sell it when I retire and move into a small flat, so that I would have a bit of a pension." Before he could answer she continued, "I will not live in your little student room".

Harriet felt Julius hand tighten on hers and the tears ran down his cheeks. " I have a lot of money saved, Harriet. I want to marry you and I will not, ever want you to live like the students do...not with you."

"Oh Julius, Harriet moved over and placed her two tiny hands on both his pudgy cheeks, closed her eyes and placed her pale thin lips against his leaving it there for a long time. It was just lips to lips. She felt Julius pull away only slightly but he placed a hand on the back of her head before their lips could fully separate, slipped the other hand to his forehead and removed his spectacles. Then she felt a gentle pressure push the back of her head forcing his lips to stick to hers. She felt a bit stifled and pushed her head back a bit. At this slight pressure Julius removed his hand from the back of her head. She pushed herself closer to him and placed her head on his heaving chest. She could hear his heart pumping hard against her ears. She looked up at him with a smile and with huge brown dilated pupils; her own glasses were on the coffee table. She did not know how it got there. He looked at her and for the first time she noticed that he had dark blue eyes but it was like looking through a jar of jelly. He squinted at her, wet cheeks. I love you Harriet. What will we do next?"

"Well Julius, I know that you may have some money but it

would never be enough for us to have our own house. Will you live here after we marry?" She asked. "Do you want to move from this cottage Harriet?" And as if he was looking at the house for the first time, he saw how small it was and how old the wall paper was. ' I have lived here all my life Julius and my mother often wished that we would win a lottery, so that she could buy a house in the country. I have often dreamed of what a house in the country would be like", she smilingly said. Julius replied softly, "I have never thought about having a house but if you want a house in the country it should be close enough so that we could get into the campus". Before she could answer he had his arm around her slim waist and she just lay on his chest sitting on his thigh as he had sat down but was not letting go of her. She continued to look up into his face with a peaceful contentment but she could still hear his heart in full drum beat although it appeared to be dropping off a bit. "Tomorrow Harriet you will come with me after work to see my banker and see how much I have saved. Only if that is alright with you?" he cautiously inquired. Still thinking of him as a poor new grad for the university pay was known to be poor in comparison with workers in the car assembly plants. "You know Julius, you should keep the little money you have and we could then share our salaries to run the house. He seemed to be pained by her suggestion and this was the first time that he had ever made a suggestion to share anything that he had. She saw his slight rejection and responded accordingly. "OK, and I will make some calls to see when we can get to the Registrar Office to post wedding bands" she said. He then asked "do you not want to marry in a church." "No! "She said., then after awhile she continued "if you wanted too I wiould but what has the church done for either of us. I mean I do not want anyone present and I do not want anyone to make us live by any rules. Besides, I do not know what religion I am and 'you' do not care for any religion, do you?"

No!" He said with some finality.

Then she quietly asked "is that alright with you, Julius?" "Yes, Harriet" was the happy reply,

"Whatever you want is alright with me, just as long as we can be together every day and every night". Then, Harriet sat up quickly but still leaning on him "Julius, what about sex...I mean, .you do not want children, do you?", embarrassed by this fort right question which just came into her head and came out of her mouth. As she looked into his eyes, his cheeks blushed into a bright red and his lips parted "I have to have some help with that eh I mean, I did not think of us having children. Is it not going to be just two of us, Harriet?"

"OK", she said business-like, "and then I must go and see my doctor and get myself on the pill which she has wanted me to take for some time. She said that it would assist me with the heavy painful menstrual periods that I continually have. This is a good time to find out."

That was the extent of their planning and discussion. It was very late when Julius decided to leave and when he eventually got up to get his coat and hat Harriet reached over to give him a big hug and she had to pull his head down to kiss his lips and it was only then that he placed his big arms around her and held her for some time, she could feel him tremble then she sent him on his way. Julius walked down the steps turning around regularly to look at her and waved and she waved back. It was an odd departure and his actions were that of one who was afraid that she would disappear from the doorway. Harriet knew that and so she waited until he was in his car before she closed the door. Julius felt for the first time an odd very pleasant feeling which was about to choke him, he was so happy that his eyes continually streamed with tears while his nose ran with a clear fluid. His face was a moist mess when he parked his car that night. The time that he arrived and when he parked his car was not lost on his landlady, who was still awake and had noticed that Julius had not eaten his supper. In fact Julius went straight up to his room and did not come back down for his meal which was still in the kitchen. When she checked his room later on that night, she could see that the bed room lights were still on and there was the sound of papers being rustled. Julius was a creature of habit and that included his house habits of turning into bed at the same time every night. She did not know what was going on but it was an odd thing to happen for she thought that she had got to know this long time tenant very well. She did not speculate for long and turned in to bed herself.

As was planned the night before Julius put on his dark suit over a clean white shirt and while he was dressing he found another surprise in himself. There was a new tie in his dresser which he had never paid any attention to but this morning he took it up and took some time fixing the knot around his neck. He looked at his good pair of shoes which he used on the odd social occasion but this time he put them on even when it was only Tuesday. He took down his briefcase, which he had carefully checked the night before for he had filled it with many of the account and letters sent to him by the bank over the years. He had never been back to the bank since that day after meeting the bank manager and that was over six to seven years ago. He took the letters and memos sent to him and just filed them in his room desk.

He had lived very frugally just as in his student days and never looked at the bottom line which showed investment returns in the hundred of thousands of dollars. His own savings which was made from his salary was all he ever looked at and that was what he based his savings on. Even so his private savings which he knew was already over two hundred thousand dollars. He had no idea what the cost of property was or what his true financial worth was but if his Harriet wanted a home in the country then they would have a home in the country.

The two University employees disappeared immediately after work and set into motion a massive undertaking for themselves. The Bank Manager became a pivotal instrument in all their plans which included being the best man at the Court House arranged matrimonial, in exactly one month to the day on posting the bans. He was the person who found them the country estate house and who brought them up to date with the true amount of money that Julius really had. It was well over five million dollars much of it invested. After buying the new Country House, which they both knew instantly that it was exactly what they wanted, a sum of money was to be deposited monthly into their account which would look after all their physical expenses leaving their salaries as 'pin money'. They actually lived off one wage, which went to purchasing their weekly grocery. With the sale of Harriet's old house their income was guaranteed for the rest of their life if they lived as they did.

SPRING TURNING

They soon settled down into a middle aged routine but there was contentment for both of them. This all occurred in the fall and winter of the year and Harriet began to treat Julius as her mother treated her father. Julius had to do nothing and he soon began to love his large screen television set which began to occupy almost all of his waking time. However, he turned to Harriet in the following early spring and said to Harriet that he did not want to work at the university anymore. He said that he had met with the banker who said that neither of them had to work for the rest of their lives if they did not wish to do so Harriet said that she would also give up her job since she wanted to spend more time with him. They did very little together but Harriet began to show Julius that there were some jobs which had to be done around the house, such as cleaning the house at least once a week, doing the laundry, shoveling the snow, cooking and washing up the dishes. Julius began to learn all these household tasks with a vigour and enthusiasm which he had never shown for anything before. Harriet took them both for counseling in sex and becoming physically acquainted with each other. While she was a bit embarrassed, Julius began to enjoy this part of their relationship but his enthusiasm did not last and it was not long before he appeared to lose his libido. Harriet tried to keep him interested but he began to lose his enthusiasm for this past time. Her monthly periods which had given her so many problems over the years disappeared once she began using the pill.

It was in the late winter and early spring that they began to become restless and were not sleeping very well and this was odd for these two individuals always slept very well. Then one night just as they had settled into bed and had turned the lights off, they began tossing and turning. The more they tried to become comfortable the more awake they remained. In the end they just laid on their backs and each knew that the other was awake. Julius looked up at the ceiling and Harriet did the same but she closed her eyes while being aware of Julius being awake. She reached over to place her arm over his huge chest, which heaved in a smooth rhythm, so that her arm rose up and down. When she opened her eyes, she saw Julius looking at her intently; she smiled at him in the darkness. Almost at the same time there was a flash of lightening which illuminated their room and the rain began to fall outside and these comforting sounds came through the open windows. In the flash of that split second they both saw an apparition standing at the doorway to their bedroom. It was cloaked in white from head to foot and it's eyes were a pale blue. They both sat up as the figure moved towards them. They hugged each other tightly but no sound came from them. Julius just watched as did Harriet. The figure stood at the foot of the bed looked at them and when the next flash of lightening burst through the window they could see the whole form staring at them Julius was choked but managed to whisper out "Who are you?". There was no reply and in an instance the figure disappeared from their room. They looked at each other and Harriet reached over to the bed side lights to put them on. Julius was searching for his glasses which he kept on his bedside table. As he fitted them on, Harriet did the same and they both got out of bed and went out of the room to check the front door of the house. The whole house was completely locked along with the windows.

Harriet was shivering and for the first time Julius reached over to actively try and comfort her by placing his arms around her tiny shoulders. They went back to bed without saying much to each other but now they fell asleep immediately and the sounds of the storm died down to a pleasant patter of rain on the windows. The next morning they said nothing to each other about the incidence but there was a change in this morning routine. The early sun revealed a spring-like weather greeting them. While the winter was not severe, once they had given in their resignations, it was interesting that no other member of staff ever remarked about their association and no one appeared to be aware that they had been married. When they left the University no one threw a party or held a coffee hour as was the custom. It was if they were not present at the university and that their work was not contributing to the efficiency of the biology department. Equally, neither Harriet nor Julius thought any more about leaving their jobs, they just gave in their resignation and left. For some unknown reason there was a true contentment on both sides and no malice was seen obvious on either side—that is of the employer and the employee.

Neither of them spoke of what they had seen the night before however, Julius awoke early and he was bright and cheerful. He showered, shaved and dressed but there was one difference he was humming, which was a very unusual thing for him to do. Non-the-less, he continued humming as he placed the tie around his neck. When he began to stay at home after his resignation he did not use a tie for any of his days away from home but on this morning he put on a very brightly coloured tie.

There was briskness, about his movements and a sense of purpose as he prepared himself to leave the house. Humming, he entered into the kitchen where Harriet was waiting with a cup of coffee, he stopped looked into her smiling eyes very deeply, took the proffered coffee and pecked her on the cheek .This was the first impulsive act of normality displayed by these two very odd individual. He sat down at the small kitchen table which was dwarfed by the high ceiling and huge size of the kitchen.

Every thing that they placed in the rooms of the house appeared to be lost and become insignificant because of the size of the rooms. Meanwhile Harriet was also smiling but no conversation took place between these two. She brought over a plate which she took from the oven where it was placed to keep warm and which was covered with two fried eggs, toasts, several rashes of bacon and some sausages. It was a very large breakfast for anyone and even for Julius who always ate heartily at every meal regardless of what was placed in front of him; this sight brought forward a very large smile from this otherwise dour man. Then Harriet spoke to him as though answering an unspoken question, "Yes, Julius it is time". To which he looked up smiled and she returned to bring an equally large plate of breakfast for herself. She sat down in front of him and they both tucked into their meal with out saying a word. From time to time Harriet looked over at Julius and watched as he hungrily ate his breakfast she approached hers a bit slower but she also ate very heartily which was very unusual for her. However, he continued his humming between mouthfuls of food. Then Harriet took up the conversation and said "Well Julius you know where to go and get our tickets?" He did not look at her but managed to say "certainly, dear". "Well" she continued "do not forget to pick up the travelers checks for our hotel, you know the bank manager said it was safer than cash". "Certainly dear", he said with a lot of charm and humming in between mouthfuls of food.

The odd thing about this normal domestic scene was this sudden behaviour and change of character of this couple. To all intents and purposes they had never discussed anything much before nor anything domestic at anytime before this morning when each individual began to speak and to behave like a normal loving old couple. Julius got up put on his coat kissed Harriet on the cheek and left the house in his car. Harriet placed the dishes into the dish washer and began to clean up the kitchen. It was about lunch time when Julius returned with a brief case which he emptied out on their bed. He called in Harriet and showed her what he had bought that morning. He had two plane tickets for the next morning, destination Las Vegas and he also had packages of clothing for both of them as well as very expensive walking shoes. He also had reservations for a double bed room suite at the King Pharaoh Hotel. This was a new theme park hotel which was built to resemble a pyramid. He also produced tickets for a coach tour to the desert region, which included a stop over at the Hoover Dam and finally a trip to a native Indian Village.

This last stop was new to the tourist tours, since these Native American Indians did not allow any outsiders to visit their reservations or village. Until now many of the Native Indians had opened up their villages to the tourists to exploit this new opportunity to increase revenue by simulating up the past history of their peoples before the white man came. It was a big draw for the travel agencies which organized tours for city folks which depicted the native Indian way of living.

This particular Native Village was a small unheard of tribe, which was not mentioned in the History of North America Indian settlements. The brochure which he showed to Harriet was a simple paper flyer that was coloured deep reddish brown. Written in bold black letters were the words—'Personalized Tour of a Native American Indian Village'. It specified a pick up time and location and the fact that only a limited number of visitors would be allowed in each group tour. Oddly enough it stated the length of time it would take to complete the tour. What was interesting about this brochure was the lack of information with regard to how they were to communicate with the tour leaders for there were no FAX or Phone numbers, no e-mail or Internet address and no location specifics. There were no logo or scenery photographs, the instructions outlined in black lettering against the red—brown paper was all that there was. Julius also showed Harriet that he had one thousand dollars in traveler checks with the accompanying receipts revealing that every thing was paid for in cash. He had no credit card receipts. Twenty four hours later Julius and Harriet walked into the foyer of the glass covered Pyramid Hotel in Las Vegas and Harriet was showing happiness and a glow or radiance which emanated from her presence.

They both went up to their room and without a word to each other, although there was a lot of smiling Harriet picked up the phone and dialed number while Julius began to unpack their suitcases. Up until now neither said anything to each other and there was no evidence that Harriet until now knew anything about any aspect of this trip which they had embarked on so unexpectedly. Harriet had taken the initiative and called the tour company. Julius said nothing as he undressed himself dropping his shirt, jacket and trousers on the king sized bed. Wearing only his underwear he went over began to the large walk-in closet and removes a khaki safari trousers and an off-white tropical short sleeved shirt, which were on pressed hangers. He dressed himself quickly and sat at the edge of the bed to put on the pair of new leather walking shoes which he had bought the day before. When he looked up Harriet was already dressed in a short safari skirt, hat and blouse of the same type of colour. All this was done quickly and without a word to each other and as they looked at each other they were amazed to see themselves in the large wall mounted mirror. They looked at each other admiringly and smiled intensely at each other as thought they were seeing each other for the first time.

They were ready for a tour and the only colour on their safari outfit was a red-brown lateral stitched piece of cloth, about a quarter of an inch in width, which was stitched across the width of their shirt pockets. No sooner had they dressed when Harriet opened the door of their room suite to the wide plush carpeted corridor holding hands. The took the elevator down to the foyer and wandered through the number of slot machines and one arm bandits where other people were sitting in their finery pulling at the handles and placing coins into the slots. There was a cacophony of sounds which was a blend of metallic and human utterances. But there was richness in the atmosphere of people having fun and the laughter pierced the air from time to time. Harriet led Julius through the entrance of the hotel where the door automatically opened to the exterior curb where the taxis and luxury cars were entering the large 'U Shaped' driveway. In the middle of the 'U' was a beautifully cultivated garden, which housed concrete and marble with numerous fountains sculptures. Harriet pulled at Julius' hands and she took them both across to look at the garden, they stood and looked mesmerized at this oasis in the middle of the desert.

There was a honking of a horn behind them and they turned around to see a small white mini-van, which had a red-brown stripe painted across the middle of the side. As they looked on, a small squat man with a dark reddish skin, black straight back combed hair stepped down backwards from the driver's seat and approached them. He looked at them and abroad smile broke across his mouth revealing even square white teeth. He stopped before them and bowed Japanese style. His eyes were oval and pale blue but they looked more like a 'goat's eyes' . He said to them "you are the last folks to be picked up before we begin the tour. Welcome to Las Vegas and our beautiful desert". They followed him to the van and he walked around to the passenger side door entry. He reached inside and pulled out a heavy plastic stool, which he placed on the driveway in front of the door. There was a sort of facetious graciousness in the action but they stood on the stool, which made it easy to enter the van. They both made their way into the back seat of the van which was the only seats which were empty. No one made any greeting comments to Julius and Harriet but there appeared to be a sort of subdued chatting between the individuals. There were two other couples in the van and Harriet and Julius brought the total to six plus the driver. The couples were all dressed in the same outfits for the men and the women. It looked as though they were all in uniform and that included the driver.

DESERT TOUR.. ..*into the second dimension*

Julius and Harriet settled into the back seat and Harriet appeared to have reverted into her quiet unsmiling demeanor and as the quiet subdued wife. She opened her purse and began feeling around as though she was looking for something specific and this went on for some time as the van sped away from the hotel. Her attention began to become quite focused on blindly searching through her purse and to involve her attention totally. Julius also appeared to have lost his spunk of the past two days and until an hour ago. He looked like the premature old man as he was, with the slightly stooped shoulders, his paunchy mid-riff and his thin hair was beginning to show. However, Julius began to look at their fellow passengers and to listen to the humming of the driver, who looked at his passengers in the large rear view mirror suddenly he coughed into the microphone which brought all the passengers to attention. He said "Welcome to the tour pf some of finest natural physical wonders of this planet." He appeared to giggle to himself as he settled behind the steering wheel. "Tell me", he said "if you can hear me clearly in the back. Is the volume loud enough?" he asked and waited for a reply.

There was a general mumbling which was incoherent and over all nodding which he took to mean approval and that all could hear him properly. Again there was that little giggle to himself. Between the microphone and his voice on the attached sell phone which rang intermittently, any vocal response from the passengers was going to a futile gesture. He was going to be the commander for the day and again he giggled to himself as though he had just told himself a joke and of course he was in control so he was just enjoying himself. He began by pointing out the different casinos and various landmarks as they travelled out of the city of Las Vegas. But strangely none of the passengers appeared to be interested in the main reason for this city to be here in the first place. His voice dropped a bit as he outlined the itinerary for the day journey through the desert but he rambled on for a bit about the 'new tour company' which had just started business recently and they were the second group of chosen tourists to be participating in the venture. His commentary had become a bit more enthusiastic as he explained how the tour company began to exploit the newness of this new Indian settlement.

He continued to give a bit of the history of other companies, which had tried to make deals with these Indians but with little to no success. He said that this was a small tribe which lived on the great plateau and mesa of the Grand Canyon and little was known of their culture, religion, their beliefs or how they survived on this waterless terrain, with it's rocky and gravel soils and tree-less landscape. Soon the passengers settled down to the movement of the van and everyone became silent as did the driver. He interrupted their reverie from time to time with descriptions of the landscape which was the same sand and beige colour. There were some scrub bushes but the undulations of rock and sand covered hills as well as an endless range of treeless mountains in the horizon all made for a rather uninteresting and bleak scenery.

Many of the passengers appeared to find a quiet peace in somnolence while others appeared to listen intently from time to time at the droll commentary of the driver. They were soon in the middle of desert country and it was odd for from time to time the driver slowed his vehicle to avoid and to cross over swathes of sand which had blown onto the road just as the snow did in the north of the continent. When the van slowed down, it was possible look at the small clumps of vegetation many of which appeared to have small clusters of flowers. Then again they passed by fenced off areas which had electrical stations and what appeared to be television towers. Apart from these man-made communication towers bearing large transformers, the rocky hillocks took over and the stark landscape held little interest to the travellers.

Suddenly the van stopped and pulled towards the curb of the road, the microphone cackled a bit and soon everyone was awake and they listened to the soft voice of the driver said, "Behind the hills', which he pointed to in the distance, "there is supposed to be a secret air force base belonging to the US Military. It is thought that they deal with unknown flying phenomena and off planet research. No one is allowed within a twenty mile radius of that base, which is protected night and day by patrolling military police with guard dogs and high tech equipment which are hidden around the area," he concluded with the same guttural chuckling to himself. "It has happened in the past that a few individuals have gotten close enough to use high powered lens cameras to take pictures of the enclosure but they were soon found and their film was taken away and discarded." He sat quietly as his little band of individuals listened to his attempt at stimulating some humour into them but all he got was a quiet respect. He concluded "neither commercial aircraft nor small private planes are allowed into that district, all of which are patrolled by the military and their traffic sounds can be heard from time to time but rarely seen." While the others were dozing off including his wife Julius looked ahead in the van and he could see the features of the driver in the oversized internal rear view mirror. He knew that the driver could also see his passengers through the same mirror, which he did by taking short sharp upward glances in the device. He had an apparent continuous smile on his face which broadened from time to time revealing the short square white teeth. Slowly, Julius turned his attention to the other passengers in the van. First of all there was a single woman who was sitting next to the driver and whom he had not seen before but she was a short plump blond woman. In the seat immediately behind the driver were two women, who looked like a mother and daughter and he had never noticed them before. They were rather slim but as the younger woman looked towards her adult companion, he saw the dark hair and slim neck of a woman in her twenties whiles the dyed hair of her companion was all that he could see, there was the occasional cackle or gravelly tone in response to a quiet question from her younger seat mate.

In the seat immediately in front of Julius was a rather fat woman accompanied by a slim old man. The woman appeared to be uncomfortable with the heat in the van, for the driver had turned down the air conditioner. The man had his head bent for most of the time and to all intent he was asleep all the time. Next to this couple was another female passenger who appeared to be oriental. Her hair was black but there was evidence of grey strands interrupting the smooth back swept hair style. For the first time Julius became aware of all the individuals in the van but more importantly he was the only young to middle aged male apart from the drive whose age it was difficult to judge. This brought a smile to his face and he had a guilty side glance at Harriet who was fast asleep and had her face turned away towards the window of the van. He then noticed that all the women were sitting with their heads turned towards the window nearer them and they popped up their heads when the driver continued his droll commentary about the outside geography or other worthwhile structure. He turned his head to look through his window and saw bright sunshine on the outside; there were no clouds along the rocky, sandstone hills which sped away in the distance as the van entered deeper into the Arizona desert. The scene outside soon became hypnotic and as Julius listened to the intermittent drone of the drivers voice, which was undecipherable, he soon nodded off.

With a jolt they all became awake to hear a chirpier voice of the driver saying "Well!, folks please take the elevator down to the bottom of the Dam, where you will be met by a guide, who will show you around the bottom of the mighty Hoover Dam as well give you a bit of the history and statistics of how twentieth feat of modern endeavor was constructed and what an engineering achievement it was for it's time". He was standing with the passenger door wide open which allowed a dry hot air to enter their cool world. The small plastic stool was acting as the first step to the outside of the van which was parked in the large concrete driveway. On one side of the driveway, was a high concrete wall but from the van they could all see the water which was held back behind the dam. They entered into a large cavernous building all of which were made of the same concrete and was unpainted.

They entered and appeared to be overwhelmed by the enormity of the building. He ushered them into the hallway in which there were a bank of elevators but it was strange that there were no other folks around. Harriet asked the driver " Are we the only ones here?" He replied, "No Mam, there are others on tour at the base of the dam and you will join them soon" as he gently placed his hand on her back steering her and the others towards the bank of elevators. They were ushered into a large elevator which moved silently downwards. They all remained silent and in seconds the door opened and on leaving the elevator they found themselves in a large open area surrounded by great cement surrounding walls. There was a lot of back ground noise which sounded like huge machinery working away and all was coming from behind the walls. As the little group tightened into a firm bunch, all of whom were staring upwards at the massive walls and saying nothing for they were all awestruck a loud voice shook them into attention "Welcome to Hoover Dam". Facing them was a woman in a blue uniform approaching them from across the opposite floor and she was smiling broadly. "You must be the next group that I was told to expect". Julius and Harriet stood closely together and Julius thought that if that was the guide she looked like an air hostess. She stood in front of them and appeared to look into each of their individual faces with her pale smiling eyes. "Good day, you are about to see one of the wonders of the world which was all man-made" Her smile caused everyone to smile as well and this was not a group who found smiling to be easy. They all listened intently as the voice gave statistics of the amount of cement used to make the structure, the billions of dollars that the Dam generates in bringing hydroelectricity as well as regulating water to the farms many miles away. The guide went into the value of this priceless resource as drinking water for many millions of people. Julius stood at the back of the small group and he thought that he could hear everything that was said by this very attractive guide. He began to pay attention to her light brown hair, her red lips, rounded hips and slim figure and he did not know whether he was fantasizing but she appeared to be looking directly at him. Harriet must have felt the same effect for she held onto Julius' hand even tighter which was really a reflex action on her part. Neither of them had ever shown any interest in other people so this was a new feeling which was developing in both of them.

'The whole mighty Colorado River has been brought under control and blocked by this massive concrete and steel structure. It ends up as a trickle as it enters Mexican territory." For the guide was concluding her speech to an audience who did not ask any questions and just stood quietly for the whole tour. As she went closer to the huge columns of concrete, which stood like massive obelisks towering away above them, all eyes looked upwards to the sky. Then one by one they reached over to touch these columns and they could feel the mighty vibrations of power which was harnessed and kept under rein. They all felt like small ants touching the columns and Julius, who was the last to reach over, could feel the power of the vibration entering through his hands into his shoulder. He appeared to have let go of Harriet hands, as he was quietly thinking about power, so that he was brought abruptly by a voice which said "Dr Kane, please do not remain behind". Julius jumped up on hearing his name and looked around to find that the group had moved away towards the elevator and he was left standing away from the group. Before he could get his bearing and move forward the lovely guide was by his side and she whispered to him "was there something that you wanted to know, Sir?" He nodded smiled back at her and followed her as she briskly moved towards the now receding group. She turned around to say "we must move quickly so that the next group can be accommodated. Besides you still have the journey to the Indian Village which is going to be exciting," she continued. "I wish that it was my turn to go. I must work for quite awhile again before I get the chance to go on that journey" Julius just mumbled but had no idea what she had said or of what she was talking about. "Is it not exciting for us to open up the Village. It has been a perfect front and protection for us for so long. Only now can we be free to take the visitors with us. But we have schedules to meet and strict rules to follow". All of this chatter was lost to Julius as he hurried to meet up with the group. They reached the elevator and bunched together and almost immediately the elevator opened and they all entered except for the guide who waved smilingly at them. Some of the group waved back but no one said thanks or good bye. The elevator moved rapidly to the top and almost instantly the door opened and they found themselves in the large entranceway, where their guide was waiting.

He beamed at them and said loudly "was this not exciting for the time it was built? came his rhetoric question. He just went in front of the group and opened the front doorway to let them out into the sunshine. The van was parked right at the entrance way to the building and they all stepped on the plastic stool to enter. The driver went to the front seat and turned on the air conditioning but turned around and said "would any of you like to use the facilities before we get on our way?" It was strange that he was making that offer now and not when they were in the building. Again there was an inaudible murmur which must have been in the negative for he just turned around started the van and continued "Great then let us be on our way". His passengers said nothing to each other and they all seemed to settle down for this part of the trip

DREAMS OR A FANTASY?

The driver for the first time went quiet and when Julius looked at him through the rear view mirror, he could see that he had taken off his dark sun glasses and his 'goat like blue eyes' appeared more prominent. As if knowing that he was been observed he looked up suddenly and caught Julius looking at him intently or so it seemed since Julius was wearing his pebble glasses. Julius did not know what to do and then he caught a 'wink' from the driver who appeared to whisper to him alone, "why do you not join the others and have a nap, Mr. Kane" Julius jumped in his seat for the words just appeared to come into his mind but it was if he was been spoken to directly. When he moved his head to look over at his wife she was fast asleep and so were all the other passengers. He looked back at the staring blue oval eyes, who was looking at him directly but this time there was a smile. Julius nodded to him and almost immediately as he had began to reach over for Harriet's hand he felt a wave of drowsiness sweep over him. Harriet just held onto his hand and he felt even more secure and it was just the bit of comforting that he needed so he went to the land of 'nod'.

Julius was smiling to himself for he saw in his dreams a beautiful pink sunset and he could see both him and Harriet holding hands and looking up at the beauty of the scene in front of them.

Then Harriet looked up at him took his hands and showed him a blanket laid out on the grass on top of a look out point where they had come to enjoy the sunset. It was an odd sunset for he had noted that two moons had begun to appear in the early night sky but he was focused on his wife. She took out a picnic lunch and then she began to pour him a coffee with the cream and sugar just as he liked it. He saw himself focus intently on the cup offered to him and he smacked his lips as he always did. She had her cup as well and he saw himself just enjoying this little repas'. He must have transferred this through his hands for Harriet tightened her grip on his large hands. He went even deeper into sleep and made himself comfortable by sliding over to lean on her shoulder or close enough so that he could feel more of her close to him.

He saw a young couple in his dream that were also holding hands. The man was burley had big brown eyes for he was also wearing pebble glasses. The woman was slight with a slightly brown to blond hair but her eyes were a pale blue. In fact, the eye was the same as the drivers for they had that oval and paleness in them like that of a goat. They both turned to him and were waving to him. Julius felt that he was unsure of whom they were waving to, so he saw himself look around and there was no one else. Just then he heard the woman say "Julius, it is us, your Mum and Dad". Julius looked earnestly at the couple and then he thought he had seen an old black and white photo at his grandma's place but it was in her bedroom which he had seen by accident one summer.

He never really thought of what his parents looked like and he never asked to see photos since his grandma was not very communicative and she had put down his curiosity so often he never bothered to pursue any such topics again. He looked back at them and then he heard his mother say, "You have done very well Julius and we are very proud of you". His mother then continued "Harriet is a very nice girl and I am glad that we found her for you. Do you really love her Julius?".He heard himself say "Of course, I love her but you did not find her for me I found her for myself. You died and left me alone," he said hotly and he thought that he never ever said anything so rough before to anyone. Just then Harriet hand again squeezed his and he heard her say to him, with a mild rebuke "Now Julius! That is not the way to speak to your parents".

He was astonished for he was standing holding Harriet's hands and facing this couple who were his supposed parents. He looked down at her and Harriet was pulling him forward to the couple and he just followed her. He then saw Harriet hold out her hand to Julius mother and say, "It is a pleasure to meet Julius' parents." The woman shook Harriet's hand and then turned towards Julius father and say "Harriet meet your father-in—law , this is Josh Kane". Harriet turned towards Mr. Kane and also shook his hands. Julius was so confused and said loudly "Harriet come away from them I do not know them. Yes they do look like the photo at my grandma's house but they left me. Do not speak to them" and he found that he was pulling Harriet quite firmly away from his dream persons.

"Now Julius, do not be so hard on us we were called away and the accident was the only way for us to leave. We left you with enough support and we have always looked after you when we could but it was very difficult for us to get away. Grandma was the next to leave and she was very angry at being left behind to look after you" came the explanation and at the same time a gentle scolding from his mother whom he was beginning to be attracted to but his father said nothing for he was just looking at what was going on. Then Josh spoke up "Now Julius, we had little choice in the decision to leave earth. We were successful in having you. I did not know much about the occupation until your mother told me of the need to integrate and to have children. You cannot imagine how proud we were when you were born. Even as a baby you looked like me and we were very proud to be your parents. We know that we had to leave you to grow up as a citizen and be successful." Josh looked at the mirror image of himself and Julius saw an older version of himself and then he began to understand but Josh continued " We thought that we would be left alone to bring you up but the temptation to tell you everything as you grew up would have been to strong to hold back. Our superiors knew that and so they took us away. It was not the best way to to remove us, nor the most pleasant but they had to make our exit permanent, for you were too valuable and important to our whole project. Please try and understand but do not worry for we shall soon be together."

"What do you mean that we shall soon be together?" Asked the startled Julius and again he felt the hand of Harriet in his. "Do not worry son, just stay on the tour".

As both Harriet and Julius stood looking at his smiling parents they heard another voice interrupt "Harriet, Harriet, my goodness Len, look at our beautiful girl!". Harriet turned around and both Julius and Harriet stood looking at Harriet's mother and father. Julius knew that they were her parents for he had seen their wedding photo which Harriet kept on their living room mantel place.

Harriet let go of Julius' hand and ran forward to meet her parents. Her mother was dressed the same way as Julius' mother in a pale beige suit with a red brown bar which ran across the top blouse. "Mum", she heard herself shout out in surprise. "Dad! My word!

Look at you both! You look so well. Meet my husband, Julius," said the excited Harriet. Julius had reached her side and stood looking at this very slim brown eyed woman who was dressed in the same outfit like his Mum. He then looked at her father, Len who held out his hand to Julius to shake. Julius found himself looking at this slim tall blue eyed man, shaking his hand which was warm and who was smiling at him encouragingly. His eyes were the same as that of the driver. "Hello Julius, your parents said that you had met our Harriet and had hit it off. Good lad, we were so pleased to see you both so happy for the first time. But you had to have a true earth upbringing." Harriet's Mum reached over to kiss him on the cheek and for the first time in his life Julius was surrounded by love from two couples and he just could not cope. So even in his dream he was shaking with tears running down his chubby cheeks. He looked at his parents and said "I do not know what to call you. I have never had to call anyone Mum or Dad"

" Do not worry Julius we shall be with you on your journey just get comfortable calling us Mum and Dad like Harriet is calling her parents and when we meet you will know us. I know how hard it must have been with you son but it is all coming to an end now." Harriet was holding her mother and fathers hands and he also found that he was moving to be closer to his parents. His mother reached over to him and he soon felt her hug him like Harriet does and he felt his father's hands on his back".

Julius knew the feel of true love by touch. Then both pairs of parents stood up and said to them stay close to each other for you will both have the same dream. We do love you both. Good luck for the time being.

In an instant, Julius opened his eyes and looked over to Harriet who was smiling at him and he was with her. Both their cheeks were wet with tears and their hands were damp. Harriet reached up to him and kissed him on the lips saying " we are going home at last, Julius"

The loud speaker crackled and they could all hear the driver say, "Well folks, we have travelled into the middle of the worlds greatest natural phenomenon. Yes," he giggled to himself, "we are on top of one of the tallest mesa in the middle of the Grand Canyon". Here the itinerary will be for us to meet our Indian Guide at the hardware store up ahead". When Julius and Harriet looked around the other passengers were awaking while they saw that some were wiping their eyes. No one was speaking but all appeared to become attentive to the sound of the driver's voice. Julius sneaked a look at the large rear view mirror and sure enough the driver was not looking at the road ahead but rather looking at his little band of travellers. No one asked how they had got to the of one of the tallest mesa which was an 'up jutting' of a full mountain which appeared to be in the middle of the grand canyon splitting it down the middle so that the water flowed around this mesa and met on the other side of it and continued into a large flow of water.

The little van pulled up in front of a wooden shop which looked like a structure out of an old western movie. The long rambling structure had a few individuals in front of it some of whom were sitting on the veranda some were moving around the building. There was an old Ford car parked in front of the store and looked like it came out of another era—the nineteen fifties. It had the long fins on the back and it was painted white except for a long band of a red-brown band painted around the middle of the exterior. The little van looked so small when it parked in front of the store. The driver ran quickly to the side passenger door, opened it and placed the plastic step on the dirt ground outside the van for the middle and one seat back passengers to come out. Lastly, Julius and Harriet came out and all the passengers appeared to be holding their lower backs in order to straighten out. They all gathered around the driver, who turned his oval blue eyes to look at them all. He then began to explain where the toilet facilities were pointing to the back of the store. He then suggested that they all buy some bottled water for there was going to be quite a walk or hike to the village. He said that they should not purchase any food as they will be fed when they come to the village. He also said that it was a pleasure driving them and he again giggled to himself as he said that he wished he was coming along with them.

At this time he said that he will go and find the guide and a couple of mongrel dogs came closer to look for handout of food from the travellers. The driver shooed them away with a loud shout and a wave of both hands in the air. The dogs must have had this done to them many times so they took off to the positions under the wooden veranda of the store. The ladies headed off to the out houses on the back of the store and the two men followed more slowly. Julius walked with Harriet still holding hands. He noticed that he was breathing easier and they both appeared to be very happy and they literally glowed in the sunshine. After relieving themselves the other passengers again each pair stood next to each other but no one was speaking they were awed by the silence and majesty of the height and power of the Canyon walls which surrounded them. Harriet nudged Julius and they headed off to the store to get a bottle of water as they were told to do. They were followed by the others but when they got into the store which front appeared to be built open for there were no doors, they went directly to the fridge and took out a bottle of water. The label was white with a red-brown label around the middle of it. They paid a store keeper who was smiling at them with the large blue oval eyes. He also wore a head band of the same red'brown colour. His shopkeeper's tunic was an off white tunic which was also kept tidy by a red-brown sash around the middle of his shirt. The little band of tourists found their way back to the van and stood around looking at the area which surrounded them but still noy saying anything to each other. There was one distinct change which had taken place and it was the fact that every one appeared to be well rested and for some unknown reason they all appeared to be contented.

Julius and Harriet were looking at the opposite side of the chasm which was the Canyon itself and they just appeared to be so small relative to the surroundings. As if by some unknown instinct Harriet held onto Julius arm more tightly than ever to give some sort of anchor to her in these stupendous surroundings. When they looked around the other fellow travellers were also viewing in different parts of the opposite side and making their own private comments and observations either to themselves or to their accompanied partner.

THE GUIDE, INDIAN VILLAGE & BAT CAVE

The looked a very small group of seven and then there was a the giggle nd then came the loud voice of the driver which shocked them all so they turned around almost in unison at the sound of his voice " Ladies and Gentlemen I will like to introduce you to your Guide." Standing behind the driver was a very tall statuesque male who was of a dark skin but he was standing in front of the now receding sun so that only his shadow could be seen blocking out the light. He moved forward towards them and then he raised his right hand in greeting. They could all see him now and they shuffled about so that the sun was not in their direct vision. He wore a head band of the now familiar red brown colour with a white top shirt but which had no buttons. He wore a pair of blue jeans and sandals with no socks, which revealed long skinny toes on very dark brown feet. His hair was very black and straight and was tied back into a very long pony tail. This man was something out of a Geronimo movie. His skin on closer examination of his face was rough but his eyes were what held their attention. They were very large and oval but they were a striking bright blue colour. His cheek bones were high up on his long face with a very high forehead and as he walked towards them he dismissed the driver, who just wondered off and all eyes were focussed on this man who was to be their guide.

He began by welcoming them "welcome to the Mesa of the Asakis Tribe. You will not find our names in any of your books. This is the first time that we will allow any outsiders on earth to visit our village. We have been here for many centuries and we were found by a visiting group of Spanish Europeans about two hundred years ago but they soon left us for while they were surrounded by water they could not find a way down to collect it and many of their brave ones tried to lower themselves down to the bottom of the Canyon but they soon perished. Those soldiers left us for they could never get our people to tell them how to get the water. Since then you should know that we made some very powerful friends from the outer world. They have shown us how to keep the other people out and how to survive better" He stopped and went around each of his visitor and when he reached each one he stared into their eyes and the visitors all met his eyes directly. When this was finished he got to the front of the group and said tersely, 'Follow me. Do not take any photos of the Mesa or of anything from now on. Do not lean over the edge to have a better look for we have no protective fences. Many people have come as far as the store but when they tried to play at the edge many have fallen to their deaths." The little group followed with Julius and Harriet bringing up the rear. The tall majestic figure in front of them took them down a dirt tract which lead from the flat top where the store was and after the first bend the group could hear nothing of the dogs or people which they had left behind. The Guide stopped and looked at them and in a very confidential tone he looked at them and came closer to them. They topped and looked up at him. He smiled and then said "I will show you the wonders of our desert but I ask that you all have a drink from your water bottles, which will make the travel lighter on your feet. Again no one asked for any reason but like a group of school children they opened their bottles and drank heartily. When they had finished they saw that the guide had also drunk from a flask of water, which was carried on a hook attached to his brown belt but turned towards his back.. He then stooped down and showed them a small scrub or clump of grass but pointed out the small pink mini flowers which at the end of each stem.

Until he had shown them this minuscule cluster of efflorescence they would all have passed this little shrub. Then the group began to look at the little shrub clumps of vegetation but he was in front and again he stopped but this time he raised his hand up for them to stop, which they obediently did. He went forward towards the left of the path next to a huge rock and which had a larger hard wiry grass attached to it. He used his height to raise himself quietly up the side of the rock and peer down into the grass from the top. He pushed his hand downwards and with a quick snatch he pulled back his hand which had a snake the colour of the desert sand. They all pulled back as he clambered down towards them for the snake had wrapped itself around his forearm but he had the head trapped firmly between his thumb and the other fingers. He looked at them and drew them closer to him again then he went down on one knee. Look at his small fangs as the mouth of the snake remained open. He then pointed out that this snake was poisonous but in all the history of his people no human had ever been bitten by this snake.

He also said that the village Shaman caught these snakes and made potions from the poisonous glands, which were on the top of the head. He showed them the bulging sacks on top of the flat head and he continued that these potions or medicines cured his tribe of many illnesses. The snake remained quiet in the vice grip of the powerful hand and the guide stood up and dropped the snake into the same patch of grass. He continued and again he showed them another small and to all an otherwise insignificant plant but when one looked closer one could see the individual beautiful bright blue single flowers. At this last stop Julius went over to the shrub looked down at it and pinched off a bit of the leaf. He crumpled it between his fingers and smelled it. The guide had stopped and looked at what Julius was doing. Julius raised his fingers with the crumpled leaf towards Harriet who bent her head to smell it then nodded and smiled "yes, it smells like an onion". Before Julius could move the others moved in held his hand and had a whiff and this included the guide, who smiled broadly at him. The Guide then placed a big hand on Julius' shoulder and said "Tell me Dr Kane can you identify any of these plants?" Julius thought for a moment and said that it was not his specialty but he could perhaps with a little time key out their identification. Harriett hurried up to catch the end of the conversation and to place her hand into Julius', who was feeling a sense of proudness at this show of his Botanical prowess.

The guide stopped many times but even though it was summer in this part of the south west, the sun had began to disappear but just as this happened the group came into a camp. It was a ramshackle of a wooden house from which smoke was emanating and the smell of

BBQ meat was pervasive. As though by an unseen signal, long tables which were stacked near the entrance way were moved together by a number of silent young native Indians who moved quickly and un-smilingly. The group of visitors stood aside to let these young men and women set up the supper table but Julius was pulled away with Harriet next to him towards the end of the clearing where all the activity was taking place by the Guide. He took them both towards the edge of the cliff and let them have a look at the endless depth which was the Canyon. When Julius looked up he could see the opposite wall but there appeared to be a cable which crossed from the side that they were on to the opposite side. On their side he followed the line back to a rusting iron enclosure. With out asking the guide said "that was built a long time ago to remove fertilizer from the opposite side. If you look carefully you will see a cave where the cable enters the opposite side wall of the canyon". Julius looked and he pulled Harriet closer so that he could point it out to her. For the first time Julius looked at the guide and asked, "how or who, found the deposits of fertilizer". The guide continued to look over the canyon wall and absentmindedly said "yes, it is the accumulated guano left over pos-sibly eons ago by the bats of the desert that have made the cave their home. As you can see it is very difficult for any predator to gain entry and that includes man" He turned around and found that his group were clustered around him and he good naturedly smiled and said "Let us eat you must be very hungry for you have not eaten anything today". They looked at each other and for the first time nodded again in silence at each other. They went to the table and a number of the young men and women placed paper plates with plastic knives and forks wrapped in white serviettes which also had the red-brown band of colour,

Plates of hot boiled corn came on the table with open sauces of butter. A plate of sliced meat which looked and smelled like beef, were also placed in the middle of the long table. Cans of coca cola, sprite and water was distributed to each one as they pointed to the can they preferred. Then the young women came around with large forks and placed large helpings of meat, salad and one corn cob and one bread roll on each plate. Without much encouragement the small group of tourists dived into the food with more energy than they had shown all day. They ate noisily and quickly and in between there were the sounds of slurping as the pop was consumed. As the main plates were emptied there was a continuous re supply coming out of the wooden shed. Then the guide sat down and began to help himself and as he did so the activity of the servers stopped they surrounded the table and when he had served himself the workers all joined in the feast.

It was Julius who broke the silence and asked a very strange question, " Mr. Guide, Sir…. when do we leave for our destination?" Everyone except the guide stopped and all eyes turned towards the Guide who took a mouthful of food, then looked up at Julius but at all of them and said. "As Soon as we finish and have a toilet break, we shall have the desert, which will give us all the power to travel to our landing site". No one asked any questions and Julius just muttered a thank you and they all continued eating again. In the stillness of the early evening all that could be heard was the sound of the supper and that was not much since the plastic made very little sound. The other members of the tribe were so young noted Harriet who began to look around at the village surroundings. And they all had those strange blue eyes which was odd since they were living in one of the hottest, brightest and driest part of the world. One would have imagined that they would have had black or brown eyes she thought to herself. Then as if by some unknown force Harriet looked up to see the Guide looking at her intently and then he gave that broad toothed smile "You are quite right Mrs. Kane as if he had read her mind. You are quite correct in thinking that we are the crossbreed of another tribe, No, it is not the Spaniards but it is with the off world group, whom you will meet with later on tonight.". Harriet blushed and Julius just smiled and reached over to hold her hand.

THE SPEECH, THE JOURNEY BEGINS BUT THE ITINERARY ENDS.

As the food was demolished by the group of travellers, the dirty dishes was taken away by the youths of the village who also ate heartily and quickly. Then the Guide came over and stood at the head of the table. He looked them over and said. "Have you eaten enough of the wonderful food grown in the dessert Ha..Ha..?" And his solemn face broke out in a wide mouthed grin, showing the square teeth and bright blue eyes. "You must enjoy all that this beautiful blue planet has to offer. We take the air that we breathe as well as the essence of all life needs—such as the water for granted as though it will be with us forever. So drink deeply and relish the meal which you have just eaten for you will have different rations for the next little while."

The guide then stood at the head of the table where the seven visitors/tourists were sitting and as he did so they all turned to look at him. The other youth of the village could be heard tidying up in the wooden shed and when they were finished they came around and stood in a semi-circle behind the Guide., who raised his hand to give a signal of welcome to the young native Indians, to join them. As they were being assembled a few brought several lots of wood and placed them in a pile next to the Guide, who in turn stooped down and placed a lighted match into the dry kiln which ignited. He then stood up to his majestic height in the late twilight and began,

> "You were all contacted by the 'Visitor' who has been keeping watch over you for most of your lives. You are the offsprings of successful mating between the out worlders and earth's best breed. Each of you are a capsule of intelligence, human—emotion(s), genetic hybrid vigour and you have all had the experience of a 'human life', free of 'off world' input or contamination, which make you a pre-

cious resource for our home planet. Your lives have been planned so that you had to develop the survival instinct in this planet. It is time to bring our venture to a close for we have given knowledge to this civilization which has started the process of Space Travel. It will not be long before this fairly intelligent race joins us in the exploration of the Universe. Our people must never trade the spirit of adventure again in exchange for the loss of emotions such as love, jealousy, hate, sympathy and yes—fear. We have reignited all these traits in you the hybrids and you will take it back to our home land so that they can be transferred into our population.

It was just by accident that we were forced to land on this planet, actually 'crash' and we lost two of our crew. The Earth people just wanted to know more about us and the knowledge which we had. Luckily we got to know the Leaders of the world and it has taken over seventy earth years to come to this stage. The Leaders are all gone but our plans have been left alone to mature and we knew that this would happen. Luckily we split up after the crash and found this little known Native Indian tribe so that we could integrate into their gene pool without much notice.

Earth people had a primitive science and we traded knowledge and stimulus to that endeavour but they have exceeded our expectations, especially in this country. We did not wish to cause any imbalance of power so we made sure that growth and information was shared by informing the other countries. However, the primitive instincts of this population is still out of control and while we needed to have a jolt of their instincts to bring us back to a reality, this population is about to destroy itself. They are not working for the common good.

They cannot regulate their human resource in time for they will out live their limited survival requirements. It is time we do not interfere anymore and leave them to themselves. Our planet has a new gene pool and so we are now guaranteed a greater survival of our race and it because of this people. Some of our hybrids will remain to intercede if there is blockage in their continued development and to observe their adaptability to their probable extinction. These volunteers for this part of the mission know that they also run the risk of termination as well, and they are akin to the warriors known as the 'kamikaze or suicide pilots' but we feel an obligation to record the end of Planet Earth.

Our youth will assist you in travelling across the Canyon using the old cable system which removed the mine of fertilizer. That cave leads to the underground trail which ends up in our zone and is protected by the forces of this country. Tonight, we must hasten to take you there but our youth will look after you. One of the short comings of our hybrids is the loss of physical strength in a few of the mentally developed so we will provide you with lots of assistance for this under ground journey. Unfortunately, we cannot use any mechanical equipment since their sensitive radar and satellite spy system would detect such underground movement. Over the years the desert has strengthened our physical stature and we have nurtured this in our village youth. They are conversant in both speech and telepathy and so they will be able to know your needs—do not be afraid."

After this lengthy speech, the Guide turned around to face the young native group exposing his back to the tourists. It was now quite dark and for the first time the small group turned to each other and began to introduce themselves to each other. Both Harriet and Julius were smiling and extending their hands to the others and introducing themselves. At an unseen signal they were surrounded by the native youth who placed a hand on each of the tourist and took each couple down to the rusty cable elevator shaft. The travellers were assisted aboard the large iron bucket in the now dark night and almost immediately the large bucket launched across the deep Canyon. They could see over the edge of their trolley where the water glistened like a coil of silver at the bottom of the canyon. They felt the cool air on their faces and Harriet stole a quick glance at their young native, who remained silent except for the now fluorescent blueness of his eyes. As the bucket entered the cave on the opposite side of the canyon wall, they were in total darkness and all that became visible was the blue light which emanated from the eyes of the native guides. Harriet held Julius' hand even tighter and she could feel his reassuring squeeze back on her fingers.

When they were allowed to disembark in the inner depth of the cave, their eyes were becoming accustomed to the darkness and they could see some of their fellow travellers. Again each of the member felt the hand of an accompanying native youth, who began to lead them in the dark. The floor felt smooth and they could feel that they were going down an incline. After a time Harriet could see a pale light in the top of the corridor in which they were moving but they were like those of a firefly. Julius and Harriet were aware that they were beginning to break out in a sweat and were becoming tired. Just as they began t give some resistance to the hands of their native guides, they came to a stop and were again silently loaded into another iron bucket, which began to move downwards. It picked up speed and they could feel their ears beginning to hurt with the rapid increase in pressure, however, just as it was becoming too painful, the bucket-trolley stopped suddenly and they were moved out onto a platform of some sort. It was still quite dark but they were all beginning to see a bit but the piercing blueness of the eyes of the young indians gave out so much fluorescence that they appeared as beacons to follow. It was a strange comforting feeling to be so close to these silent and strange peoples, who took the responsibility of their charges so diligently and effortlessly.

Another short walk and then entering another underground trolley which again descended in a downward motion, this exercise was repeated two more times and was followed by a horizontal movement not unlike that of a small train or the mine mini rail ore carrier. All this was done in the dark and in silence apart from the shuffling of shoes and the scraping on the metal buckets when there was loading an unloading of the guides and passengers. Suddenly, the silence was broken by the small whine as of a very far away engine and this sound developed becoming louder and louder. It appeared to the group that they would soon stumble into a jet engine at the next turn in the tunnel but they did not for it appeared as though they had passed the sound and it was coming from behind them.

It was awhile before the silence intensified again but the blue eyes were around them and this gave some comfort. After this last walk, they stopped and one of the guides turned to face them in the dark and said "It will not be long now before we get out of this underground passage way. The last part of this journey will be on a mine rail and you will stand in a small ore cart. Shield your eyes a bit for although it is still night time, the light from the air field will hurt them. I must prepare you for the last part of this journey. In the early morning there will be a shooting star which will appear to arc across the sky. You will be on that ship and will be on your journey home but there is a mixture of gases which you must breathe before you leave to go into space and so you will be kept for awhile in a prepared section of the vessel. You will feel sleepy and you will fall asleep but this essential for you to be prepared for deep space travel. There is a side effect which you will notice in all of you but it is not dangerous, so try and relax through out the rest of this trip. Please follow me and the guides will look after you for they can see clearly in the dark.

The small obedient group moved forwards and from time to time one of them would feel the gentle touch of one of the guides who moved them away from unseen obstacle on the ground. Harriet continued to hold onto Julius' hand and she could feel him place his arm around her shoulder in the dark when they had to stop. She felt safe and a deep love for this man appeared to become stronger. She did not understand or question why they were on this trip but she had a strong premonition that they had to do what they were doing. Julius appeared to be truly happy for the first time in his life, even more so than when they both fell in love months ago. She knew that there was something special about Julius but never tried to decipher what it was. She just knew that they were 'soul mates' who had found each other. She also knew that something great was going to happen when they had got together and so she quietly looked after Julius as though he was the 'crown jewels' which she had to protect. She felt a latent happiness which was about to burst forward in her and this brought about a great excitement but she had to control it and to quiet herself so she could be with Julius when he needed her. With these thoughts going through her mind she hooked up his arm even closer to her and she smiled in the dark for she could hear him wheeze close to her ear and place his wet lips on her cheek.

The group entered into a wide space in the mine which was dimly lit but they could see the small ore cart which they entered with their silent blue eyed protectors. Then the voice of the one who had spoken to them earlier said as they were all aboard, "To assist you with the light which will definitely hurt your eyes, one of the guides will place a black band over your eyes for the next part of the trip. Do not be alarmed we will make sure you are not hurt". Almost immediately, each of the travellers were bind folded but they could feel the arm of one of the guides holding their hands. The small ore wagon began to move silently for there was no engine so it could be assumed that they were moving down hill when the brake was removed. Unknown to all they were entering the different dimension.

After a short interval, they could hear sounds of other people moving around. The wagon jad stopped and they were all moved quietly by the hand onto the ground. They then felt their guides hold their hands and move them walking in a definite direction. Even through their blind fold they could see that there were large lights around them. Harriet looked downwards through a slit of her blindfold and could see the ground which looked like they were in daylight. She held onto Julius' hand and arm but kept her head down so she could see her feet and that of Julius moving as they walked. She could not hear voices but there appeared to be a lot of movement of heavy equipment and of lights. She was also aware that they were in the middle of he group who were all walking with guides in a distinct direction. Then she felt the hard ground give way to a metal like floor and they were also moving into a closed area. She could not see very well as the bright lights appeared to have been removed, all there was now was darkness.

The young leader's voice again broke the silence and said "It will not be long before we remove your blind folds, please bear with us for it is really for your own safety". As he completed the last statement there was a clang followed by the sound of an elevator on the move, as though a huge door had closed and there was silence which had blocked out all the new sounds that they were becoming used to. Again the voice of the new leader came softer almost as a whisper "There is a special mixture of gas which is about to be released into the chamber, please breathe normally and relax on the seats just behind each of you". Almost as if by command the travellers felt behind them for a hard but smooth surface which they were assisted to sit themselves down. There was a sigh of relief and of relaxation for them all and within seconds they all appeared to be slowly drifting off and to breathe slowly and noiselessly some appeared to have gone to sleep, all but Harriet, who still continued to look through the bottom part of her blind fold. She could see a dim light on the dark floor which appeared to be of a metal like surface. She felt that the air had changed and it had a sweetish taste to it, which while not unpleasant was different. She still held onto Julius' arm and hands and he appeared to be asleep.

There was a stirring sound and the seats all appeared to adjust backwards very slowly so that they were in a lying down position. The sound was not unpleasant and it even caused them all to relax even more. The sweet smell of he air was becoming even more intense then the voice of the leader came back to them "When I give the order to remove your mask, do so slowly. Do not be alarmed or be disturbed for there will be a change in some of your physical appearance which will show first in the eyes. This test will reveal all those who have successfully had the off worlders traits. It was about thirty minutes when the voice said, "Please remove your blind fold .and slowly look around you but do not try to get up from your place, you will not be able to move yourself for the next hour or so"

The blind folds were removed and when Harriet looked over to Julius she was stunned to see that his eyes had turned into a bright fluorescent blue and was glowing as he turned his head towards her. She looked at the others and they were also blue. The eyes of the guides appeared be even bluer and more fluorescent than before, the she heard Julius say "Hello Harriet, your eyes have remained brown. You are not one of us." He stared at her and the warmth and affection which he always showed to her could not be seen by her, but he was still holding her hands in a very affectionate way. She said smilingly "Julius you look beautiful with out your glasses and those blue eyes suit you" . She then continued, "I guess the gas did not work on me but that is alright some of us has to be different, isn't that so Julius?"

"Yes Harriet" he replied and continued "you will always be my Harriet and in coming with me I shall have brought the greatest of all gifts from Earth to our people and our planet It is in the form of a living capsule filled with the greatest of all emotions—'Love'—. It is you Harriet. You are coming to a planet and a world which is very different from all that you have known, Harriet. Because of our blue eyes we now have the knowledge of what we are and what was our Mission over five decades ago. We are going home to bring back some of these basics to our population, are you willing to give up all your past for this new adventure Harriet for we will not be coming back?". Harriet remained silent as Julius spoke to her but his blue eyes were not like the Julius she had come to know, none the less, she was with the one person that she trusted and truly loved and she slowly replied "You are the one I love Julius and where ever you go so will I as long as we are together forever". She then pulled herself to a sitting position as did Julius and as they turned around they found that they were in a very large cabin by themselves for as they were speaking they were aware that the other travellers were moving out into an aisle outside the cabin. They went through to the aisle and almost immediately one of the young Native Indian youths appeared in front of them and standing straight said "Please follow me to your quarters, Commander!" Julius raised his right hand up to his head in salute as though he had done this before and said very confidently "after you officer but please show us where we are now". The officer moved towards the cabin from which they had just left and pressed a button lever on the wall. The wall parted to show a clear window and receding in the blackness of space was a blue planet fading away in the distance.

The End

THE AUTHOR :

Having left the Caribbean and his home of Trinidad, over the forty plus years ago, Darryl Leslie Gopaul finds that with age (his final frontier) that his childhood memories recur with a vividness that is becoming of his "anec-dotage"

He explains "that these stories were embellished for the fear effect on this virgin audience, there is no doubt. However, my maternal grandfather was bed-ridden because of a gangrous toe and we, the grand children, were sent into his room to keep him company. 'From his four poster ornate bed and in his white silk pajamas, we were his susceptible and gullible audience.

Professionally, Darryl is a well established Medical Microbiologist, who has travelled extensively around the world lecturing and is author to many scientific publications and scientific posters. He has been the Leader of an Ambassador group of Scientists to the Mid East and was present with the Ambassador Group, when the revolution in the former USSR and the fall of communism took place. Today he lives in Canada with his wife and two daughters.